monsoonbooks

WESTERN CHANT

Barbara Ismail spent several years in Kelantan in the 1970s and '80s, living in Kampong Dusun and Pengkalan Cepa, studying Wayang Siam and the Kelantanese dialect. She holds a PhD in Anthropology from Yale University, and is originally from Brooklyn, New York.

Western Chant is the sixth in Barbara Ismail's series of Kain Songket Mysteries based in Kelantan. The first book in the series, *Shadow Play*, won Best Debut Novel at the SBPA Book Awards in Singapore and was shortlisted for the Popular Readers' Choice Awards in Malaysia; the second book in the series, *Princess Play*, was shortlisted for the Popular Readers' Choice Awards in Malaysia.

For more information about the author and her books, visit *www.barbaraismail.com*.

Kain Songket Mysteries

(published and forthcoming)

Shadow Play
Princess Play
Spirit Tiger
Moon Kite
Spinning Top
Western Chant
Little Axe

WESTERN CHANT

Volume VI in the Kain Songket Mysteries Series

BARBARA ISMAIL

monsoonbooks

First published in 2021
by Monsoon Books Ltd
www.monsoonbooks.co.uk

No.1 The Lodge, Burrough Court, Burrough on the Hill,
Melton Mowbray LE14 2QS, UK

First edition.

ISBN (paperback): 9781912049844
ISBN (ebook): 9781912049851

Copyright©Barbara Ismail, 2021
The moral right of the author has been asserted.

All rights reserved. No part of this publication may be reproduced, stored in a retrieval system, or transmitted, in any form or by any means without the prior written permission of the publisher, nor be otherwise circulated in any form of binding or cover other than that in which it is published and without a similar condition being imposed on the subsequent purchaser.

Cover design by Cover Kitchen.

A Cataloguing-in-Publication data record is available from the British Library.

Printed and bound in Great Britain by Clays Ltd, Elcograf S.p.A.

For Shahmim

Malay Glossary

Adik Younger brother or sister.

Abang Older Brother. A term of respect for a younger man, or a man of similar age to the speaker.

Alamak An exclamation, much like 'My Goodness!'

Alhamdulillah Thank God.

Angin Bertiup The wind blows: the equivalent of 'people say'.

Astigfirullah An expression of unpleasant surprise. In Arabic, 'I seek forgiveness from Allah.'

Ayah Father

Baju Kurung A long traditional blouse, which comes almost to the knee. It is long sleeved with a split collar. Traditionally worn with a sarong or a long skirt.

Batik Wax print cloth, commonly used for women's sarong.

Bomoh Traditional healer and purveyor of magic and spells.

Che Mister

Cik Miss

Dikir Barat Literally, 'Western Chant', an improvised song about a village or political situation made for entertainment and competition.

Hidung Mancung Chiseled nose.

Intan Berlian Diamond, used as a term of affection.

Kain Songket The queen of Kelantan fabrics. Woven of silk with geometric patterns made of gold. It is commonly used for weddings and other special occasions.

Kakak Older Sister. A term of respect for a younger woman or a woman of a similar age to the speaker.

Kampong Village.

Keropok Crackers or puffy chips made from fish, squid or prawn.

Kopi Peng Iced Coffee.

Lusa The day after tomorrow.

Mak Mother.

Mak Cik Aunty. A term of respect for an older woman. Also carries the meaning of a businesswoman and pillar of society.

Onde-Onde

A type of Malay Cake: a rice flour ball with molasses syrup in the middle and coconut flakes on the outside.

Pak Cik Uncle. A term of respect for an older man.

Pak Long Eldest Uncle: a term for the eldest of a parent's siblings.

Parang Machete.

Pasar Besar Main market.

Rumah Tukai A house made of plaited bamboo screens.

Sarong A tubular skirt worn by both men and women which ties around the waist and comes to the ankles.

Semangat Life energy.

Semoga dia tenang disana May he (she) be at peace there: rest in peace.

Shariah Muslim religious law.

Talak Muslim pronouncement of divorce. A couple can remarry if the husband pronounces one or two talak, but three means the divorce is permanent unless the wife marries and divorces someone else.

Teh Tarik Literally 'pulled tea', which is poured from one cup to another in a high arc. Often sold on the street and served in a plastic bag with a straw.

Tukang Karut The lead singer of the dikir barat troupe.

Malay Idioms

Bagai duri sebatang terbuang
Like a single thorn thrown away: something of no importance.
Bagai kepiting batu
Like a rock crab, which has strong claws and a hard shell. A miser.
Barang dimana ditiup angin, disanalah dia chondong
Like a tree which leans whichever way the wind blows. To be adaptable in order to take advantage of every opportunity.
Belah dada melihat hati
Open my chest and see my heart: I swear (the equivalent of 'cross my heart and hope to die').
Biar puteh tulang, jangan puteh mata
Better white bones than white eyes: that is, better bleached bones in death than white eyes in humiliation.
Cerdik, tak akal
Clever, but not wise. Often used of children being cunning.
Dari jauh orang angkat telunjok, kalau dekat diangkat mata
From afar, people point, from close, they raise their eyebrows: said of an object of shame and derision.
Dia makan nangka, kita kena getah
He eats the jackfruit, we get sticky (fingers). Something unfair.

Diajar anak harimau makan daging

To teach a tiger cub to eat meat: to encourage someone on a path they may be inclined to anyway, which will not serve them well.

Empat gasal, lima genap

Four is odd, five is even: someone who is being contrary.

Enggang sama enggang, pipit sama pipit

Hornbills go with hornbills; finches go with finches. Each goes with its own kind.

Intan dikalongkan ke leher anjing

Putting a diamond collar on a dog: spreading pearls before swine.

Itek dengar gemuruh

A duck listening to thunder: utter bewilderment.

Itek diajar berenang

Teaching a duck to swim: telling an expert how to do it.

Kain basoh kering di pinggang

His wet sarong must dry on him (because it's the only one he's got).

Kaki untut dipakaikan gelang

Putting a bracelet on a diseased leg: drawing attention to things you don't want noticed.

Kasehankan raja berusung

To feel sorry for a prince carried in a litter: because you imagine him to be ill. Don't waste your sympathy.

Kerbau cucuk hidung

A kerbau with a ring through its nose: someone who can be ordered about.

Kubur kata mari, rumah kata nanti

The grave tells you to come, the house tells you to wait. Someone on the verge of death, pulled both the die and to not die.

Kurang kurang bubur, lebih lebih sudu

The less porridge the more spoons: to make a big fuss over a trivial matter.

Masam muka macam nikah tak suka

As sour faced as an unwilling bride.

Memanjat pokok cekur, boleh jatoh mati

Even climbing a cekur (a creeping vine) one can fall to one's death: finding exaggerated danger in a task.

Musoh di dalam selimut

An enemy under the blanket: a betrayer. Often used to mean an unfaithful wife.

Rapuh mulut

Literally, 'fragile mouth': one given to babbling and blurting secrets.

Sebab mulut badan binasa

Because of the mouth, the body is destroyed. To talk too much.

Tak terpagut di ayam, tak tersudu di itek

Chickens won't peck at it; ducks won't put their bills to it: something utterly worthless.

Tua Tupai

From the saying '*Tua, tua tupai tak tidur atas tanah*'; old like an old squirrel who won't sleep on the ground, because the females are up in the trees.

Chapter I

Amin leaned over his coffee cup at the small roadside stall, drawing thoughtfully on his cigarette. He'd been hired to provide the entertainment at a circumcision ceremony in the small kampong of Tapak Gajah, near Bacok, and he was there to collect material as unobtrusively as possible.

He was a popular singer of dikir barat, an impromptu singing performance originally from Southern Thailand, a primarily Malay region with many connections to Kelantan. It concerned local affairs or the political situation: the lyrics were funny, sharp and usually specific to the locality. Amin made it his business to snoop around the village in which he would perform, to spice his songs with local allusions. Snoop would not be a word Amin would comfortably use, however: investigate or research, something more academic would be appropriate, but those who ended up in his crosshairs might disagree.

This was Amin's second day in Tapak Gajah, and he already felt the eyes of the village upon him. He'd sat at the tiny stand on the Bacok road, slowly sipping coffee and smoking cigarettes, talking with the men who stopped there during the day. He overheard conversations, eavesdropped on gossip, and began to fix in his head the social constellation surrounding him. Naturally, he'd never poke fun at the family that hired him: they would remain out of his songs except for a positive message at the start and a hearty thank you. Others of course, would find themselves satirized, but Amin always strove to be funny and pointed but not vicious. It was not fully a matter of decency, but of business as well, as who would hire a dikir barat *tukang karut*, or leader, who made any situation worse and left this audience resentful and possibly furious? It was meant to be a gentle ribbing rather than a verbal evisceration.

'You're going to sing at Che Nasir's party, aren't you?' asked the owner, pouring coffee for both of them. 'I heard you'd be here.'

Amin acknowledged that he was. 'Just trying to feel the atmosphere here and find out what's going on,' he answered mildly.

'Have you heard anything good?' he leaned over the miniscule counter, holding his cup.

Amin shook his head genially. He wanted to hear gossip, not spread it. 'Have you?'

The man laughed. 'Not too much happens around here,' he told him. 'Such a small place, isn't it? We don't have any scandals.'

'You're lucky, then, to have such a town,' Amin replied. 'There's always something, though, isn't there?' He took a large slurp of his coffee. 'But you're right, there isn't much.' He nodded to punctuate his comments.

'We aren't like Bacok, or even Kota Bharu,' the man continued, bringing up the town nearby and the largest city in Kelantan. 'You know, streetlights and paved roads and such.' He waved a hand at the rutted dirt road that ran to the kampong, requiring drivers of cars and motorcycles to weave slowly around the potholes or find themselves inside one. 'You have to want to come to Tapak Gajah,' he informed him. 'Nobody just passes through for the fun of it. This road's a mess: driving anything over it at night is dangerous, really. On a full moon it's alright, but otherwise? You can't see where you're going and if you hit a hole, you're in the dirt. It's the government,' he said, with growing enthusiasm for his subject. 'The federal government is punishing us for voting opposition, and they don't spend any money here.'

Amin nodded. Kelantan never voted for the Barisan Nasional, the coalition of parties that ruled Malaysia's federal government and most of the states. Kelantan, ever different, voted reliably in the early 1970s for PMIP, the Pan Malayan Islamic Party, though a local rival Islamic party was also on the rise. It was widely believed that the central government refused to spend any money on Kelantan to punish them for their orneriness, and their refusal to vote as most other states did. In a way, Kelantan enjoyed its isolation, encouraged by the lack of roads to the rest of Malaysia (a two-lane highway up the East Coast was the sole artery, and it was often flooded during the rainy season), and the dearth of business for the largest companies. Kelantan for the Kelantanese explained the political situation, and if it meant the state lagged behind in electricity and water and roads, well then, so be it.

The owner held forth on this political philosophy for several long minutes, wiping the counter as he continued to damn the

Barisan Nasional and extoll the PMIP, while allowing the new rising Islamic party, PAS, might also be worth considering. This was standard fare in coffee shops throughout the area, and Amin had not only heard it many times before; he'd often given the same speech himself. He hardly needed this kind of information to include in his performance: it was a staple of Kelantan entertainment and always guaranteed audience approval.

He was searching for, hoping for, low-level village gossip, which he could weave into his songs and have them pinch, but not sting. A real scandal would be too hot for him to handle and would guarantee to affront someone. Just garden variety gossip would do.

The coffee bar was beginning to fill with several fishermen coming back from their boats. They nodded politely and asked for their coffee and snacks, clearly tired after a long day's work. Quietly, they ate and drank, while the owner droned on about politics with no one listening. At last, one of the men interrupted and asked Amin what he was doing.

'Just here, you know. I'll be performing at Che Nasir's party …'

'I've heard about you!' he smiled and interrupted again. 'Dikir barat, right? I can't wait. Digging for dirt, eh? Good place to do it,' he nodded. 'Trying to find out what goes on in Tapak Gajah. Not much, and that's the truth. You're going to really work for it, I'm afraid. But still,' he added with a grin, 'there's always something to find, isn't there?'

Amin agreed, but though everyone assured him there must be something, he hadn't yet heard about it, and no one seemed to be either volunteering or talking about any scandal in particular. True, he'd overheard fishermen grousing about their captains, and the occasional husband complaining of his wife, but how would this be different from anywhere else? He could hardly base an evening's entertainment on the fact that captains of fishing boats seemed to think their crews could work endlessly without a break. That was five minutes, and then he had the rest of the evening to fill.

He tried to keep himself from becoming impatient, since no one wants to chat with someone who isn't willing to spend the time making it interesting. So, he smiled and bantered with the men, none of whom gave him any material, and as it became late, they left to go home and take their well-earned rest. Another man slipped onto a stool as it emptied out, an older man with a full beard speckled with grey and his hair tucked up under an improvised turban made from an old sarong. Although he wore faded clothing, it was of a good quality, and something about the way he held himself led Amin to assume he had some money.

He ordered a coffee and examined the depleted assortment of cakes before picking one. He stirred his cup in a thoughtful sort of way for several moments, and then turned to Amin and introduced himself.

'You're here for the celebration, aren't you?' he asked. Amin nodded and acknowledged he was. 'Dikir barat, right? I've always loved it.' He nodded and smiled. 'I'm Che Zulkifli,' he informed him, giving his name formally. 'I have a *keropok* factory in the village. It's small really, we make prawn and fish crackers, you know, the usual kind. Nothing fancy,' he said into his coffee cup.

Amin smiled pleasantly, unsure of what his reaction was supposed to be. 'Do you know Che Nasir well?' he asked politely.

'Oh, I know him alright,' the newcomer said. 'Yes, it's a small kampong and we all know each other.'

'Are you from here?'

'Oh yes, born here, grew up here. Never lived anywhere else really. I'm used to Tapak Gajah. I know all of it.'

Amin thought this was an odd comment but decided not to pursue it. The man made him uncomfortable in a way he couldn't explain. Not that he was rude or discourteous in any way, but there was something …

'I could tell you stories about this village. I know all of them. Even those about your employer.' He gave a sideways smile, a self-satisfied expression. 'Oh yes, I could tell you a great many things.'

Though this was just what Amin was seeking, it made him uneasy to have it offered in this way. He preferred to overhear things or listen to them as part of a larger conversation. He was suspicious of people offering him information privately or promising him great scoops on fellow villagers. After all, he wasn't a newspaper reporter digging for a story: he just sought local colour as it were, and not to be drawn into anyone's particular grudge. And whatever Zulkifli was offering, it sounded to him like someone getting even.

'Ah well,' he replied lightly, 'I don't want the whole history of Tapak Gajah. That's too much information for me!' He motioned for another cup of coffee.

'But really interesting,' Zulkifli muttered. 'There's a lot going on here.'

Amin regarded the coffee shop landlord, hoping to learn something from his face. He returned the look, raising his eyebrows but saying nothing.

'Come and see me tomorrow,' Zulkifli suggested, getting up to leave. 'You can find the factory easily enough, and I'll be there.' He walked off without further comment, ambling down the dirt road.

'What was that?' Amin asked.

'He's a strange guy sometimes,' the owner said, striving to be non-committal. 'He's a big shot around here, his factory does very well. There aren't many people he likes, though.'

'Why?'

The man shrugged. 'It's the same way with his whole family. I don't think they like anyone very much.'

'I've never met anyone like that,' Amin said, gazing down the road where Zulkifli had disappeared. 'Who didn't like people, I mean.'

'They're all cold like that. No friends, really. I can't imagine living that way. But,' he added practically, 'you can hardly say anything about that during a dikir barat!'

'Absolutely,' Amin agreed. 'I've no interest in that.'

'Still, Zulkifli might be something you could use. There's lots of talk about him in general. As I said, he's a strange sort and I don't say that because he's never done anything, well, strange.'

'Like what?'

The man thought for a while, as though struggling with a

23

desire to talk and a desire to keep quiet. Naturally, the desire to talk won out. 'He's got a lot of money; he might be the richest man here. But do you see how he dresses? An old sarong on his head, and a faded one around his waist. Whatever he's wearing seems to be all he's got: *kain basoh kering di pinggang* – if his sarong gets wet it must dry on him. Is it necessary? No, indeed. But that's the way he is.'

Amin fought to appear absorbed. After all, wealthy people who were too cheap to even dress normally was not a bombshell. That would do for one line, a throwaway really. Though actually, he wasn't sure he wanted anything to do with Zulkifli, so perhaps it would be wise to leave him out of the proceedings altogether. The man chattered on, while others came for a break in the day.

'Investigating Zulkifli, are you?' an older man asked, having gotten the gist of the monologue. 'Maybe that's not the best idea.'

'Why?' asked Amin, though he was inclined to believe him.

'He can be a bit odd,' he answered quietly, without much emphasis. Amin offered him a cigarette, which he happily accepted. 'Hassan,' he introduced himself briefly. 'I just don't think he's the kind of person who will take well to being mentioned in dikir barat. You don't want a fight on your hands, just a pleasant evening where everyone enjoys themselves, isn't it?'

'Exactly,' Amin agreed. 'Just fun.'

'If it's anything having to do with fun, it won't involve Zulkifli,' he advised. 'Find something else to sing about.'

'Any suggestions?'

Hassan laughed. 'Not much happens here.'

'So I've been told.'

'Correctly, then. But maybe …' he assumed a meditative expression.

Amin was hopeful. Maybe something he could use would actually be whispered.

'We had a big deal about a sawmill someone was thinking about putting up here. The same people who did that in Kampong Laut. But Zulkifli threatened to sue, even though they wouldn't be on his land.'

'Why?'

'He said he didn't want the disturbance. People were really unhappy about that, I can tell you. Think of the jobs we could have here! All kinds of people went to talk to him to ask him to stop fighting it, but he wouldn't. Disturbance? What kind of thing is that when all your neighbours want it?'

'It's an interesting story,' Amin said lightly, thinking it was anything but. He'd already decided he didn't want anything to do with Zulkifli and using that would be an excellent way of inciting him. And maybe he'd threaten to sue. 'But really, there's Zulkifli again …'

'You're right,' Hassan murmured into his coffee cup. 'It's hard to think of anything that doesn't involve him.'

Amin reluctantly got up from his stool and stretched his back. This had been a disappointing mission into the village. He'd gotten no usable material and had spent a good deal of time here drinking substandard coffee. It was time to try for another post. The market, perhaps. The women of Tapak Gajah might be more forthcoming than the men. He could only hope.

He called his goodbyes to the men and wandered through the kampong to the small afternoon market which sold the fish as they came off the boats. He bought some to bring home for dinner, why not? He was here and the fish could not be any fresher. He ambled around the small booths heaped with the day's catch, which were all manned by men. But the few vegetable stalls in the corner were all run by women, and he squatted in front of an artistically arranged pyramid of cucumbers to speak to the proprietor.

'You're the dikir barat guy,' she said briefly after inspecting him up and down. 'I saw you in the kampong trying to pick up some stories, right? Not succeeding too well, it seemed to me.'

'No,' he admitted, 'not too well.'

'You shouldn't talk to the men,' she advised him. 'They all bring up these political type stories which could get you in a whole lot of trouble.'

'Zulkifli?'

She shrugged and hopefully regarded a woman passing by with a small basket of fish. The woman stopped and examined a cucumber on the very point of the edifice. 'How much?' she asked.

The seller smiled. 'Two for 50 cents,' and began wrapping them in newspaper, ready to go if they were paid for. She was handed her money, the cucumbers changed hands, and the woman cheerfully turned back to Amin. 'You should just hang around the market tomorrow afternoon,' she directed him. 'There's a lot to see and hear. You have to pick it up yourself, because I'm not handing you any stories,' she said politely but firmly. 'But I've told you where to find them.'

***

Amin knew excellent advice when he heard it, and the next morning he came together with his wife to scout the market. He reasoned a woman might hear more in this arena than a man. A man for the coffee shop, a woman for the market.

Although Amin overheard some interesting tidbits as he strolled around, he saw his wife in deep conversation with a group of women on the far side of the area. She didn't seem to be overhearing the affairs of the village as much as eliciting them, and it was a friendly and animated crowd. There were smiles and laughter and intense discussion: Amin was proud of his wife for her ability to get along with almost everyone, and how she could turn a common enough dialogue into an absolute talkfest. She'd have all the information he'd need gathered up after this visit, after only an hour or so's worth of time. It was a real gift.

A few men began to gather on the outside of this assembly, drawn, no doubt, by the animation and good-natured repartee. For no reason he could name, he began to feel uneasy, wishing the men would leave the women alone. He drifted over to find his wife and take her home, though he could not say why he felt this was imperative. The crowd now seemed to become darker, with raised voices instead of laughter, and a good deal pushing beginning in the centre of the gathering.

Suddenly, there were screams, and everyone seemed to draw back toward the edges of the group, covering their mouths with their hands, shocked. Amin moved quickly, pushing his way to the middle where two bodies lay with their blood running into the street. It was his wife and Zulkifli, and they were both quite dead.

Chapter II

Hamzah, the chief of police at the Bacok station, stood in the middle of the main road waiting for the Kota Bharu men to arrive. He turned his hat around in his hands, though he was trying not to appear anxious. What a mess he'd found! Two dead bodies and no one remembered anything. And the husband seemed like he might just die himself at any moment.

When he'd received an unintelligible call, full of emotion but short on details, he'd come right out, since Tapak Gajah was about the only clear information he received. Everyone in town, so it seemed, was in a wide circle around the two corpses, whispering to each other but afraid to touch anything. That was good luck anyway, since the crime scene, if you wanted to call the market that, was untouched. Everyone remained where they were, though the fish sellers were grumbling since their catch was not getting any fresher as they stood there, waiting for the capital's professionals.

The two newly widowed spouses sat next to each other on a wooden bench beneath an awning. Amin was frozen, staring wide-eyed at his wife's body, unable to take in what had happened. Zulkifli's wife, however, seemed to be taking it fairly calmly, absently fanning herself with her headscarf, turning to see if the police were finally arriving. A woman came with a tray of tea, which she graciously accepted, but Amin didn't even notice her as she urged him to drink.

'Can you imagine?' murmured Halimah, Zulkifli's widow. 'It's an extraordinary thing, this. I can't believe it myself.' She took a sip of tea daintily and shook her head. 'Not in a million years. Killed right here in the evening market. Surrounded by fish!' This seemed to make things worse, though the woman listening to her could not see how.

'When they called me over, I didn't believe them,' she continued calmly. 'I said to them, "What are you talking about? How could he be dead right here in Tapak Gajah?" These things don't happen here, or at least,' she corrected herself, 'they shouldn't. Killed right here and no one knows why, or how? I don't know what the world's coming to, I really don't.' She swallowed the rest of her tea and was immediately given a refill.

Two of her neighbours had come over to sit next to her and try to comfort her. They thought briefly of rubbing her arms and shoulders and holding her hands, as they might with someone else, but didn't dare touch her. They were thankful she was so calm, exhibiting no signs of grief or pain, which might be embarrassing to deal with. So far, things seemed to be going in as decorous a manner as could be hoped for in a double murder, and the citizens of Tapak Gajah were grateful for that.

At last, the Kota Bharu delegation arrived, led by Police Chief Osman and his right-hand man, Rahman. They'd seen murders before, so this held no horrors for them. In fact, they'd seen quite a bit worse, so they were unshakable. They knelt on either side of the bodies, carefully examining the wounds. Amin's wife had been slashed near the heart and stomach and had bled into the ground. Zulkifli had been strangled.

'Whoever did this,' said Rahman, with his hand on Zulkifli's shoulder, 'really knew what he was doing. He snapped his neck like a chicken's. See that?' he pointed to his head, lolling unnaturally on the ground.

Osman nodded. 'Strong, I'd guess. And at least as tall as Zulkifli. A man, I'd say. But she was slashed. Was that a different killer, do you think?'

'I think it has to be,' Rahman answered slowly, lifting the shoulder he'd been holding and observing the arm held under the body. 'I think I've found at least one murder weapon.' He carefully brought the arm out and laid it straight out from the shoulder. He dug again under the body and immediately reached back to find a cloth. He then cocked his head and peered behind it, reaching in carefully and coming out with a knife. He held it in his hand and passed it gently to Osman. It was a *parang,* a machete ubiquitous in any Malay kampong and used for any number of tasks. It was streaked with blood.

Osman sat back on his heels. 'Was he walking around the kampong waving a parang? How could no one notice?' He stared unhappily at the knife in his hand. 'Why didn't he use a regular knife?'

'Maybe he didn't have one, or at least have it handy. I don't like this at all. All these people were here, and no one can tell us what happened?'

'We haven't asked them yet,' Osman said reasonably. 'We've got to ask them first. Someone must have seen him coming here wielding a parang. It doesn't happen every day.'

He stood up slowly, and Rahman did the same, unhappily contemplating the woman's corpse. 'I don't understand this.'

'We'll understand it when we've done the interviews,' Osman said briskly. 'Let's get it going.'

Hamzah's men organized the grumbling villagers to give their statements. Many were complaining they had to get home, they hadn't seen anything, they didn't know anything, and besides, their fish would be worth nothing if they didn't get it sold right now. Couldn't they sell it while they waited?

'Two people just died, and you're worried about fish?' Hamzah asked them. 'Surely some things are more important …'

The grumbling did not stop; it went underground and Hamzah could see that the answer to his question was yes. Nevertheless, it seemed wrong to have his witnesses bargaining about fish while they waited to talk about a murder.

'No,' he said shortly, annoyed. 'Just wait till you're called to talk to Police Chief.' He swept an angry eye over the crowd, which did not seem to affect them at all. Possibly because most had their heads down whispering to one another, paying no attention to him at all. Fish, indeed!

Osman sat down with Amin, appearing grave and sympathetic. 'What a shock,' he began. 'What happened?'

Amin stared at him for a long moment, unable to put together a sentence. Osman offered him a cigarette and lit it for him. He waited, and then asked again. This time, Amin swallowed, and tried to articulate how his world had collapsed only an hour or so ago.

'That's my wife,' he began, the cigarette hanging out of the corner of his mouth. 'She's dead. I didn't see it, you know. She was talking to some of the women, and I saw it was a very ... good conversation, you know. Laughing and talking and very relaxed. Then suddenly there was an uproar and people were huddled around there. I didn't know what happened. I pushed my way through because I was worried, it was in the same place where she was talking. And there she was, lying on the ground, covered in blood. Just in an instant. How can that be? This morning she was fine, and now she's gone. I don't know. The kids ...' he trailed off. Osman could well believe his confusion.

'Do you know what the conversation was about?'

He nodded. 'It was about my dikir barat.' Osman was blank, and Amin continued. 'I'm a dikir barat singer, and I was hired for a circumcision here in Tapak Gajah. Well, I did what I always do, I hung around here to pick up some local gossip I could use in my songs. At the coffee shop, you know. Listen to the talk.' He stopped speaking and stared off into the distance. Osman cleared his throat to try to bring him back to the here and now. Amin started, and resumed his explanation. 'I sent her to talk to the market women. Sometimes the women really have the information and of course it's easier if a woman talks to them. Sometimes they don't want to talk to a man. It's not because they're shy, it's because they think we're stupid.' He nodded at Osman, who nodded back. He could certainly attest to that.

'She was helping me, you know. And it seemed to me from

where I was standing that this conversation was going well, and that she was getting a lot of stuff I could use. I was just going over to get her so we could go home, just going to get her.' He sighed. 'And then there was the crowd and all that.' He turned to Osman. 'And now she's dead.'

Osman nodded again and lit his own cigarette. It didn't seem that Amin was going to be a lot of help, but it did reveal how quickly this must have happened, almost before anyone noticed it. 'Did you hear anything you thought was interesting?' he asked Amin. Ferreting out relevant gossip was part of his job, and to have someone else actually doing it for him was a gift.

Amin beheld a tree nearby, as though he thought it was the most fascinating thing he'd ever seen. 'Her name is Yati. Yati binti Ibrahim.' He stopped speaking and then resumed.

'There wasn't much that was interesting,' he replied slowly, 'but people were warning me away from Zulkifli. I don't know what it was about him that they thought was so important, or such a secret. Everyone said how rich he was, but he was dressed like a beggar. Really old and faded sarong and another even older one used as a headscarf. He was something the cat would drag in. And then when he left the other men said he was wealthy, as if that would be the big secret, but you know, a lot of wealthy men won't spend a dime. *Bagai kepiting batu*, like a rock crab, with strong claws and a hard shell. That's not too much to add to the performance.

'But it was the way they talked about him. Warning me not to make any comments about him because it would be better if he were left out of it. No one said it right out, mind you, or said what would happen if I said something, but it was very odd. And he asked me to come and see him, which is even odder. I couldn't figure it out. No one asks you over to their house to offer dirt on their neighbours. At a coffee shop or the market, it's ok, but you don't sit down to make a meal of it. Well, I never had a chance to go to see him, but if I'm honest, I'm not sure I would have gone anyway. He was a little creepy. And then, now he's dead.'

'Did people dislike him?'

Amin shrugged. 'I don't know. I'm not from here so I don't really know much about these people. It would be better if you asked someone who actually lives here. But someone certainly didn't like him, did they?'

Osman nodded again. 'Thank you, Che Amin. We will call you if we need to speak to you again. We probably will, because right now I don't even know all the things I want to ask. One more thing; did you or your wife know anyone here?'

Amin shook his head. 'We've never been here. I've never heard of it. Why would you? We're not from the Bacok area, you see. Kubang Kerian. In this little village, I don't know anyone.'

'Did your wife?'

'No.'

'The only time you've seen any of these people is what, yesterday? And your wife, today.'

'That's it. And I hope I never see them again.'

Chapter III

Cik Minah was sitting on the porch of Maryam's house in Kampong Penambang. Maryam was somewhat surprised to see her: she was a cousin, of course, but a distant one, and not often given to visiting without a holiday or ceremony to bring her all the way to the Kota Bharu area. She arrived in a taxi from Bacok and came to the house as determined as any commander. She was well dressed and heavily jewelled, as befitted an unannounced visit from so far away. She seemed to be just about controlling herself and keeping things polite and quiet. She and Maryam traded courteous niceties and Maryam graciously offered tea and coffee and sent her youngest son Yi to her cousin Rubiah's house to bring back both Rubiah and her fabled cakes.

Finally, Cik Minah came to the point of her visit. 'Yam, we've heard all about your detecting and working with the Kota Bharu police, you're famous, you know! And I'm so proud to be your cousin and tell people about it when they bring up your name! The most horrible thing happened in Tapak Gajah and now I feel it might be my fault and I need your help!'

'Now, Nah,' she soothed, 'you must tell me all about it. And Rubiah, too, she's a wonderful sleuth herself and we always work together. Start from the beginning.'

Minah took a deep breath and tried to keep the story organized. 'You know about Johari's circumcision, it's coming up and we're hoping to see you there, and of course we're planning the party. I hired Che Amin for dikir barat; have you heard of him? He's very well known in the Bacok area, and I believe he's well known all over Kelantan. Anyway, we arranged it and he was hanging around the kampong like these dikir barat people do, to pick up the local stories and such. And when he's doing that, his wife is at the market talking to some women and gets killed by a village man, Zulkifli! He slashes her with a parang, and she falls down dead right there in the market. You won't believe this, but he is then immediately strangled and dies. Two people dead in the market at one time. In Tapak Gajah!'

She halted momentarily to have a sip of coffee and accept a proffered cigarette. She turned to both Maryam and Rubiah as they all lit their cigarettes to gauge their reactions and was gratified to see they were shocked.

'We'd heard something about it,' Rubiah said. 'I didn't realize it was you, Nah. *Alamak!* Then what?'

'The police came, of course, and pulled over everyone who'd been in the market. But you know how these things are. So many people were right there, right next to her and no one saw anything until she hit the ground. And then someone killed Zulkifli right away, but no one saw that either. It has to be one of the people who was there, of course it does. But I hear no one is saying anything.'

'Why would that be?' asked Maryam.

'I think it's because Zulkifli wasn't well liked, and really, no one wants to give up his killer because they're secretly glad he did it.' She blew out the smoke from her cigarette for emphasis. 'They're all protecting whomever did it.'

'How do you feel about it, Nah?'

'Well, honestly, I didn't like him either. Not that he ever did anything to me, you understand, or that I'd ever consider killing him.'

'Excellent,' said Maryam dryly. 'I'm glad to hear it.'

'You know what I mean,' Minah said, unfazed. 'He was a difficult man to like. Very snooty, and about what, I really don't know. He had some money and used to lord it over everyone. He liked threatening people with the courts. Always telling people who said things he didn't like or did things he didn't like that he'd take them to court and ruin them. Kind of an idiot, that way, *semoga dia tenang disana,* may he rest in peace,' she finished carefully. No need to stir up the dead.

'And you think someone may have wanted to get rid of him?'

'Someone did get rid of him, it's a fact. So, since it was my party, I want to get to the bottom of this. I feel responsible. I mean, it wasn't my fault, but the woman who was killed was there because I hired her husband, so I think in some way I am bearing the sin and I don't want it.'

Maryam nodded and carefully selected one of Rubiah's cakes. She and Rubiah were close cousins and had been together all their lives. While Maryam ran a stall selling Kelantanese fabric in the *pasar besar,* the main market in Kota Bharu, Rubiah had a tiny coffee and cake stand on the second floor of the same market. Though small, it was known throughout Kelantan for the superb quality of the cakes. Rubiah always seemed to have a wide selection on hand even at home and shared them generously. Minah did not let the opportunity to sample them go to waste and picked out her favourites while she told her story in the lively style favoured by the whole family.

'We have to find out who killed Zulkifli so I can get this off my conscience,' she said firmly. 'I want to be practical, although of course, I'm very sorry it happened. But if it hadn't happened around someone I hired I wouldn't be worried about solving it. Well, naturally I wouldn't, but now I have to. You see that, don't you?'

Maryam and Rubiah both nodded. It was true. It was now Minah's responsibility in a roundabout way, and it went without saying she'd want to discharge this responsibility as quickly as she could. They'd help; she was a relative, and they couldn't resist a mystery like this.

'We'll talk to the police,' Maryam assured her cousin. 'Don't worry about it anymore. We'll let you know as soon as we've found something.'

After sharing some more family news, and congratulating each other on new grandchildren and school graduations, Minah rose to take her leave. All three shared a certain family resemblance: they were middle-aged mak cik, older, wiser women who were the backbone of Kelantan society and commerce. All had lovely dark brown eyes, though Rubiah's were hidden behind academic style glasses. Maryam had a snub nose and full lips, while Minah had higher cheekbones and greyer hair than the other two, the reason for this not being of particular importance. But all three held themselves with a sure knowledge of their worth and pride in the job they did, be it their success in business or raising their children.

They said their goodbyes affectionately, promising to see one another soon. As Minah left, Maryam turned to Rubiah. 'And Osman hasn't come to ask us about this! What is he thinking?'

'Maybe he wants to give us a rest,' answered Rubiah. Of the two, she was less enamoured of their detective careers. 'It's a good thing.'

'We're going to get involved anyway,' Maryam pointed out. 'We've got to help Minah.'

'True, but he didn't know that. You know, fatherhood may be making him more independent.'

Maryam rolled her eyes at that. Some chance. But she wanted to be polite about him, for she was really quite fond of him, and so she made a noncommittal noise which could be interpreted as positive. Osman had come to Kelantan several years earlier as a green young policeman who spoke only standard Malay. He was from Perak, on the west coast of Malaysia, an area much more mixed with Chinese, Malays and Indians than Kelantan, which was overwhelmingly Malay. The general opinion of the West Coast on the East was at best doubtful, and Osman had a difficult time at first. Maryam and Rubiah had met him and taken him under their capacious wings, nearly imprisoning him in the process, but they all became close and the women had helped in a variety of cases. They weren't planning on this one, but the call of a relative could not be ignored, and they were prepared to help the police, and Osman in particular, once again.

They went into Kota Bharu in the evening, right after dinnertime so Osman would not think they were anticipating an invitation to eat. They called from outside of Osman's police housing, and were greeted by his wife, Azrina, holding their new baby, Azman.

'Come in,' she cried eagerly, happy to see them and happy to have a chance to show off her baby. They'd seen him before, but he was of an age where every week brought breathtaking changes. He was making noises now, and his eyes were open and alert. Maryam and Rubiah made much of him, fighting to hold him and congratulating his mother on her assiduous attention, while taking care not to attract evil spirits to the child.

'Little babies are best,' Maryam said, holding him close. 'They always smell so good.'

Azrina nodded happily. 'He's sleeping better now, almost through the night now.'

'Is Osman helping you?' Rubiah asked. Azrina was a teacher at Sultanah Zainab High School and had professional responsibilities of her own.

'Oh yes,' she assured them. 'And of course, my sister's come from Perak to help. My mother just left.' She paused for a moment. 'Osman's mother is anxious to come and I'm sure she will,' she advised them, leaving out the 'whether I like it or not'.

Maryam could understand her trepidation, given what she'd heard about Osman's formidable mother. Silently she wished Azrina good luck in avoiding her now that her first grandchild had arrived. It seemed impossible she wouldn't be in Kelantan as a whirlwind of activity, displacing Azrina as the primary caregiver and offering comparisons between Kelantan and Perak in which Kelantan would not come off well, and then offering to bring the baby back to Perak and civilization with her. Azrina had much to anticipate.

They were ushered into the living room with many cries of welcome, ensconced on the couch and provided with coffee, cigarettes and fruit. Osman, previously thin as a rail, appeared more substantial, and it was possible to imagine him as an older man with a good deal more weight on him. Well well, thought Maryam, he's really getting older.

'So good to see you,' Osman said after hellos were said and news exchanged. 'It's been too long.'

'Very busy?' Maryam asked.

'Yes,' Osman replied, intuiting something was coming at him. 'Yes, a lot of new cases.'

'My cousin Minah lives in Tapak Gajah …'

'She's your cousin?' Of course she was. Maryam had relatives all over Kelantan. 'She was sponsoring a dikir barat for her son's circumcision …'

'Yes, I've heard.'

'I guess she called you.'

'She asked us to help out. She feels responsible in some way because she hired the man to perform, and now his wife is dead under what you would call suspicious circumstances. She wants it cleared up so that she doesn't bear the sin.'

'I see,' he nodded.

'If possible,' she said politely, 'we'd like to help you.'

About ten years fell off Osman's age as he spoke to her. He could feel it going and was powerless to stop it. He agreed it would be incredibly helpful if they were to assist the police.

Maryam was pleased at his response and the subtle change in his demeanour. 'We could go to Tapak Gajah and interview the people who were at the market at the time,' she suggested. 'Maybe they'd speak to us more easily, since we aren't official.' She gave him a sweet smile.

'We spoke to most of them already. No one remembers anything,' he said morosely. 'You've never seen so many people who couldn't remember who was standing behind the victim no more than half an hour after it happened. I don't think they'd remember if they were actually at the market except that's where we were standing at the time.'

'They're always like that,' Rubiah sighed. 'No one knows anything at first.'

'But they remember later, right, Mak Cik?' asked Azrina. 'Maybe I can go with you,' she added excitedly. Azrina had her own ambitions to be a detective.

'What about Azman?' Osman interjected, worried. 'You don't want to just leave him.'

'I'm not just leaving him,' she replied. 'My sister's here to watch him. What do you think?'

'My mother wants to come from Ipoh to stay with the baby,' Osman turned to Maryam and Rubiah. 'I think my father will come too.'

Both women remained expressionless. Finally, Rubiah said, 'That would be nice,' ambivalently. 'They've seen him in Perak, haven't they?'

'Oh yes, we were there, of course. But they'd like some more time with him, and with Azrina back at work they thought they could really do a lot for us.'

'Sometimes it's easier if the wife's parents come to stay,' Rubiah offered up as an objective opinion. 'You know, so they get along better.'

'No,' answered Osman heartily. 'My mother and Azrina get along so well, it isn't a problem. It will be nice to have her here, you know, cooking and all of that stuff.'

A glance from Azrina made him try to walk back his statement to little avail. He then turned to Maryam and Rubiah with relief, hoping to save himself with another topic altogether. 'Have you been to Tapak Gajah before?'

'It's a very small place,' Rubiah replied. 'There's really no reason to go there …'

'Unless you have family there,' Maryam gently corrected.

'Of course, for family,' Rubiah continued. 'We may have been there once or twice to see Cik Minah. Not much to see, I'd say.'

'They don't do a lot there,' Maryam continued, 'not like Kampong Penambang. We have *songket* weaving and *batik* and then we're so close to Kota Bharu, so we have the city …'

'And Tapak Gajah is close to Bacok I guess, but it's not a place you'd just visit to see it,' Rubiah concluded.

'Yes,' said Osman.

'We'll have to be going there,' Maryam said resignedly. 'So, they've already told you they don't know anything.' She sighed. She hated when witnesses started with that. 'Someone knows something.'

'We agree,' Osman answered, reaching for his son and placing him on his lap. 'They're all covering for someone, or think they are. Everyone was pretty much standing on top of one another so it's impossible they were all struck blind just at the right moment.'

'I gather no one liked Zulkifli particularly.'

'I didn't find anyone. Even his wife seemed to take it well. I think her attitude was that she wouldn't have harmed him, but if someone else had then that was the end of it. She didn't seem very curious as to who this might be. When I asked her, she said, "What does it matter? He's dead now and it won't change anything. No, I don't care who it was." That's quite a comment from a wife now, isn't it?'

'Remarkable,' Maryam replied. 'Do they have any children?'

'Two grown boys,' Osman said, dangling one of Azman's toys in front of him. The baby tracked each movement and tried to grab for it. 'And a daughter, who's moved away to Tanah Merah, to get as far away from her father as possible, I gather.'

'Do you think his wife killed him?'

'She wasn't even in the market, so no.'

'Maybe she paid someone to do it,' Rubiah said hopefully. 'You know, to get rid of him.'

Osman viewed her doubtfully. 'It doesn't seem likely. I think there were several other people at the market who'd also be glad to have him gone.'

'Did they owe him money?'

Osman shook his head. 'I don't think so. Everyone agrees he was too cheap even to lend money. He liked to hold on to it.'

'Sounds lovely,' Maryam commented. 'Well, we promised Minah so that's that. We'll be going to Bacok tomorrow. Can we have a car?'

Osman was momentarily stricken, but he obeyed immediately once he'd pulled himself together.

Chapter IV

Thinking back, Osman's interviews in Tapak Gajah had not been among his most successful. Amin's demeanour wrung his heart – Amin dreaded the trip back to the house he'd left that very morning with his wife, only to return without her. How would he break it to his children? What would his life be like going forward? He couldn't even think.

Osman could not imagine such devastation happening to him, it seemed such a brutal way to destroy a life. He stood in place absently watching nothing in particular, now reluctant to turn back to the investigation. It all seemed so hopeless.

Rahman had culled a witness from the herd and ushered him over to Osman. 'You've got to talk to him,' he announced when he was close enough not to shout. 'He saw it!'

'What did you see?' Osman asked him. He was a middle-aged man who'd been selling fish, burned dark by the sun and though wiry, seemed extremely strong. He stood shyly next to Rahman.

'Well, I was right behind him …'

'Sit down first and let's start from the beginning.'

'Can we get some coffee?' he asked Rahman as an aside. This could take some time, and there was no reason to be thirsty while answering. Rahman went off to arrange refreshment, and Osman examined his witness.

'Are you a fisherman?'

The man nodded.

'From Tapak Gajah?'

He nodded again. He seemed intimidated by Osman's rank and importance, or perhaps he could not easily understand what Osman was saying. Osman did not speak the local Kelantanese dialect very well. His standard Malay was difficult for some Kelantanese to decipher, and at times like these he depended upon Rahman, a local man, to translate for him. Mercifully, Rahman soon returned and began interpreting.

'Where's he from?' asked the witness when Rahman sat down.

'Perak.'

'Aah,' he said as if it explained a great deal. And now he was ready to tell what he'd seen.

'My name is Awang Suleiman, and I'm from here. I work on one of the boats, and today I was helping sell some of the catch here at the afternoon market.'

'Do you always do that?'

He shook his head. 'We take turns. That way you get to go straight home sometimes. Anyway, today I was selling what we had left, and I was at the end there,' he pointed to his table at the end of the row of several. 'I was listening to the women talk. They were laughing about village stuff, you know, what people did.'

'Do you remember any of it?'

He sat and thought. 'It just didn't seem important,' he prefaced his recital of gossip. 'But let's see, they did mention Pak Ngah, who's just married a younger woman. You know how the older women feel about that. A second wife. It won't last. They were laughing at him, calling him *tua tupai,* an old squirrel chasing young girls. They're really tough when they get started on a guy.'

'I've heard,' said Osman shortly. 'What else?'

'Not too much else that I can remember?'

'Anything about Zulkifli?'

Awang frowned at him. 'Why do you ask?'

'No reason.'

'No, they didn't. But it wouldn't have been likely; generally, people here don't like to talk about him.'

'Why?'

'Just so,' he said, beginning to be uncomfortable. 'He's a rich guy, no one wants to get on his bad side.'

'And how would you do that?'

He was definitely squirming now. 'Just talking about him. He didn't like it. He thought people were criticizing him.' Awang seemed to have remembered that Zulkifli was dead and would no longer be an object of fear, or at least discomfort. 'He could be mean, and you know, he had shares in some of the boats and could make sure you wouldn't get a job on one if he thought you were talking about him.'

'People must have disliked him.'

'Oh, they did. But no one wanted to fight with him either, because you'd lose. You'd be out of a job or someone in your family would, or he'd threaten to take you to court and think of the trouble that would be! And someone like me wouldn't have time or money to get into one of those fights.'

'I gather he's done this before.'

Awang nodded. 'Yes, so we've seen it already. We know what would have happened. But now, of course, everything will be different because he's gone.'

Well, there was an excellent motive. It seemed from what his one witness said it would apply to the whole village. He sighed, thinking of endless interviews.

'And his wife, will she keep up the tradition?'

Awang shook his head. 'She's not so bad. I can't see her spending all day driving people crazy like he did. It's more likely his sons will take over, and they're alright. Things will probably get easier,' he finished cheerfully.

'Did you see anything when the murders happened? Was there anyone you recognized close by?' Osman continued.

Awang turned to Rahman and said in rapid Kelantanese, 'I don't know if I should say. What if I'm wrong? Maybe it would be best to see what happens.'

'See what happens? What does that mean? You have to tell what you've seen. You said you'd seen something. What was it?'

Awang turned and regarded Osman as if deciding whether he should say anything. Apparently, he decided he should, and took a deep breath. 'I think it was Zulkifli who killed the woman.'

'What? Why?' The two policemen were shocked. 'Did he know her?' Osman asked Rahman, who shrugged. 'Amin said they didn't know anyone in town.'

'Why would he kill her?' Osman demanded. Awang, who'd become more relaxed, crawled back into his shell. It was his turn to shrug.

'I'd never seen her before, so I can't say. I don't know anything about it.' He gazed pleadingly towards Rahman to save him. 'That's for the police to find out.' He began to take on a decidedly sullen aspect. 'I'm sorry I ever said anything. Do you see what's happening to me! Now I'm supposed to know why he did it.'

'Not at all,' Rahman soothed him. 'He's just surprised. So am I, come to that. He doesn't really believe you know why.'

'Because I don't,' he said, not cheering up at all.

'How did it happen?' Rahman asked, taking over the questioning.

'He just came up behind her while she was talking and slashed her across the chest. It happened so fast I didn't even move. No one did. I'm not sure all the women talking even noticed it at first, that is if they weren't looking right at her. And then she kind of fell to the ground, all of a heap, and everyone started screaming. Poor girl. What a horrible thing to do.'

'And then what did Zulkifli do?'

'He turned around,' Awang continued. 'Like he had finished what he wanted to do and was going back home. I saw his face, and he was calm. Not angry, not … bloodthirsty. No, just like a man who's finished his job and now wants his dinner. I stopped paying any attention to him and started towards the woman and suddenly Zulkifli fell also. I didn't pay any attention to him, I thought he tripped or something. Though after what I'd just seen, I wouldn't have done anything for him even if I'd known he was dead or going to be very soon. He deserved it. Don't tell me about the law, I know you're going to. But after what he did, I can't say it bothers me much. Me, I wouldn't even hunt for whoever did it.

It isn't worth the time.'

As a policeman, he could not take that view. 'Justice has to be done,' he replied, wondering whether it already had been. He put the thought aside and kept on with his work.

'So, you saw no one near Zulkifli when he fell?'

'I didn't see it. There were quite a few people, the women and all.'

'Was the market that crowded where you were?'

Awang shrugged again. 'Not so much.'

'Just a few women gathered, talking.'

He nodded.

'How many stalls were there? Were they all for fish?'

'All fishermen. Let's see, I think around five? I'm not sure.'

'So then, there are five stalls lined up, and then a few women selling vegetables, right? How many shoppers would you say?'

'I don't know. A lot of people buy the fish for their dinner each evening. You know, it's so fresh if you can buy it just when the boats come in.'

'So, there were a lot of shoppers?'

Awang suspected where this was going and refused to be brought along. 'I don't know,' he repeated. 'I wasn't paying attention.'

'Ok, so, you're at your stand. Were you serving anyone?'

'When?'

'When you saw Zulkifli.'

Awang relaxed again and eyed Rahman's shirt pocket and the cigarettes therein. Rahman dutifully produced them and lit one up for each of them. Awang sat on the wooden bench and took a deep drag. 'I'm selling my fish,' he began, starting to enjoy the story, 'and like I said, there were a few women over at the end there and they're talking about stuff in the village. And then, I see Zulkifli walk up. Not hurrying, not anxious, just walking regularly, and he pulls out a parang and slashes her. Like it was nothing! She falls, and suddenly he falls, but I have to admit I didn't care about him. I still don't,' he added.

'I ran over after I realized what happened and everyone in the market did the same. I think some people stepped over his body to get to hers. No one paid it any attention for a good few minutes.

'And you saw no one near Zulkifli when he fell?'

'I wasn't paying any attention.'

Rahman nodded. He had a feeling no one in the market had been paying attention and if they were, they wouldn't say. The fishermen were the most likely to have seen the killer if anyone had, so he dismissed Awang with a promise to question him again and called over another one of the fishmongers.

Their next possible witness was a tall, lanky young man, probably new to the crew, who came to them and sat down with absolutely no expression on his face. Rahman tried to put him at ease by offering a cigarette, which he gladly accepted but appeared no happier afterward.

Osman cleared his throat and started the questioning, hoping this boy would understand him. They used Standard Malay in schools, didn't they? Osman thought his Kelantanese had improved tremendously, but sometimes still felt awkward conducting interrogations in it. The boy eyed him warily.

Osman introduced himself and Rahman, which seemed to

leave their witness completely unimpressed. When prodded to introduce himself, he began his story, haltingly, watching Osman to see if he understood and mutely appealing to Rahman when he was sure he didn't.

'My name is Dollah bin Awang,' he began, as Osman sighed at the sheer number of Awangs, father and son, he found in Kelantan. 'I just started working on a boat. I'm the most junior, you know, so I get stuck with selling the rest of the catch in the afternoon.' He was resigned to his job for the foreseeable future. 'I was just selling fish this afternoon like always, and I saw there was a group of women talking, in front of the vegetables. They were laughing, but I wasn't listening to what they were talking about. Probably men. They're usually making fun of men when they start laughing like that.' He seemed resigned to that, too. 'Then, all of a sudden there was a scuffle, sort of, people were suddenly moving, and I saw one of the women, the one who wasn't from here, fall to the ground. Then Zulkifli fell also.' He appeared satisfied with his recital and applied his attention to his cigarette.

'Was Zukifli there the whole time?' Osman asked.

He shook his head. 'I don't think so. No. It was just the women.'

'When did he show up?'

Dollah thought for a moment, trying to picture the scene in his mind. 'I don't know. It seems to me the first time I saw him was when he fell.'

'So, he had just shown up at the market?'

Dollah nodded and exhaled. 'I don't remember seeing him walk into the market. It's kind of a small one, anyway, just fish and vegetables, though people from Tapak Gajah like to come there to get really fresh fish.'

'Did you notice Zulkifli talking to the woman?'

'No, I wasn't really watching them. Watching any of them, I mean.'

'What were you watching?'

'Nothing.'

'Nothing?'

'Just inspecting the fish, you know. I wasn't really interested in anything going on there.'

What a witness, Osman thought to himself. He suspected most of them would claim the same complete inattention to everything taking place not five feet away from them.

'But you noticed Zulkifli falling.'

'Yes.'

'Who was near him when he fell?'

Dollah sat and thought, 'I don't know.' Osman almost awaiting it. 'Maybe it was Che Ali. I remember he was there. Whether he was right behind Zulkifli I can't say, but he was nearby.'

'And a moment earlier, was Zulkifli behind the woman?'

He screwed up his face in a pantomime of thought. Osman braced himself for the inevitable answer. 'I don't know.'

'Thank you,' Osman told him. 'Please give Che Rahman your address, we may need to call you again.'

Dollah nodded and loped away, relief obvious in his every move.

'Let's get this Ali here and see what he says.'

Ali was a middle-aged man who'd been shopping at the market. He was a carpenter from Tapak Gajah and shopped at the afternoon market most days to get food for dinner. He was an established householder with a wife and children, two of whom were already married with children. He was not at all intimidated by the police.

He sat down on the bench and offered cigarettes all around. 'Do you think we might be able to get some coffee?' he asked Rahman, and not waiting for an answer, he waved over a young boy hovering on the edge of the crowed and sent him for coffee. It appeared moments later, served by the man who ran the shop and was happy for any excuse to hear the details of what had transpired.

'What a shock!' Ali said ruefully, shaking his head at the pity of it all. He took a sip of his coffee and seemed to feel better. 'That poor woman. I'm so sorry for her.'

Osman, too, was drinking his coffee and wondering why he hadn't thought of ordering it. Too busy to get any more, he guessed. 'Not sorry for Zulkifli?' he asked.

Ali smiled and shook his head. 'Not really, to be frank. He wasn't such a nice person. In fact, to tell the truth, I think this whole kampong will be happier without him. Should I not say things like this? Maybe not,' he answered his own question. 'But you'll soon find it out so it might as well be said. He spent his time making people unhappy, or at least uncomfortable. Anything that was said about him, and I mean just about anything, would make him threaten to sue, or fire, or harm them somehow. That type of man. Very unpleasant. Unloved. I doubt his own wife is that broken up about it. Well, she may have preferred he died in some less public way, but the fact that he's gone isn't going to cause her much pain. I don't think so, anyway,' he qualified, but didn't seem as though he believed it needed it.

'Really,' Osman commented.

'Yes. Well, there's always one in any kampong, isn't there? Someone who puts himself over everyone else. Well, that was Zulkifli. And mean, though I know you shouldn't say anything ill of the dead. In that case I shall be quiet.' He smiled again.

'Was there anyone he was particularly mean to?'

'Just about everyone, at one time or another. Maybe not too seriously, but enough to embarrass them. Take me, for instance. Do you know what he did to me?'

Osman shook his head.

'Well,' Ali began, 'he accused me of stealing from him. Stealing what, you ask? Some coconuts from his coconut plantation. What does he think I am? A ten-year-old kid on a dare? Did he think I was climbing up trees to pick some coconuts when they're cheap enough in the market, and,' he paused for dramatic effect, 'I have my own coconut trees. Why in heaven's name would I pilfer his?

'But he embarrassed me so much with his accusations. *Kurang kurang bubur, lebih lebih sudu:* the less broth, the more spoons. Such a small matter to make such a fuss over, though of course it was no matter at all since I had nothing to do with his damned coconuts. But he talked about it endlessly and even threatened to go to the police! I ask you: have you ever heard of anything so stupid?' He shook his head, remembering. 'But he used it to humiliate me, and that's what got me. That's the kind of man he was.'

He lit another cigarette from the butt of the first and blew the smoke out in a philosophical way. 'You know what they say: *Biar puteh tulang, jangan puteh mata*: better white bones than white eyes, better death than humiliation. Someone must have taken that to heart when it came to Zulkifli. Someone he'd been torturing, I guess.'

'Any guesses as to who that might be?'

'Could be anyone. There's no one he wouldn't treat badly.'

'But has he taken on anyone in particular lately?' Osman knew Ali knew exactly what he meant but wasn't going to provide a name if he could help it. 'How long ago did he accuse you of stealing?'

'Me?' answered Ali in a tone of injured dignity. 'That was a while ago.'

'And since then?' Osman was losing patience quickly.

'Well, I'm not sure …'

'Listen, Che Ali,' Osman began. Rahman noted the signs of Osman's temper rising and was poised to intercept it if necessary. 'I'm asking you nicely who he's been attacking. Either you can answer me nicely here, or we can go to the police station in Kota Bharu for a longer chat. Tell me which you'd prefer.'

Ali was nervous for the first time, as though he hadn't realized Osman was the police chief and could demand cooperation instead of requesting it. 'Well,' he cleared his throat. 'I have to think.'

'Go ahead,' Osman invited him, and walked over to confer with Rahman. 'This Zulkifli probably attacked the whole village at one time or another. People who do that usually do it to everyone. It's a bad habit.'

Rahman nodded. 'I believe our witness will come up with several more names. I doubt he wants to be the only one as a noted victim. Where was he anyway, behind Zulkifli?' He walked back to Ali, who was deep in thought.

'Were you behind Zulkifli in the market? Did you see him?'

'I don't actually recall,' he said. 'I was buying fish, of course. Was he there? He could have been, but I don't know that I took any notice of him.'

'Did you notice when he fell?'

'Yes, of course,' he answered, remembering the scene, and no doubt, calculating the possibilities. 'I think I was looking to the side to see him.'

'Who was behind him?'

'I'm not sure. I was watching at Zulkifli, not behind him.'

'Sometimes,' Rahman offered, 'if you try to remember what happened you find you notice what you didn't think you did.' He stood patiently next to Ali as if to encourage him to reach back in his memory to see what could be uncovered.

Ali was clearly trying. 'It's hard,' he admitted. 'I can picture him falling …'

'The market wasn't that crowded, was it?'

'No,' he said thoughtfully. 'Not so many people.'

'And you were in front of the stand …'

Ali nodded. 'I was.'

'Who was in front of you?'

'The shopkeeper.'

'Right!' Rahman congratulated him. 'And Zulkifli to your

side, you said?'

Ali nodded. 'Now, turn around in your mind and peek at the back of Zulkifli, who do you see?'

Ali closed his eyes to indicate thought. 'Yusuf,' he said triumphantly. 'Yes, Yusuf was shopping, and he was behind him.'

And that's as far as the Kota Bharu Police Department had gotten.

Chapter V

Just as Minah had dressed for her visit to Kampong Penambang, her cousins dressed for theirs to Tapak Gajah. They sailed into the village the next day in their air-conditioned police car, with Maryam's son-in-law Rahman at the wheel, and exited the car in a blaze of high-quality batik and heavy gold jewellery. It was imperative they be taken seriously, as women of worth, and one of the best ways to signal that status was a display of well-crafted gold.

They stopped at Minah's house first, to get their bearings and as much background as possible. Rahman came in with them, and Minah fussed over him, asking about his wife Aliza and tempting him with a variety of sweets. As if he hadn't been stuffed full of some of Kelantan's best cakes before he left, thought Rubiah, and then corrected herself. That was not a good way to start off the investigation. Surely Minah's impressive spread of cakes was a sign of her respect and affection, not one-upmanship with Rubiah's cakes. Which were no doubt better anyway.

Minah gave them the details as she understood them. Amin's wife was standing with a group of women where there were a few vegetable sellers. Apparently, it was a lively discussion punctuated by a good deal of laughter, though even those who participated in it could not remember the details of what was said, save that Zulkifli was never mentioned. There were a few shoppers seeking fresh fish, mostly men. Zulkifli was seen wandering into the market, and no one acknowledged taking any notice of him. Suddenly, with no warning, Amin's wife fell, slashed with a parang wielded by Zulkifli. Before people realized what had happened, Zulkifli himself fell right next to her, strangled. Everyone jumped back at that point, having seen absolutely nothing, not even who might have been standing behind, or at least next to, the murdered man.

'That's what you know?' asked Rubiah. It seemed so unlikely.

'That's all anyone's admitting to,' Minah replied. 'Someone must have seen something. And still there's no explanation about why the woman was killed. She's not even from here.'

'No one knew her?'

Minah shook her head. 'No, everyone agrees she'd never been here before. Even her husband says so.'

'Strange,' said Maryam. 'We need a motive for her death, and a murderer for his. It seems, from what I've heard, there are plenty of motives around for killing him.

'There certainly are. He was not well liked.'

'Anyone in the market could have done it – the men, that is. I don't see one of the women strangling him. Was he tall?'

'Pretty average,' Minah said. 'But taller than most women.'

Maryam nodded. 'Anyone you particularly think we ought to talk to?'

Minah thought for a moment. 'Maybe you can start with Che Ali. He already spoke to the police, but I don't think they got too much out of him. Everyone was very vague when speaking to the police, you know. I hope they'll remember a little more when they talk to you, given that you're doing it for me. You never know, though,' she reflected. 'Sometimes, people don't remember anything.'

'You mean they don't say anything. They remember well enough,' Rubiah commented.

'True,' Maryam agreed, rising. 'We should start right away, Nah. We want to get this taken care of as soon as possible. By the way, when is Johari's circumcision?'

'It was supposed to be this weekend, but now we've put it off. It didn't seem right to go ahead with it when people have been killed. We've got to wait.'

'You're right. It would been the wrong thing to do,' Maryam continued. 'Point us the way to this Ali's house, and we'll get started.'

***

Minah took them out on the porch and pointed to a large house not too far away. It could be seen from Minah's porch, though there were several fruit trees which screened part of it. They walked down the well-worn dirt path to the house, which was surrounded by an immaculate yard bordered by bright flowers in large dragon pots. A teen-aged boy was sitting on the steps with two friends, a tray of cold drinks next to them. Maryam called out to them, wishing them a good morning and asking if it were Ali's house.

One of the boys rose immediately and politely asked her name, then went up the steps into the house and emerged with a man obviously his father, who came down to meet her.

'Hello, *Kakak*,' he greeted her. 'Welcome.' He folded his hands in front of him and waited for her to tell him why she was there.

'I have come on behalf of my cousin Cik Minah,' Maryam began. 'Cik Rubiah and I are here assisting the police in their inquiries about the two deaths in the marketplace. Cik Minah has specifically asked for our help in solving this crime.'

'Aah,' he said. 'A good thing. This will hang over the village until it's taken care of. Come in, come in,' he urged them, ushering them into the house and scattering the boys on the stairs. He offered them seats on the living room set, and briefly called into the kitchen to ensure snacks would be arriving. Rahman blended quietly into the background, letting Maryam and Rubiah take the lead.

'Well,' Ali began jovially. 'How can I help you?'

'Perhaps you could tell us what happened in the market that afternoon,' Maryam said amiably.

Ali eyed Rahman, clearly recognizing him from his first interrogation. 'You were here already,' he stated. 'I remember you.'

'I was,' Rahman agreed. 'I'm here now with Mak Cik Maryam and Mak Cik Rubiah who are helping us.'

'Letting them take the lead,' Ali said somewhat snidely.

'Officer Rahman has very kindly offered to come with us to give us help and protection,' Maryam interjected smoothly. Rubiah was quite unprepared to hear her give credit elsewhere, especially to imply that Rahman was helping them. She'd really mellowed, Rubiah reflected. She couldn't imagine Maryam making this kind of comment even a few years earlier.

Having set him straight on that matter, Maryam continued. 'As I was saying, could you tell us what happened in the market that afternoon?'

Ali leaned back, preparing to hold forth on what he knew. He began with why he had gone to the market, the kind of fish he'd been hoping to find, though he had been sadly disappointed, and what kind of fish he'd had to substitute. He then explained how he planned to have it cooked for dinner. Maryam believed he was trying to bore them to tears before saying anything of interest, hoping they would no longer be able to pay attention after he droned on about the relative merits of grilled fish versus curried fish and what kind of vegetables he favoured for the latter. Rubiah wondered when she'd been quite so bored and could not remember. Luckily, coffee and cigarettes were presented, no doubt to help them stay awake in the face of this onslaught of irrelevant data. She downed one cup almost immediately and was ready for another; she feared falling asleep on the sofa to be spared his whole testimony, which so far promised to tell them absolutely nothing.

Maryam burst in, unable to control herself any longer. 'Che Ali,' she implored. 'Could we please get to the part right before you saw the woman fall to the ground? We're very interested in what happened at that time.'

He seemed affronted, as if he had so much more to say on

the cooking of fish and choosing the freshest one. With a regretful sigh, he fast forwarded to the time when he noticed Amin's wife falling to the ground. 'I was choosing my dinner, really not paying attention to anything around me, and I noticed that a woman had fallen, and Zulkifli was standing behind her. He'd slashed her with his parang, and she was bleeding very badly. Then, immediately after that, Zulkifli fell as well.'

'Did you see who might have been behind him?' Maryam asked, with the same hope the police had had when they asked the same question.

He moved his eyes over to Rahman, and answered, 'As I told the police, I think Yusuf was there. I can't be completely sure, but I think so.'

'Who is Yusuf?' Maryam asked.

'Yusuf lives here and works at a lot of things. Sometimes a carpenter, the family has some rice land, some coconut land but really, not much. All these together don't make much of a living for a grown man, I'm afraid.'

'He's a carpenter at least sometimes – has he ever worked for you?'

Ali considered this question, as if the answer would be a matter of opinion rather than fact. 'Indeed, he has, as a helper. Occasionally.'

'Was he competent?' asked Rubiah, suspecting he was not.

Ali was pained. 'You know, I think he may have talent, but he doesn't pay attention long enough to really be good. He's old enough to be a carpenter on his own, you know. Must be twenty-five or so. When I was that age, I was working for myself, and was married, with a child. Yusuf is still a child himself, living at home with his parents, doing odd jobs here and there. He hasn't grown up yet, and I'm not sure he ever will. He's happy being a kid and having no responsibilities.' It was clear Ali had no respect for this kind of life, but neither would any Malay adult. There was a time for childhood to end and adult obligations to be assumed. 'I told him as much,' Ali continued. 'I don't think he liked hearing it, but maybe it was good for him.'

'Did he say anything when you told him that?'

'He just sat through it, like he must have sat through his parents giving him the same lecture. Didn't say much of anything but he wasn't very happy either.'

'Would he have anything against Zulkifli?'

'I don't really know. I don't know they had much to do with each other, they're a whole different generation. Zulkifli's closer to my age – we weren't far apart in school. Yusuf is about the age of my son, so I can't see them being friends.'

'Did he ever work for Zulkifli?'

'He might have. Zulkifli has a lot of different things going on. He owns some businesses; Yusuf might have worked in one.'

'It seems like in a village of this size everyone would know where everyone else worked,' Rahman interjected. 'I could tell you that about everyone in my own kampong, which is a bit larger than this.' He sat quietly, waiting for the answer.

'I suppose you're right: maybe I just don't want to get too involved.'

'You are already,' said Rubiah, trying to hide her impatience. 'Everyone here is involved. You've had two people die at once in your market. You can't pretend to ignore that.'

Ali was glum, as clearly that had been his preferred course of action. 'You're right of course. I can't do that.'

'Although you'd want to. So would anyone.'

Ali cheered up slightly, since someone else echoed what he himself had been thinking.

'But, we can't. And I think it would be best if you were to really cooperate, telling us all you know, so this can be solved and life return to normal.' Maryam regarded him sternly, waiting for his reaction.

'Yes, I see that.' He still wasn't happy. 'Yusuf worked for Zulkifli. He has a small keropok factory in town, you must have seen it. It's the only one here. A lot of people in the kampong have had jobs there – part time jobs mostly, they don't pay very well and therefore people come and go. They work for a little while and then get something else: they get onto a boat crew and go fishing, or do some carpentry, make batik. A little of this and a little of that, like many kampong people. *Barang dimana ditiup angin, disanalah dia condong:* like a tree which leans whichever way the wind blows. They have to be ready to do any kind of job, right?'

'Did he and Zulkifli get on? Or were they fighting with each other?' Rubiah ignored his homily on kampong employment to get back to the matter at hand, which she felt he was doing a good deal to avoid, and she was curious why.

'Well,' he hesitated. 'I don't think Zulkifli had a lot of respect for him. He was a hardworking man himself, say what you will about him. And I think he thought Yusuf didn't take his work seriously enough ...'

'How do you know this? Did Zulkifli tell you that's what he thought?'

'Not in so many words.'

'Did you speak to him often?' Maryam pursued. 'Were you good friends?'

'Well, not so much good friends ...'

'Then what?' Maryam leaned forward to catch the answer.

'It's just, well, I just ...' he sputtered, not wanting to give a straight answer, though Maryam wondered what would be so incriminating about admitting you were a friend of Zulkifli's. After all, they grew up and continued to live in that village, they went to school together – what could be more natural? Yet Ali was choking on the actual words, so reluctant was he to say them. She almost felt sorry for him, but not quite.

'What's the problem, Che Ali,' Rubiah continued, clearly following Maryam's train of thought. 'Why don't you want to admit you were friends?'

'We weren't really, you know. Yes, naturally we knew each other, as you say we both grew up here, but we were never close.'

'But he did tell you how he felt about Yusuf.'

'He may have mentioned something.' Ali was willing himself to stay calm.

'And that was ... ?' Rahman prompted him.

'He didn't like him. He thought he was useless and immature. Not an adult. As if everyone else hadn't come to that conclusion.' Now that he'd started talking, it was all coming out as fast as he could say it. 'He came to see me about it, as if I were Yusuf's father. Go talk to his family! I told him, why are you coming to me? As though I could give Yusuf the lecture he needed. That's for his parents to do, isn't it?

'Giving him a job, Zulkifli told me, is a complete waste of time. *Intan dikalongkan ke leher anjing:* putting a diamond collar on a dog. I agree, I made the same mistake. So why come and tell me?' Ali seemed much calmer now that he'd said it, though Rahman thought it was odd he seemed so angered by it. It didn't seem that important, but clearly, Ali had some connection to Yusuf which made him rather touchy.

'And did he go to talk to Yusuf's parents?' asked Maryam.

Now Ali shrugged, perfectly at ease. 'I really don't know,' he admitted. 'I never asked. It's nothing to me, you see.'

Maryam rose. 'Thank you for your help, Abang Ali,' she said politely. 'I believe we'll be going to Yusuf's house now, it seems he's the next important witness for us.'

Ali seemed both relieved for them to go and a bit put out that anyone else would be considered an important witness. They left it to him to work out his conflicts and went to see Yusuf's parents, who lived not far away, though to be fair, nothing in Tapak Gajah was that far away.

Chapter VI

Yusuf's house was a world away from Ali's comfortable gentility. It was a large, rambling house with several grandchildren in the front yard, playing games and raising a cloud of dust. Laundry hung along the sides of the house, some fishing nets lay on the porch awaiting repairs, and voices issued from inside the house discussing an upcoming dinner, a misplaced paring knife, the reason the nets were not yet completed and appeals to see what the kids were doing. A lot going on, but it seemed friendly and high-spirited.

Maryam, Rubiah and Rahman stood at the bottom of the stairs, while a crowd of children gathered watching them and jostling for a good viewing position. They giggled among themselves and were particularly interested in Rahman's uniform. An older man came outside; Maryam assumed it was Yusuf's father, who ushered them up the stairs and provided seats on the porch and the promise of cold drinks. Rahman turned and made faces at the children below, sending them into gales of laughter. They were shooed away when their grandfather returned so there could be adult conversation without a peanut gallery observing.

He introduced himself as Hussein, Yusuf's father. He sat down easily and waved his hand over a collection of cold soft drinks, urging his guests to drink. He seemed pleasant, yet underneath he seemed tense, and Maryam noted that only he came to the 'meeting', not Yusuf.

'You're here about Zulkifli,' Hussein opened the discussion, getting right to the point. 'I heard you were here to see Ali.'

'That was fast,' Maryam said. It was out before she could grab it back. She didn't feel it was polite to say it, but Hussein seemed unfazed.

'The kampong grapevine,' he smiled. 'I probably heard it before you even got up the stairs.'

'It's the same everywhere,' Rubiah agreed.

'But you're here to talk about Zulkifli,' he circled right back to what he assumed was the topic at hand.

'Well, actually, to talk about Yusuf.'

Hussein sat silently.

'I understand Yusuf worked for Zulkifli,' said Rubiah carefully. 'And for Ali.'

His father grunted and lit a cigarette, offering one to the assembled group.

'So, he did, didn't he?' Maryam asked again, clearing her throat.

'He did,' Hussein answered shortly.

'Was it ... successful?' she asked.

'Successful? What do you mean?'

'Did it go well? Were they both happy with his work? Does he have a good relationship with them?'

'He didn't get fired, if that's what you're asking,' Hussein said. 'He still works for them. For Ali, I mean, he can't work for Zul. Anyway, if your question is whether he was a good worker they wanted to keep and would he likely make a go of either profession, the answer is probably not. It's my own son, you know, and I don't like saying this about him, but I don't think either man was pleased with him. He doesn't tend to be diligent, I would say. He works, but he doesn't put all his energy into it. Perhaps it's our fault. He's the youngest and he's a bit spoiled. We made things easy for him, and he hasn't grown up yet. Not married, though we've tried. We thought a wife would make him settle down and take some responsibility. But the possible wives want to see him grow up before they marry him, and they don't see that. The parents we spoke to were of course polite, but nothing came of it.' He sounded sad.

'How will he become a man if he doesn't take on a man's work? It's a little here and there: carpentry, sawmill, fishing crew. Choose one, I told him, and do it well. You're no child anymore, living with your parents, unmarried at your age. My wife defends him, and says he needs time, but he's had all the time he needs. This is it! Look at his brothers and sisters,' he waved a hand towards the troop of children standing around the stairs watching the visitors. 'They've got children of their own, and work of their own, and houses of their own.' He gave his cigarette a disgusted glare. 'My grandchildren will get married before Yusuf does.'

'Did he ever argue with Zulkifli?'

'Everyone who deals with Zulkifli argues with him. He can

argue over nothing. He likes it,' Hussein affirmed. 'Not like other people. He wants for an argument, he digs for it.' He shook his head. This was not the Malay way, which counselled easy social relations and a minimum of overt quarrelling. People would go so far as to actually agree with one another publicly just to avoid a scene, with no intention of carrying out what was ostensibly concluded. Politeness and an avoidance of embarrassment was a hallmark of kampong culture, and to actively seek out discord was not only rare, it was close to unbearable.

'He must have been difficult,' Maryam said diplomatically.

'Impossible,' Hussein corrected her. 'Think of the problems he made here in Tapak Gajah, starting fights with people.' He shook his head unhappily. 'And Yusuf would just lose his temper. I could hardly blame him, dealing with Zulkifli, but still, if you need the job, you have to guard your tongue, isn't it?'

He studied them for confirmation, and they nodded. It was the unfortunate truth about working for other people: you were forced to put up with their vagaries and even their rudeness. Maryam and Rubiah reflected how much easier it was to work for oneself. Maryam didn't think she could ever have a boss. She was born to be one, not to cope with one. She brought her attention back to Hussein, who was still deep in his interpretation of Zulkifli's personality, which was not shown to best advantage.

'You can ask anyone here, and they've had some problem with him. Could be a small one, that really doesn't matter too much, or a business issue with some money involved. But everyone's had something. How his wife bore it, I will never know. Maybe she paid him no attention, but he could be loud, and tough to ignore.'

'You didn't like him, either,' Rubiah added.

'Of course not. How could you like him?'

'How did he make his money?' Rahman sought to rescue the conversation from psychological analysis to a motive for murder, though he realized one might easily lead to the other. Nevertheless, he thought he understood the depth of Hussein's distaste for Zulkifli, and it was time to move on.

Hussein lit another cigarette and finished his drink. A grandchild had clearly been sent out to bring home cakes and they had been duly plated and put out for the guests. Rubiah thought they were of surprising high quality and designed to eat a few. Maryam followed suit.

'He got some of his money from his father, who owned a fishing boat. Probably he got it from his father. You know how these things go. And his sons will get the factory and whatever else he's got and won't have put themselves out at all for it.'

'How many children does he have?'

'Three. Two sons and a daughter. The daughter's moved away with her husband to Tanah Merah. Both the sons are here. They work together, but let's see how long that lasts now that they both can inherit. They're a contentious family, all of them.'

'Is Yusuf at home?' Maryam asked.

Hussein nodded glumly. 'Yes, he is. I'll get him.'

He turned around and shouted through the opened door for someone to get Yusuf. A few moments later, the man himself appeared at the door, his hair still wet from washing, a clean sarong and a button-down shirt over it. He appeared exceptionally neat.

Maryam wasn't sure what she envisaged: a weedy man-boy with a torn t-shirt and a wary expression, or a sullen teenager who'd just woken up, but Yusuf was none of those things. He was a well-built man with excellent manners and an air of confidence. Hussein was a handsome older man, with, Maryam noted, excellent bone structure, and Yusuf resembled him, with large, bright eyes and high cheekbones. His hair was combed back, and his clothes were spotless, and he wore a welcoming smile.

He greeted them, and his father, and sat down, whereupon a nephew immediately placed a coffee cup in front of him. He absolutely did not have the air of a profligate, unemployed slacker. Maryam did not know where to begin, but Yusuf helped her.

'I hear you are helping the police, Mak Cik,' he began. 'You must be asking about Zulkifli's death, aren't you? That's what I heard from the kids, anyway.' He smiled again. 'Please ask me whatever you need to.'

He leaned back and took a cigarette from the tray on the floor where they sat, with an appropriately attentive expression as he awaited questions. Rahman began.

'You were in the market that afternoon, then.'

Yusuf nodded. 'Buying fish for dinner. It's right off the boats.'

'Were you near Zulkifli?'

'You've seen the market. It's quite small – anyone who was there was near anyone else.'

'Let me be frank, Che Yusuf. I mean, were you right behind him? Someone killed him, strangled him, as I'm sure you've heard.

And that person would of course have to be right up against him.'

'I was next to him, yes. Let me think. It wasn't really crowded but then again, everyone is up against the tables, so it's all bunched up. If you're asking if I was close enough to strangle him,' he lifted his eyebrows at Rahman, clarifying if that was indeed the question, 'then probably yes. Did I strangle him? No. Why would I? I saw the woman fall and at first couldn't really figure out what happened. I certainly didn't think she was dead! Then I saw the blood, and I just stood there, shocked. The next thing I know Zulkifli falls down next to me. Dead also. I turned and got out of the way as fast as I could. I'd never seen anything like that, people getting killed in front of you and behind you. I never want to again!'

'How well did you know Zulkifli?' Rahman asked.

Yusuf shrugged noncommittally. 'I know him. I grew up in this village and he's always been a fixture here. And, as I'm sure you know, I've worked for him in the keropok factory.'

'How was that?'

Yusuf made a face. 'I didn't like it. It isn't a big factory, but it's very noisy and he was always pushing people to work faster. With all the machines and equipment, I was afraid someone would get hurt.' He thought for a moment. 'Lots of sharp blades and very slippery. It's a dangerous place.'

'Where else have you worked?

'On a fishing boat. Doing some carpentry. I've worked all around really.'

'How did you like fishing?'

'It was alright.' Yusuf did not seem particularly interested. 'It's very hard work, you know. Pulling nets and carrying in the catch. You have to get up early and sometimes you don't get home till late, till after the catch is sold. And you're out in all kinds of weather, so it can be fierce. The ocean can get rough around here.

'We usually pulled into Pulau Perhentian on the way back. Those islands, you know, off the coast, near Terengganu. That was nice. They're very pretty.'

An odd comment, Maryam thought. Most fishermen were concerned with their catch and how much they'd earned, not whether the islands they stopped at to keep their nets free and pack up the fish were picturesque. It was a strange perspective he had, and the way he spoke it was clear neither of the jobs he described were much to his liking.

'Did you work with Ali when you were a carpenter?'

He nodded. 'Yes, I worked with him.'

'How did you like it?' Maryam prodded.

'I didn't really. Ali can be very difficult, I found. Always criticizing, always asking me to work faster. You know, you can easily injure yourself with those tools; you've got to be careful,' he said earnestly. 'I tried to keep a sharp eye on them all the time. I didn't want to cut myself, and it would be easy to do. Especially,' he said in a wounded tone, 'if someone is rushing you the whole time.' He fell silent for a moment. 'I'm still working there sometimes, when Ali needs help. But I won't be rushed, you know. If I get injured, Ali isn't going to help me. I've got to be careful.'

Maryam began to see why his father was so fed up with him.

Memanjat pokok cekur, boleh jatoh mati: even climbing a cekur (a creeping vine), one can fall to one's death. He saw danger everywhere when work was involved. Maryam could read his father's face as he heard this recitation of the jobs he'd had, and in each one lay dangers no one else could see.

'What are you doing now?' Rubiah asked.

'Well, I'm in the market for something now. Something interesting; I don't know what yet.'

'How do all these other men manage it?' his father asked, trying to keep calm. 'All these fishermen, all the men who work in the factory. Tell me, how do they manage to stay alive?' This was clearly a familiar discussion between them.

'I really can't say,' Yusuf said, stung. 'A lot of them do get hurt, you know. Or lost at sea, for instance. You hear about it all the time.'

'You do not!' his father said between his gritted teeth. 'You see men working on the ships every day for years, and nothing happens to them.'

Yusuf said nothing, but began sulking, which Maryam gathered was the way this conversation usually ended up. Anyway, she was here to find out about Zulkifli's death, not about Yusuf's aversion to work.

'So, when you noticed Zulkifli fall next to you, who was there, nearby?'

Yusuf made a show of pulling himself out of his mood and coming back to assist the police. 'Well, there was me. There was Ali. There were the people selling – they were nearby but they couldn't have gotten to anyone because the tables were in the way.' He surveyed the sky to imagine the scene again. 'I just can't picture who was next to Zulkifli. Or behind him.' He sighed. 'I wish I'd been paying better attention,' he said plaintively. 'But how was I to know it would be important?'

'Yes, indeed,' said Rubiah. 'We never know in advance, that's the problem.'

He considered her to see if she was mocking him, but he couldn't really be sure, so decided to ignore it. 'There was a woman selling vegetables, though I don't think she was actually behind him. She was sitting behind her vegetables,' he explained. 'But she might remember. It's Mak Cik Khadijah. Maybe she'll remember more,' he added hopefully.

She could hardly remember less, Rubiah thought to herself. Perhaps a woman was at least paying attention, though it seemed a long shot. Nevertheless, after ascertaining where to find her, they rose to leave.

'I hope you find whoever did it,' Yusuf said sincerely, gazing into their eyes. 'Whoever did it should be brought to justice.' His father longed to slap him but didn't dare do it in front of all of them.

With pleasant smiles and many expressions of thanks they walked down the stairs and waded through the thicket of children at the bottom. As they walked through the kampong, Rubiah asked, 'Did you see his father's face? I had to feel sorry for him.'

Maryam nodded. 'I know. That man will never hold a job. And he seems like such an upstanding person.'

'Until he starts talking.'

'Do you think he might have done it?' Rahman asked.

'Of course,' Maryam answered. 'But strangling someone like that, it could be treacherous. You could strain your wrist. We ought to ask Zulkifli's wife about that.'

Chapter VII

Zulkifli's wife was serene. There was no outward show of any emotion approaching happiness, but there was a bit of relief. She greeted them without any emotion at all, introduced herself as Halimah, then sat them down on the sofa and let her daughter-in-law accept their condolences and serve them yet more coffee and more cakes.

She lit a cigarette and offered them to Maryam and Rubiah. Rahman declined and smoked his own. They sat in silence for a few moments after the daughter-in-law retired to the kitchen.

'My daughter-in-law,' she explained unnecessarily. 'Razaleigh's wife.'

They nodded, 'You have two sons, don't you?'

Halimah agreed she did. 'Johan is the younger one. He isn't married yet. He lives here or stays with his brother.' She was then content to smoke her cigarette in silence.

Maryam reflected there was an epidemic of young men of marriageable age who remained single in Tapak Gajah. For such a small place it was surprising to hear of two of them in one afternoon.

'We are here helping the police to find out who ...'

'Killed,' she suggested, helpfully.

'Yes, your husband.'

'Yes, I heard about you. You're detectives.'

'Yes.'

'He was strangled, wasn't he?'

'That's what I've heard.'

'Right there in the market in front of everyone.'

'Yes.'

'But no one saw it.'

'No one's come forward to say they saw anything. It's very perplexing.'

'Maybe not. He wasn't very popular, you know. A very argumentative man. Picked fights with everyone.'

'But not with you.'

'Not anymore,' she said with a straight face. 'I've been married a long time and I've lost my taste for his arguments years ago. He may as well have argued with the hens outside as with me. I couldn't even hear him speak.'

Maryam didn't quite know what to say to that. 'But after all, you've been married …'

'A while,' she interrupted. 'And if you're going to ask me how I put up with it, I paid no attention to him whatsoever. I put the food on the table and if he wanted to eat, he did, and if not, I took it off the table and gave it to the goats. I never asked him why he didn't eat it or if he liked his dinner. I did the laundry, after all, you can't leave dirty clothes around. I threw his clothes on his bed and if he wanted to fold them, he could. If not, he didn't.

'You're wondering why we didn't divorce, aren't you? It's

simple. I didn't know where to go. As for why he didn't ask for a divorce, I don't know. If I were in his position, I certainly would have. But there's no understanding people. Maybe he liked having someone he couldn't fight with. Heaven knows he fought with everyone else.

'He wasn't always like this. When we were first married he was much like everyone else, maybe a little more litigious, but a lot of men like being in court and playing lawyer, so I didn't think anything of it. Little by little he got worse and lost all his friends. Even his family found him hard to take. I don't blame them. I went to see my family alone, or with the children. I didn't bring him along. He wouldn't have gone anyway; they didn't like him.'

'How was his relationship with his children?'

She lit another cigarette and had a sip of coffee. She was perfectly at ease. 'Not good. It was fine when they were little, but when they got older the same thing happened with them as with everyone else. Fighting all the time, threats of lawsuits, you name it.'

'Lawsuits about what?' Rubiah was confounded, what would you sue your own children about?

'Oh, how he was writing them out of his will, how he would prevent them from ever having any of his property. He played one son off against the other. I told them not to pay any mind, once he died, he couldn't bully them, and he wrote and tore up so many wills ... it was crazy.'

'Did he leave a will now?'

'Of course. Left everything to me and to the kids, just as it should be. I told them they needn't have worried. The boys will take over the keropok factory, his share in some fishing boats and some land. My daughter will also get some land. I'll be fine.'

Maryam believed that with no trouble at all. She wondered briefly whether this composed woman would have kept a will which allocated the property as she saw fit and tore up any others Zulkifli may have written. She couldn't quite blame her, no one wants to see their own children disinherited by someone like that. Still, would it be a basis for murder?

'I imagine your sons were quite resentful about his intimidation,' Rubiah continued while Maryam was considering.

'Of course,' Halimah answered easily. She wasn't taking any chances in lying. 'Can you blame them? He held his money over them like a whip.'

'Did he do the same to you?'

She smiled for the first time. 'He might have if I had showed any interest. But he had nothing on me because I didn't care. It's very liberating.'

'But what would you have done if he'd divorced you?'

Now she laughed. 'Taken all of his money I could get my hands on and left. I don't have anywhere to go, as I said, but I suppose I could have bought a house somewhere. But he didn't, did he? He knew I didn't care. And I still don't,' she ended emphatically, lest there be any doubt about how she felt.

'I understand that,' Maryam murmured.

'Do you know if he's had any arguments with Yusuf, who worked for him?'

'I know Yusuf. Not likely to hold a job, I'd say. I don't doubt for a moment he had arguments with him, he was no exception.

I don't know if it would have led him to kill Zulkifli.' She leaned back in her chair and examined the pattern on the couch.

'If I understand the situation correctly,' Halimah summed up, 'no one saw who killed Zulkifli though he died in front of all the people in the market, and so far, no one's said a word about who it might be either. What does that tell you?' she asked. 'No one cares. Or, let me correct myself, no one wants the killer to be found. A public service, you might call it. I know you think me very cold,' she said, nodding at Maryam and Rubiah in turn, and flicking her cigarette ash into the saucer of her coffee cup, 'but I try to be realistic. It makes life less painful; don't you think?'

She studied them, awaiting their opinion. Rubiah spoke up first. 'You're right, it does. A lot of our pain comes from having to acknowledge the stories we tell ourselves aren't true.'

'That's right,' Halimah agreed. 'And I try to keep that sort of thing to a minimum. It's how I've been able to live my life without too much sorrow. How could I stay married to Zulkifli otherwise? I don't know how people have the strength to get through life lying to themselves, I really don't. The disappointments! I suppose most people are much stronger than I am, and I must admire them for it, but I'm not able to do it.

'Do you think me cold?' she asked Maryam directly. 'I'm sorry if you do.' She stopped for a moment as her daughter-in-law appeared to change her cup and saucer for a new one and pour her a fresh cup of coffee. She then poured for all in turn and left, still silent. The service in this house was excellent, Maryam had to hand it to Halimah.

'It isn't coldness. It's quite the opposite. I've neither the imagination nor the strength to pretend things are as they aren't.'

'I don't think that at all,' Maryam didn't realize she believed it. 'I think it takes more strength to refuse to tell yourself happy stories and confront things as they are. There's no escaping.'

'There's no need to, either,' Halimah replied, clearly quite happy to pursue this philosophical discussion. She tapped her cigarette again on the saucer, making yet more work for the diligent young woman.

Maryam changed the subject. 'Your children seem quite devoted.'

Halimah smiled. 'Maybe. My daughter's already gone back to Tanah Merah. She was here for the funeral of course, but she's a lot like me: she won't pretend to a devotion she doesn't feel. I kind of like that about her, even if it extends to me. The boys are a bit different. They'll do their duty if it kills them. I'm very lucky about that. They'll take care of me no matter what they think of me privately. You have to admire it. I didn't do that for my mother-in-law.'

Maryam could well believe it. This frighteningly practical woman would waste no energy on caring for someone she didn't like. The world would be a very cold place if everyone was like that.

'But for your mother, certainly …'

Halimah laughed. 'Of course, I loved my mother, so I took care of her. It was my pleasure. Like my children. But my mother-in-law? No, I didn't care for her much. Too much like my husband – I guess that's where he got it from. Anyway, she had a daughter, so I thought it was a job for her and not for me. I'd only tell her what a horrible son she'd raised, and she thought he was a real prince. She told me so often enough! At first, I would just nod, but after a while I wanted to set her straight. She did not like it. You know how mothers can be with their oldest sons, or in her case, her only son. Alamak! An angel.

'Well, they got on well together. Bickering all day long, and I think they both enjoyed it. It could really get on your nerves. My nerves, anyway.' She suddenly gave a radiant smile. 'That's over with now.' She leaned back into the cushions, thoroughly pleased.

If Maryam hadn't known that Halimah wasn't at the market, she would have identified her as the prime suspect. No one was happier about Zulkifli's death than she was. Maryam would have put money on the killer himself being less happy about it. She wondered though; no one had actually told her Halimah wasn't at the market. Could she have strangled her husband there? Or more likely, as she was a small woman, and might not have been able to reach up to properly do the job, might she have hired someone to do it?

When Maryam emerged from her reverie, she found Rahman had taken over the conversation and was asking about the two sons and whether he could speak with them. Halimah agreed they could, though warning Rahman they were adults, and she couldn't speak for them. She directed them to Razaleigh's house, in the same compound. Fatimah, Razaleigh's wife, had been doing duty as serving girl, and offered to take them over to her home.

She whipped off her apron as they walked down the stairs and smoothed her clothing. 'Alamak,' she said as soon as they were out of earshot, 'I'm not the maid! She should hire someone to do all the service and washing up and all that. She asks me and my husband tells me to go, but I'll tell you, I'm not that thrilled about it. I've had enough!'

They had already arrived at her house, a smaller version of Halimah's, and she called to her husband as she walked up the stairs. 'There are detectives here to see you!' Razaleigh walked out of the house and guided them to chairs on the porch. As they sat down, Fatimah went into the kitchen.

They all offered their condolences to Razaleigh, who accepted them politely, then waited for whatever questions were forthcoming. When he had given their whereabouts for the time of their father's death (both brothers at the keropok factory), Rahman asked what their relationship was like with their father.

'Well, he was a very difficult man. Even when we were kids, though it's gotten worse as he got older and so did we. I'm sure everyone's mentioned how much he loved an argument. It was no different with us; maybe it was worse, because he could try to frighten us by saying he would take away our inheritance. You can only hear that so many times before you stop listening, though.

'He was a good father when we were little kids,' he reminisced. 'Took us to work with him sometimes. He was very loving. But as soon as we hit our teens, he changed. Then we were the same as everyone else, just targets to attack. I don't know why he was like that. He isn't the same with his grandkids. He's neither nice nor not nice: he pays them no attention. I guess he's too involved in his lawsuits and his feuds.'

'Can you think of anyone who might want to kill him?' Maryam asked.

'Anyone,' said his son firmly. 'Anyone who's ever had the shortest conversation with him probably wants to kill him.'

'And you?'

He shrugged. 'I can't kill him because he's my father. But if he weren't, I certainly would.'

Maryam thought this family might take frankness a bit too far. From a police angle, it was refreshing, but from a personal perspective, it froze the blood. 'You seem, forgive me, so straightforward. I'm glad of it, but I must admit I'm not used to people answering so honestly.'

He smiled. 'We get that from our mother. You've spoken to her, haven't you? She's never been anything but blunt. It makes some people uncomfortable, but she really doesn't care. I guess we don't either,' he confirmed. 'It might have cost us some friends, but it saved us the time of having to say the right thing instead of what we thought.'

Maryam had no doubt it made people uncomfortable; it made her a bit uneasy as well. She supposed their brand of hyper-honesty made for many fewer misunderstandings, but she was relieved she didn't have to live with it.

Chapter VIII

'What a family!' Rubiah said in the car, relief audible in her voice. 'I guess there are no secrets there.'

'Do you think she paid someone to kill him?' Maryam asked.

'No,' Rubiah answered firmly. 'First of all, she would have told you. She really doesn't care who knows, you could tell that. She wasn't putting herself out, anyway. As she said, she just ignored him and he seemed to accept it, which is strange. And secondly, I think if she wanted him dead she'd have done it herself. Waited until he was sitting down and then slit his throat. The sons might have,' Rubiah said, considering. 'They probably would have said so also, don't you think?'

'Maybe,' Maryam said quietly. There was something hovering at the edge of her consciousness and she couldn't capture it. Now it was gone.

'We should come back here tomorrow,' Rahman said. 'Let's finish all the interviews as soon as possible. People might forget, if they were ever going to talk. I've never met a group of people who saw less than these.'

'If no one liked him, they probably were happy enough to have him gone.' Maryam was struck by a thought. 'Could you have someone check the court records in Bacok? Let's see if he was actually starting a lawsuit instead of just threatening one. That would be an excellent motive for someone to want to be rid of him before he cost them more money than they had.'

Rubiah nodded approvingly and Rahman agreed. 'It would be interesting if any of the people we spoke to had a court date with him but didn't mention it.'

'His wife would have mentioned it, I think, though I can't see him suing her.'

'Why not? Surely not for sentimental reasons!'

'There seems to be precious little sentiment in that home. Can you imagine, the daughter's already gone back? Bored, I suppose, in Tapak Gajah …'

'Back to the metropolis of Tanah Merah. Naturally. One could hardly blame her.'

'Some people are addicted to excitement.'

Rubiah laughed. In her opinion there were no cosmopolitan centres in Kelantan other than Kota Bharu. Tanah Merah? Please.

'No, really. Leaving your recently widowed mother?'

'Who doesn't care at all? I don't think that's much of a problem.'

'I wonder how she felt about her father?'

'Her mother said she was just like her. Therefore, I deduce she did not like him particularly, but most of all, she didn't care. About anyone. Well, maybe her own children, and her husband if he was very nice to her. Otherwise, probably not. I'm just curious why you would marry someone like that?'

'Could be an arranged marriage. The family has money,'

Maryam suggested. 'The boy's family might have thought it was a solid match. Not everyone may have known they had no blood in their veins.'

'They've probably found out by now.'

'Yes, I feel sorry for her mother-in-law if she thought she'd get any care from this new wife. She'll be lucky enough not to get poisoned by her.'

'That seems harsh,' Rahman interrupted. 'Maybe she's nice to her husband's family.'

Maryam and Rubiah both began laughing. 'Oh, Rahman,' said Maryam. 'You're so trusting.'

Rahman silently fumed, but he knew there was no point in arguing. They thought he was naïve anyway, no matter how long he'd been on the police force or how old he was. They didn't have to believe him anyway for it to be true, he soothed himself. He could be right even if they didn't think so.

***

The search of Bacok's courthouse came back in two days – as Rubiah said, it was Bacok after all and how much could be going on in its legal world? Well, a few cases, certainly, and much to their delight, one brought by Zulkifli against Ali.

'And to think he didn't mention it!' Rubiah exclaimed. 'Did he think that no one was ever going to check?'

'Probably not,' said Maryam. They were already on their way back to see Ali and confront him with what they'd found. 'I can't wait to hear the story.'

They sat comfortably in Ali's living room once more, waiting calmly to hear what he had to say. At first, he had nothing. He goggled at them as though he could simply not understand what they were saying. He began sputtering, and his wife brought in tea and gave it to him at once, then sat down to see what had so upset him.

'Well. I don't know … a lawsuit in the Bacok courts … how would I?' Then Ali fell silent, probably deciding it was best to get a story organized rather than make it up as he went along. He sipped his tea while shooting sideward glances at the two women, which made him appear shiftier rather than blameless. Maryam cleared her throat, and Ali made up his mind to speak, albeit reluctantly.

'I knew there was a lawsuit,' he began.

'Yes,' interrupted Rubiah. 'We saw your signature on the document.'

'Well, yes, I guess you did. Anyway, as I was saying, I knew there was a lawsuit, but I thought it pretty frivolous.'

'What was he suing you for?' asked Rubiah.

'Can't you see it on the document?'

'I'd rather you explained it to me,' Rahman answered in his most official voice. 'It will be clearer.'

Ali became annoyed, then decided that wouldn't help him. He arranged his face in a polite expression and addressed Rahman. 'It was a little thing, really. A small disagreement over some land boundary between our two fields right outside the village. Nothing much.'

'Why did he bring suit?'

'Because that was what he did. Always. Go back a little when you're searching court records and you'll find he sued a lot of people.' Rahman had instructed Din, the most junior policeman on the force, to do just that and had found Zulkifli's name all over the records, going back years. The clerks in the court all knew him well – he was their best customer.

Rahman nodded. 'I saw that. But yours was the most recent.'

Ali shrugged, trying for casual air, but failing. 'Yes, but I knew it was just the usual with him.'

'Did you think about settling?'

Ali became belligerent. 'Why should I settle? He was just trying to get a little more land for himself, chiselling it off my field. That was what he did. And then, if you wanted to avoid the whole court problem, you'd settle, and he'd get another bit of land. If you didn't, well, you'd go to court, which was what he enjoyed most. I don't enjoy it; most people want to keep away from it. But he was happy there.'

'So, what did you do?'

'I told him to go ahead and take it to court if he wanted to. I wouldn't just settle. I didn't believe the boundaries were wrong, or that he actually owned another foot or two from the fence. I'll fight it, I told him. I won't hand him some of my land just to get him off my back. He'll call again next year with the same story grubbing for a bit more, and this will go on endlessly, like blackmail. I've seen him do it to other people and I won't allow it.'

'Who else did he do it to?'

'Another man in town, Mat Yin. After three years or so, Mat

Yin had enough and said he was ready to go to court to fight what Zulkifli was asking now, and everything he'd asked in the past. It was a big lawsuit. Zulkifli lost! Oh, it was a great day for Mat Yin. Everyone laughed at Zulkifli – it drove him crazy. First time, I think, someone really fought back. Mat Yin hired a lawyer and everything.' He smiled, remembering.

'Don't bother thinking that Mat Yin killed him,' he advised Rahman. 'It would be more likely the other way around. Anyway, Mat Yin moved away to live with his daughter in Terengganu.' He said it as if he'd moved to the far side of the moon.

'Were you going to get a lawyer, too?'

Ali squirmed a little. 'Well, I was waiting to see what happened. I didn't know whether Zulkifli would go forward with it, or whether he'd back down.'

'Did he ever back down?' Maryam asked.

'Well … no. But you never know.'

'And now,' began Maryam.

'Yes, now it's all over. But listen,' Ali reminded her, 'I'd hardly kill him just because of a lawsuit. It would be ridiculous.'

'People have killed for less,' she answered mildly.

'Well, I haven't.'

'Good to hear,' Maryam assured him. 'Perhaps it isn't only one thing, though. Perhaps it's a combination of things that make people murder. I've found that, investigating various crimes, and I know Officer Rahman has as well. This could be just a part of it.

'Anyway,' she said, rising, 'We just wanted to clear things up about the lawsuit. Thank you for doing that for us. If we need to speak with you again, we'll come back. Alright?'

'Of course,' he nodded, not relishing the possibility.

***

'I don't think he did it,' Rubiah announced. 'We're wasting our time asking him.'

'Really,' Maryam commented. 'Who do you think did it?'

'I don't know yet. Probably his son on the instructions of his mother. But whoever did, I don't think it was him. He didn't really have reason.'

'The lawsuit?'

Rubiah waved the lawsuit away with her hand. 'Not important enough. Annoying yes, but not enough to kill for. We should dig elsewhere. We're just scratching the surface here.'

Usually Rubiah was the one trying to get each case over with as quickly as she could, and to that end Maryam expected Rubiah to support the nomination of the easiest candidate. It was not often Rubiah dismissed suspects out of hand. 'Rahman?' she asked. 'What do you think?'

'I'd have to agree, although I can't say for sure. But I don't see that much of a motive here, unless there's more we still don't know about. I wouldn't mind taking spending more time on Yusuf though.' He opened the car door for them. 'But now, I need to get home.'

Chapter IX

Rahman also had a baby to get home to. He and Aliza had a girl only two months earlier, named Sharifah Aini after Rahman's favourite singer. At first, Aliza resisted the name, thinking it odd to name a baby for a celebrity whose name everyone would recognize. But she did like the name itself, and her husband seemed so set on it. In the end, she found herself quite happy with the baby's name, and once heard, people never forgot it.

At two months, she was an easygoing child, with a light dusting of feathery black hair and big brown eyes which always had a slightly mystified expression. Aliza and Rahman thought she was the most beautiful baby ever seen, and they doted on her. Rahman, who had been devoted to his job, now avoided overtime if he could. He no longer wished to work as he had in the past, immersed in his cases. Now, he let work wait for the next day so he could be with his family.

He could not believe his luck. He was still astounded each time he came home to find Aliza was his wife. She had become a head-turning beauty, just like her sister Ashikin. And smart! A high school teacher and apprentice detective to boot. He could discuss his work with her, and she was really interested. She could help him, as she helped her mother and Rubiah. And Sharifah Aini, well, she would be as beautiful as her mother, and just as smart. He could see that in her already. Possibly a singer as well, like her namesake. Rahman never thought he'd find anyone whose singing he admired more than hers, but if his daughter should inherit that talent, it might happen. And if she didn't, he really didn't care.

Maryam and Mamat spent a good deal of time at the house, helping with the baby. Both felt more comfortable doing this at their daughter's houses rather than at their son Azmi's. Not that Azmi's wife wasn't unfailingly polite and friendly, welcoming them when they came, but Maryam felt it easier to work with her own daughters rather than a daughter-in-law.

Nuraini, Ashikin's eldest daughter, was now approaching kindergarten, but her attitude toward attention going to other children when it should be directed at her had not changed. She now had more children to keep her grandparents away from. Mamat, who never disciplined her in any way, began to get testy if she tried to banish Sharifah Aini from the room when she visited, or drag Mamat away to concentrate on her. This was a new development Nuraini did not care for, and it was happening not only with Mamat, but with her uncles Yi and Rahman.

Rahman too had taken a very lenient attitude, saying nothing to Nuraini but playing with the boys in spite of her sulks. But when she began to show her jealousy of Sharifah Aini, he could not ignore it. One afternoon, Ashikin, Aliza and Maryam were summoned to Maryam's living room by ear-splitting shrieks, which were issued by Nuraini when Rahman gave her a stern lecture about caring for the baby and not being selfish. Nuraini could not believe anyone would actually have the temerity to talk to her that way, and her only reaction was a full-blown tantrum. And her grandparents, with all the adults in her family, backed him up.

'Aini, I told you about caring for the children younger than you are, your brothers and cousins,' said Ashikin, trying to hide her exasperation. This was one in a long line of lectures she'd delivered on the same subject, and she was losing patience rapidly. But the biggest shock for Nuraini was Mamat, her constant defender and greatest fan, joining in the chorus.

'You're growing up now. You must learn to control yourself and stop screaming. She's a baby, and you're her older sister. You can't ask people not to care for her. That's not nice.'

The screams had abated as soon as other people entered the room, for she was sure they would rescue her from Rahman and his scolding. But no! They continued it. All because of these babies, which Nuraini had never asked for and could not really understand why she was called upon to be nice to them. First it was Zakaria, her younger brother and then Yunus, her second younger brother. Now Sharifah Aini. When would all this end?

Rahman still seemed stern, and even Mamat was not pleased with her. No one offered to take her for ice cream or order Yi to play with her. They crowded instead around Sharifah Aini and showed her to Nuraini (as if she hadn't seen her before) to illustrate how sweet she was and how Nuraini should be excited to now have another girl to play with when she was older. Nuraini bought none of it and, instead, burst into tears.

They'd all been talking about it for years, and Maryam had soothed Ashikin, telling her it would soon end, and Nuraini would get over it on her own. But now that seemed a vain hope, and someone, she feared, would have to step in and let the child know that this was no longer tolerable. After all, she'd be starting school very soon, and though her grandparents might be willing to put up with all kinds of queenly behaviour, her schoolmates never would.

She began to explain that to Nuraini, who seemed stunned. 'School? What do you mean? They won't like me?' And the wailing began again.

'That's enough!' her mother thundered, frightening her into silence. 'Really Nuraini, everyone's tried as best they can to never scold you even when you were treating your brothers badly. You can't do that anymore. And, you can't start on your little cousins. It's time you changed your behaviour, young lady, and now's a good time to start.'

With that, she took Nuraini's hand and led her out of the house and back to her own. Nuraini was too shocked to make any noise, and went along silently, but Maryam knew that Ashikin's house would be the site of an explosion later in the day.

Rahman shook his head regretfully, holding Sharifah Aini close to his chest, resting her head on his shoulder. 'It's too bad Nuraini's so stubborn about all this. She's refused to change at all. I can't have her treating Sharifah Aini badly,' he said by way of apology.

Mamat shook his head. 'You were right,' he said. 'It's just

difficult. And see this little *intan berlian,* this diamond!' He held his hands out to take Sharifah Aini, already asleep again, so he could hold her and walk with her on the porch, pointing out the birds as she slept.

'I think he's partial to his granddaughters,' Maryam commented in a low voice to Rubiah. 'Have you noticed how he acts with Nuraini and Sharifah Aini? He's very nice to the boys, but he never fawns over them.'

Rubiah nodded. Abdullah was the same. 'Maybe they feel more comfortable acting that way to baby girls. They think baby boys have to be manly.'

Maryam sighed. 'At least he's gotten a bit stricter with Nuraini. She needs to be curbed.'

'It's already starting. Wait till she goes to school.'

'I just don't like the way she treats her brothers. At best she ignores them. At worst she pushes them away. It isn't right.'

'I wouldn't worry about it,' Rubiah patted her knee. 'I think Ashikin is about to erupt.'

***

At the market the next morning, Maryam sat ruminating upon her pile of batik fabric, carefully smoking a cigarette so that ash would not fall on any of her fabrics. She had a stall in an excellent location in the main market, the *pasar besar,* in Kota Bharu, the centre of commerce for the state. She sold *kain songket,* Kelantan's famous woven silk with geometric designs in gold thread, made in Kampong Penambang, and batik her brother Malek made. She was an excellent businesswoman and made most of the family's income.

She contemplated the shoppers wandering through the aisles. The fabric sellers were in the building itself; it would not do to have any of their stock rained on. While batik was fairly affordable, kain songket could run into astronomical sums, and must be protected. In a ring around the building were foods: a section for fresh fruits and vegetables, a section for take-out foods prepared by the sellers, and another section for fish. Almost all the shopkeepers were women except for those who sold fish, who were almost always men, shouldering heavy boxes of fish and ice. The shoppers were almost always women, since they were believed to be much better with money than men, and a male shopper was often greeted as an easy opportunity to overcharge. They seemed to feel it beneath their dignity to really bargain and were in a hurry to get out of the market and back to the coffee shops ringing it, which were their own purview. Or as many of the women considered it, a comfortable place to do nothing and talk while their wives were making money. Perspective is everything,

Several women stopped to examine batik sarong. They were alone, and seemed busy, which could often mean a quick sale as they were here to buy and not to browse. She sold four sarong in quick succession with little effort, which was always welcome. She strained to identify anyone shopping for a wedding, seeking for songket in quantity, but couldn't see anyone fitting that description. It certainly didn't happen every day, but it was always great when it did.

As noon approached, the tide of shoppers began to ebb, with only a few remaining. Maryam began to anticipate sitting with Rubiah, who often came downstairs, loaded with cakes and coffee to sit with Maryam for a while.

Before Rubiah could appear, however, a woman drifted by and felt the thickness of the kain songket. 'I'm just browsing,' she informed Maryam. 'My daughter's getting married …'

'Congratulations!'

'Thanks, and I'm beginning to shop for the songket we'll need.'

Maryam nodded sagely. A wedding needed a lot of songket. 'You're looking for the best quality,' she informed her, reaching in back of her for the best songket. She didn't keep it out front because she didn't want people touching it if they weren't serious buyers. This was very prime stuff.

The woman's eyes widened when she saw the bolts put before her: lush, thick fabric with the dull sheen of first quality silk and intricate patterns make of solid gold wire. Even from a distance they winked luxuriously. Maryam had pulled out a muted cream; not quite white, but certainly not beige. The gold sparkled as the fabric moved.

'Alamak!' the woman exclaimed. 'That's lovely!' Then she clamped her mouth shut as if she'd already said too much. You were supposed to find fault with the fabric to drive the price down, but it was clear there was no fault here. The only question would be how much she wanted it.

'What colour were you thinking of?' Maryam asked, to get her talking again.

'Well, it's funny you brought out this one,' she answered. 'I'd been thinking white, but this is, I don't know, softer.'

Maryam agreed. 'White can be harsh. This glows, you see. It sends a nice light onto the face.'

Rubiah appeared at her side, laying down her burden on a stool. She smiled at the woman. 'Wedding?'

'Uh-huh,' the woman said absently, lost in the cloth. 'Can I hold this up against you?' she asked Rubiah. 'Just to see how it frames the face.'

Rubiah smiled. She'd been called into service before. She held the fabric up under her chin and assumed a pleasant expression.

'I see,' said the woman, clearly smitten by the silk. 'It does kind of … glow.'

'Would you like me to put it aside for you?' Maryam asked. 'Then you can bring your daughter to see if she likes it.'

The woman seemed reluctant. 'No,' Maryam assured her. 'No money now. I'll just make sure it doesn't get sold in the meantime. When would you like to come back?'

'Umm,' the woman thought. '*Lusa*? The day after tomorrow?'

'I'll be here,' Maryam smiled. 'And I'll put it away safely.'

'Thank you! I'll see you in two days then.'

Maryam smiled and nodded.

'She'll buy it,' commented Rubiah, after she left.

'She will,' Maryam agreed. 'It's really lovely songket.'

'Well, let's eat.'

Chapter X

'You know what's gotten lost here?' Osman asked no one in particular. 'Why Zulkifli killed Yati. We know he did it, but why?'

The police in the station looked at one another: a pop quiz none were prepared for. Din, always hoping to be noticed, stepped up to answer. 'Because,' he cleared this throat, 'she was asking questions about village gossip, and he was afraid a secret he had would come out into the open.'

Osman stared. Sometimes Din amazed him. He was such a scrawny kid (much like Osman himself when he first arrived from Perak, but he might not consciously realize it); tall and very thin, with outsized shoulders he hadn't yet grown into. He had a nice face, Osman thought, with an intelligent expression, narrow eyes and a *hidung mancung,* a chiselled nose with a high bridge, much prized among Malays. He wasn't yet handsome, but he might be in a year or two, and sometimes he seemed to grasp the point more quickly than Osman anticipated. This was one of those times.

'I think you're right,' Osman announced, and Din blushed with pleasure. 'We think he's a got a secret. Not just any secret, but one that he'd kill to keep quiet. And kill right in front of everyone so there's no possible way he'd get away with it. It must be pretty bad.'

'Do you think his wife knows?' Din asked.

'Would she care?' asked Rahman. 'They're a pretty cold family. I spoke to them – they say what they think no matter what.'

'Do you think we could ask them about this?' asked Osman.

'We could ask,' Rahman replied. 'Whether they'd tell us this terrible secret, if they know it, is another thing altogether. How terrible could it be?'

'Terrible enough to kill for,' Osman said. 'Let's not forget, he did kill for it. Why else kill someone he'd never spoken to in his life?' He paused. 'We've got to find out who she was talking to, and what they know. That seems to be the key, don't you think?'

Rahman nodded and reached for his hat. 'I guess I'll go now.' He checked his watch. 'I can still make it for the afternoon market.' He rose to leave. 'Come on, Din,' he said, in the same tone used to call a favourite dog. Din trotted after him.

The market in Tapak Gajah was small, but lively. Several fishing crews were selling the catch they'd just brought in, and at the end of the row of ramshackle displays were some vegetable sellers, who'd artistically arranged their wares on tarps spread along the ground. There was a hum of voices as people bought their fish and perhaps stopped for a brief chat with friends. A couple of the laconic men behind their rows of the day's catch were a bit put out to be there, but the women sellers were in good spirits and very talkative.

Rahman stopped at the vegetable displays, thinking he might

take some home as long as he was here, and perhaps some fish. The woman behind an eggplant ziggurat called to him. 'You were here a few days ago with those women detectives, weren't you? What were their names?' She thought for a moment, and before Rahman could say anything she'd remembered. 'Maryam, that's it! You're the policeman who was with her!'

Rahman would have preferred to be remembered as the policeman she was with, rather than the other way around, but ... 'Yes, that was me,' he agreed. 'We were asking about Cik Yati and Che Zulkifli.'

She nodded. 'Yes, of course.'

'I still have more questions to ask you. Tell me, were you the woman who was talking to Yati right before she was ... she died?'

'We were all in a group,' she explained, straightening her eggplants. 'But she was talking to Khadijah.' She pointed to another woman close by, sitting behind a hillock of keropok bags.

'Are you talking about me?' Khadijah asked good-naturedly. Rahman bought his eggplants and sauntered over to Khadijah's domain and squatted in front of her merchandise. He realized he'd best buy some keropok as well. He hoped Aliza hadn't planned dinner yet.

'I'm back to learn about what happened when the woman here ... died,' he finished. 'Her name was Yati,' he added. 'She was talking to you right before ... it.'

'Yes,' Khadijah agreed. 'Poor thing. What a shock to us all. I've never seen anything like that.' She meditated on the bags in front of her.

'What were you talking about?'

'Oh, things,' she said vaguely. 'Little village stories. Things her husband might be able to use in dikir barat, you know.'

Rahman had the feeling she was evading him.

'Like what?'

'I hardly remember,' she said, moving the keropok bags around. Rahman paid for two, and she wrapped them up for him. He hoped that might set her more at ease.

'Can you try to remember?'

'You know,' she said, leaning forward, 'I don't really know that much. Harmless stuff. Little stuff. Not the kind of thing that people would kill for.'

'Of course not,' Rahman agreed. 'Do you have any theories on why Zulkifli would have killed her? A woman he didn't know?'

She sniffed. 'He wouldn't need too much encouragement to kill anyone, whether he knew them or not. He was mean.'

'Had he been mean to you?'

'Not to me …'

Rahman was encouraging and sympathetic.

'He fired my husband, you see, from his precious keropok factory. Threatened to take us to court, for what, we were never sure. What would he get out of us anyway? Some keropok? I won't sell his merchandise anymore. I get my keropok from a nice lady just down the road. He can keep his keropok and … He just wanted to ruin us, for fun, you see. No, I didn't like him at all. But I couldn't have killed him, because I was sitting right here.'

'I never thought you did,' Rahman assured her. 'No one suspects you of it.' But he did wonder briefly about her husband.

As if she read his mind, she continued. 'And my husband

didn't do it either,' she informed him stiffly. 'He was bringing in the boats with the rest of the crew. So don't even think about him.'

'I wouldn't.' But he'd check up on it, anyway.

'You see, my husband was hardly the only one he'd done something like that to. There are so many men here in the village he's fired and tried to bankrupt – not that it would take too long to bankrupt most of us. We aren't that wealthy out here.'

Rahman nodded.

'But almost every family has a story about how Zulkifli drove someone crazy: a husband, a father, a son. I don't know who killed him, but I'm sure whoever did had a good reason.' She glared at him defiantly, as if daring him to contradict her.

'I've heard that,' he said distantly. 'We've no clues on who might have done it.'

'And you won't get any, either. No one in Tapak Gajah is sorry to see him go, and no one will remember anything they've seen. Not that I saw anything,' she hastily added. 'I didn't. But if I did …' She left it unsaid.

'I know that's the truth,' Rahman agreed. 'But I didn't come to ask about Zulkifli. I came to ask about that poor woman he killed. Of course, we know who killed her, but it bothers us as to why he did it. Do you have any ideas?'

She did. 'I hardly know Zulkifli's secrets. I hardly knew him at all, except for what he did to people. And his wife, she's a strange one. We all give her lots of room. She's very unfeeling, you know. Very.' She brought out a plastic bag of hand-rolled cigarettes, and Rahman promptly offered one of his store-bought ones, which she gratefully accepted.

'But there are stories. Well, there are always stories in a kampong, as I'm sure you know.' Rahman did know: he was kampong born and bred. 'People say that he often took advantage of the women in the family when he was going after the men. You know, promising not to fire them, or whatever he was going to do, if he could … have … a young wife or daughter. Disgusting. But, actually, I don't know if it's true. It sounds true enough, I wouldn't put it past him. This would have been a while ago, because lately I doubt he was interested. He just cared about his money and his court cases. I don't see him chasing women, but what do I know?

'Anyway, these stories go on to say that there might have been a child, or children, depending on the tale you're hearing, that resulted from these … I don't know what to call it. And if it's true, these poor women. And their husbands, raising these children. Though a woman will love her child no matter who the father is, don't you think?' She didn't wait for his answer. 'The men, I'm not so sure. Maybe they love the child they've brought up. It's not a question you can ask anyone, can you? Even if you ask your own husband, he'll start wondering why you're asking, won't he? So, what do you think?'

Rahman was unprepared for the question, but sat back on his heels and thought about it for a moment. 'I think,' he answered slowly, 'that a man might be really angry and resentful about it before the child was born, but when he saw the baby, he might well fall in love with it as if it were his own, and never think that it wasn't. People talk about it as though it would be all a man would think about forever, but if he loves his wife and it wasn't her fault? I think he'd love the child.' Until he'd heard the question, he'd never even considered it, and he had just blurted out his answer. But as a new father, he remembered the first time he saw Sharifah Aini and how he'd adored her from the start; how she came to be was far less important than who she was. He was deeply grateful he didn't have to grapple with this for himself, but he thought a decent and loving man would embrace the baby and not give over his whole life to bitterness. Especially if the wife had participated only to save him.

Khadijah nodded and smiled at him. 'Thank you. Not that it applies to me, you see. We were way past the time he might have suggested anything to me when this whole thing happened with my husband, and my daughters were thankfully grown and married. But it's nice to know.' She gazed off into the distance, thinking.

'I don't know if what I'm going to tell you is true or not. It's just ... *angin bertiup,* the wind blows. But I did hear a while ago that Che Hamid had a lot of trouble with Zulkifli, well, that part wasn't just talk, everyone knows it happened. A big blow up. Che Hamid was hurt in the keropok factory, which had some new machine Zulkifli had bought, I don't even know what it is. We always made keropok by hand, so I don't know what you need a machine for, which by the way, is a menace to everyone here, but anyway, instead of offering him compensation, as any decent person would have done, our Zulkifli says that Che Hamid owes him for damaging the machines! Can you believe it? And the poor man could barely walk for a while. Well, that's who he was.

'Then, suddenly, Zulkifli isn't talking about damages anymore, and actually gives Che Hamid some money, which was only right, if you ask me.' She glanced meaningfully at Rahman. 'And just a few months later, his wife is pregnant, and not so happy about it. She's very glum, when she should be happy. Che Hamid doesn't talk about it. Of course, after the baby was born, a girl, they're much happier, relieved even. Maybe it's just as you say: maybe it's Che Hamid's baby after all. She kind of favours him. She certainly fits into the family; you know what I mean? Maybe you should talk to them. They live down there,' she pointed with her thumb toward the beach. 'Just be careful how you talk about it; but what am I saying? You know more about handling this than I do.'

She smiled again, silently urging him to move on and leave her to sell her inventory. 'But wait,' Rahman asked, 'did you mention this to Yati?'

'Someone may have said something,' she said warily. 'I'm not sure about that. I tend to think not. We were telling stories you laugh at, and no one would have found that amusing.'

Rahman wondered whether Zulkifli would really kill to protect a secret everyone seemed to know. The time for that was long past.

'Do you think his wife heard these stories?'

Khadijah was unperturbed. 'Maybe, maybe not. Anyone who spoke to a lot of people here would know, but she doesn't really speak to anyone. I can't imagine anyone would seek her out to tell her. No, that wouldn't happen. And I've never seen her sitting with friends, or even acquaintances, just talking. So, who knows? Who cares,' she added under her breath.

'You don't like her.' Rahman stated.

'Why should I?' she asked defensively. 'Has she ever once

tried to stop her husband from the things he did? Did she ever take anyone's part to protect them from him? No, she did not. So why should I like her? I don't even know her, but I know what she hasn't done.' She glanced at his cigarettes and he quickly offered another.

'Take as many as you'd like,' he urged her.

'I'll just take two,' she said. 'One for later.'

'Do you think everyone feels the same?'

'Most people, I'd say.'

'Do you know anyone who doesn't?'

'No, but there might be people who like her who I don't know about.' Her expression said this was unlikely.

He rose up, stretching his legs. 'Thank you so much, Kakak, I'm grateful for your help.' He smiled and backed away, almost knocking over Din who'd been standing rapt behind him.

'Let's go see Che Hamid,' he said, and they walked down towards the sea.

Chapter XI

'You found out a lot,' said Din admiringly.

Rahman smiled. Had he ever been that young and eager? Probably. It made him feel protective of Din and his puppylike devotion. 'I hope we'll be finding out more from Hamid.'

It wasn't far from the market to the beach, which was still buzzing with activity. Groups of men were hauling the boats up onto the beach, untangling nets, presenting their waiting wives with their share of the catch and any money they'd received. The coffee shop set up immediately in front of a small grove of coconut palms was doing a land office business, with its few stools taken and men sitting on upturned boxes. *Kopi peng,* iced coffee, seemed to be the beverage of choice, and Rahman ordered two, so he and Din had a reason to hang around.

They pulled up two boxes and lounged there, sipping their coffee and starting up conversations. Everyone was interested in them: new faces, and policemen at that.

'The murders,' a darkly tanned man guessed immediately, wolfing down some fried bananas with his drink. 'You want some more information on that.'

'If you have any,' Rahman replied politely.

'Not me,' the man said. 'I hadn't left the beach yet. I just heard about it second hand, you might say. Very sad about the lady. Poor thing, I can't understand why he would have killed her. But he was a cruel man.' Others who'd been listening to the conversation concurred.

'He used to have a share on a boat,' another man chimed in. 'We all stayed away from that crew. Best not to get involved with him at all, if you could avoid it.' Many of the men agreed.

'Why was that?'

'There'd always be trouble about getting your share when it was time to pay, and your share of the catch when the boat came in. He'd be here to meet the boat when it came in and argue about every damned fish.' There was a murmur of assent. 'I swear he'd count each one,' the sailor continued. 'As if you hadn't been out all day in the sun working as hard as you could, and him getting the biggest share anyway. He'd grab a fish out of your very hands! It was unbelievable, that's what it was. I'm not unhappy he's gone. No, I'm not.'

'He sounds difficult,' Rahman agreed.

'Difficult?' one of the men repeated. 'He wasn't difficult. He was a catastrophe. An evil spirit!' Most of the men laughed, though a little uncomfortably, since Zulkifli was recently dead and it didn't seem quite the thing to run him down. But the general consensus was clear, and Zulkifli would win no popularity contests among these fishermen.

'It's a shame he was killed,' the same sailor continued doubtfully, 'but I can't say he'll be missed.'

'I guess his sons will take over his investments?' Rahman

ventured.

The man shrugged. 'His sons are alright. Normal people. They'll be no better nor worse than all the other partners. I don't think they'll count the fish!' There was general laughter.

'Do you know Che Hamid?' Rahman inquired.

'Why?' asked the man, suddenly cautious. 'What do you want with him?'

'I heard he'd had some trouble with Zulkifli.'

'That he did,' another man confirmed. 'But that was a while ago, wasn't it? They haven't had anything to do with each other since then.'

'Does Hamid work on the boats?'

'Not really. But he's getting older, you see.'

Rahman nodded. Fishing seemed like very hard work. 'Does he live nearby? I'd like to talk to him.'

'Why,' asked one of the men. 'He didn't kill Zulkifli.'

Rahman nodded. He certainly wouldn't debate the issue here and now.

'I suppose you'll find out somehow,' one of the men said, and gave Rahman directions to Che Hamid's house, which was just moments from where they were. Rahman nodded his thanks, and he and Din rose to go.

'Che Hamid didn't do anything,' the man repeated. 'Just remember that.'

***

Che Hamid's house was perched precariously over the sand, the outside woven bamboo walls weather beaten and faded with sun and rain. It was a *rumah tukai,* a house made of bamboo screens instead of wood, let alone concrete, and although in the past they were quite common, now they were those of the poorest Kelantanese. There was no yard, as the houses in this area were directly on the sand, intermittently shaded by coconut palms. Rahman and Din stood at the bottom of a narrow ladder that led straight into the living room. The absence of a porch made Rahman sad, as it didn't seem right to lack such an important room in the house. So much socializing and relaxing was done there, covered from the sun yet open to the breeze, often decorated with large flowerpots and bird cages. He sighed, examining this flimsy structure that hardly embodied what he thought of as a house, and lost most of his enthusiasm for conducting an interview.

A woman came to the door to see who'd arrived. She would have been pretty – maybe very pretty – if her careworn face had some animation to it. But she projected only anxiety and exhaustion to see them standing at the bottom of her ladder.

'Yes?' she asked tentatively. 'What do you want?'

'Does Che Hamid live here?'

'Yes,' she said slowly, her eyes darting between Rahman and Din. 'Why?'

'Well, we'd just like to talk to him.'

'Why? What are you doing?'

Rahman cleared his throat, fighting the instinct to say goodbye and just go home. He'd lost all taste for pursing this interview right now. He didn't want to go into this hot, cramped little house and force these people to try to come up with tea or a drink and possibly a snack, which they would feel duty bound to provide. He did not want to add to whatever cares were already weighing this woman down, draining her of her looks and animation. And he absolutely did not want to find out anything which might lead him to think her husband had killed Zulkifli.

He was well on the way to wondering why he'd ever become a policeman, when Din brought him out of his reverie. 'Suggest we meet him at the coffee shop,' he whispered urgently. 'We can buy him a coffee and not trouble them to entertain us.'

He stared at Din with newfound respect. Of course! He wasn't thinking at all, he was lucky Din was with him and had woken him up. He nodded at Din and turned back to the woman. 'Please ask your husband to meet us at the coffee shop on the beach. We'll be waiting for him there.'

She stared at him, not replying, and he in turn said his goodbyes, and he and Din walked off, retracing their steps, with Rahman's relief making him almost lightheaded. 'Thank you, Din,' he said, putting a hand on the boy's shoulder. 'You really saved me there.'

Din ducked his head and smiled happily. Luckily, the shop had emptied out since they'd left, so they wouldn't need to conduct an interview in full view of an interested audience. They snagged the stools this time, ordered another two kopi peng and waited for Che Hamid.

He came slowly, walking with a pronounced limp. Like his wife, he wore the signs of a difficult life on his face, which was prematurely old. He had deep lines around his mouth, which was bordered by a short grey beard and moustache. He held himself as though he were in pain, whether from his leg or his back was hard to tell, but he was slightly bent and out of breath even from the short walk from his house. Rahman rose immediately and offered him a stool, which he gratefully accepted. He sat and took a minute or two to catch his breath and wipe the sweat off his face. He examined Rahman and asked in a hoarse voice, 'Who are you?'

'My name is Rahman, and this is Zainuddin. We are police from Kota Bharu, investigating the murder of Che Zulkifli in the market a few days ago.'

After a moment of silence, Din asked if he'd like coffee, and Hamid ordered the iced coffee everyone drank here, and swallowed it in one gulp. Din signalled for a second. Hamid sipped it slowly and turned to them. 'What do you want?' he asked over the rim of the glass.

'You've heard about Zulkifli's death, no doubt.'

He made an indeterminate noise, which could be a yes.

'We're investigating who might have killed him. It has to be someone in the kampong. He was killed in the market and everyone would notice someone who wasn't from here.'

He grunted again and applied himself to the coffee. He signalled to Din it was time for a third, and Din quickly obeyed.

'Why are you asking me? I didn't kill him. Do you see my leg?' he asked bitterly. 'Do you think I could manage it with no one seeing?'

Rahman did not think so, and wished he'd known about that before he went to find Che Hamid.

'And besides, he deserved what he got. He deserved worse, if you ask me. A selfish, vicious ... whatever. I worked in his factory. He accused me of ruining his machinery, or a piece of it. I'd had an accident with it, which led, eventually, to my leg being as it is. And did he offer to help? He did not.' He took another sip of his coffee and motioned for Din to pass the plate of fried bananas. 'He made it worse, hounding me to pay him for the machine. I could never afford that.' He fell silent.

'What happened then?' asked Din, like a child asking for a story.

'Why, what happens with everything he does,' Hamid replied moodily. 'He started ranting about courts and police and taking my house. I went to work on one of the boats until I couldn't really get around anymore, and that son of a ... you know would always meet the boats to make sure no one got any more than what he thought was "fair". He wouldn't know fair if he fell on it. Anyway, he'd meet his boats and then berate me in front of everyone. Every day! And I know he spoke to the captain of the boat I worked on to tell him to fire me. All these rich guys know each other, you know.

'And I know that's true because the captain told me! And he didn't fire me, which then got him into an argument with Zulkifli. There's always another argument with him.'

Hamid seemed angry and applied himself to the plate of bananas. Din and Rahman realized he was hungry; Rahman could not believe he was such a fool he hadn't realized it earlier. He got up to speak quietly with the owner, who nodded and walked off, leaving the three of them alone.

'Che Hamid, where do you work now?'

Hamid finished chewing his banana. 'It's hard for me to work now. What with my leg and all. I make batik outside my house, and my wife sells it in the morning market, or sometimes goes door to door in the kampong around here. Our daughter helps out when she can. She's my youngest, the last one at home. My other children are married, though they don't live too far away. I have two sons who work on the boats. Sometimes they give me their share of the catch to sell, but I don't like doing that, taking money from them like that. They need it themselves.'

'It must be difficult,' Din sympathized.

The owner returned with several banana leaf packages, which contained meals. He offered one to Hamid, who thanked him and opened it right there. A hearty meal of curried fish and rice, with pickles on the side. There were at least three more in the plastic bag he held. 'My wife's cooking,' he said proudly. 'She does takeout orders in the evenings.'

'You know,' said Rahman. 'I think I'll order two to take home with me, if you have it.'

The man trudged back again towards his house.

'Good?' he asked Hamid.

'She's a great cook,' he commented. 'Of course, it helps if you have the ingredients.'

'It does.' Rahman was growing increasingly guilty, for reasons he couldn't quite articulate. 'Any ideas, Che Hamid, on why Zulkifli might have wanted to kill that poor woman?' It has been his intention to ask about Hamid's daughter, and when she'd been born. He thought he'd try to find out if there'd been anything about her birth that would lead him to think she might be Zulkifli's biological daughter. But why? What would it prove? It would humiliate them all and wouldn't clarify anything about the murder. Rahman dropped the line of questioning regarding Hamid, and determined to feed him, send home meals for his family tonight, and call it a day. He couldn't face being the police just now.

'Because he's horrible,' Hamid answered bluntly. 'Though I hear he didn't even know her. Well, maybe she was asking questions about him. He really didn't like that, you know. Very secretive about all the terrible things he did. Maybe that was it? Who knows? It really doesn't make any sense – someone preparing for dikir barat wants funny stuff, not trying to be Sherlock Holmes. They wouldn't bother trying to find out something really deep and hidden, and if they found it, they'd try their best to forget it, right? This is just entertainment.'

'You're right,' Rahman agreed. He rose as the owner returned with his dinner and settled the bill. 'Thank you for your time, Che Hamid,' he said politely.

'Thank you for dinner,' he replied.

Rahman discreetly slipped a few bills into the bag with Hamid's dinner. He and Din left Tapak Gajah, knowing little more than they had when they'd arrived, but Rahman was full of anger at himself for asking questions, for hurting people, for things he hadn't even done.

'I don't know why they wanted to talk to me,' Che Hamid told the owner. 'They hardly asked anything. Well, I don't care,' he said, rising with a bit of trouble, holding his bag filled with food. 'I think I definitely came out of this a winner.'

He bade him good night and limped off, content.

Chapter XII

Rahman was moody when he returned home, presenting Aliza with his packaged dinners, keropok and eggplant.

'This is great!' she enthused, peeking into the banana leaf wrappers. 'An odd assortment, though.'

'It's whomever I was trying to talk to,' Rahman said tiredly, dropping into a chair and seeking Sharifah Aini. 'Where's the baby?'

'Ayah took her for a walk,' she answered, getting out plates. 'They should be back in a few minutes. What's the matter?'

He ran his hand through his hair, pushing it back from his forehead. 'I don't know. It was a terrible day, but I can't really explain why.'

She put the plates on the table and walked over to sit near him. 'What happened?'

'Nothing happened. I feel I just woke up, that's all. I was in the middle of asking questions, because I found someone who might have had a reason to kill Zulkifli, though it's years ago ... one of the market women told me there were tales about this guy, Hamid, who had a run-in with Zulkifli and was threatened with court. The word was Zulkifli might have asked for the wife, and that the daughter born after that time was really his. And of course, Din and I go searching for this Hamid, and we find a ramshackle house out on the beach which didn't even have a porch ... and I started thinking about how we sit on the porch all the time, and they didn't have one, and I couldn't face going into this house. Sitting in a hot, unfurnished little room with people who couldn't afford anything but would give us the last tea they had if we were there. I just could not do it. Din suggested we meet him at the coffee shop, and we did, and he limps very badly and clearly couldn't have killed Zulkifli and I didn't even want to talk about his daughter because how humiliating for him and the girl? If he raised her and loved her who cares whose she is, and I didn't want to drag it all up and make everyone miserable ... and he was hungry, you could see that, so we bought him dinner and more of these packages to bring home and I didn't ask him anything. Din must think I've lost it completely.' He stared sadly at the floor. 'And maybe I have. I don't know about being a policeman anymore, Liza. I can't keep chasing people and digging up all their secrets and for what? This guy Zulkifli, he sounds terrible. He probably was. Everyone's probably better off that he's gone. His wife is happier, his kids are relieved, and no one who saw him killed will say a word because they're glad he's dead. So who am I to interfere?'

At this point, Mamat came up the stairs holding little Sharifah Aini, who cooed at him and at her parents. Aliza got up to take her.

'She was wonderful,' Mamat said happily. 'So alert. Such a good baby!' His eyes moved back and forth, first at Rahman and then at Aliza. 'Are you alright?' he asked.

'I'm fine,' Rahman answered. 'I've just had a tough day, and been thinking. Maybe I should be something else. I don't know if I'm cut out for this.'

'I didn't foresee that,' said Mamat.

'It can happen,' Aliza shrugged. 'I think Rahman needs to think about what he wants to do …'

'I want,' he said quickly, 'not to chase down people who have enough on their hands without me interfering.'

'You didn't feel this way before,' Mamat said logically. Catching the expression on Rahman's face, he decided to retreat. 'I'll leave you two to talk it out. Have a good night, and try not to worry. We're always here if you want to talk to us.' He left immediately, most unlike his usual drawn-out goodbyes, often punctuated by a farewell cup of coffee and a long chat with both of them.

Alone again, Rahman held his daughter on his shoulder and hummed to her absentmindedly, while Aliza regarded him with concern. 'You need a break from this for a little while.'

'I may need a break from this forever, but it isn't possible right now. There are no 'breaks' in police work. I'll have to be in there tomorrow, like it or not. But here's the problem: I don't care who killed Zulkifli. I don't want to arrest anyone for it, ruin their life for killing someone who may well have deserved it.'

'Can we really make that determination?' Aliza asked him. 'Though I see your point.'

'Maybe I'm just tired,' Rahman sought to end his confessional and get back to normal living. Besides, he had nothing else useful to say. 'Let me change her diaper,' he said, getting up. 'I'll be back in a minute and we can eat.'

***

Maryam and Rubiah had interviewing of their own to do. 'Can't we bring people from Tapak Gajah here?' Rubiah asked rhetorically. 'I'm tired of going all the way over there.'

'They might not appreciate it,' Maryam advised. 'Still, it would save a lot of trouble.'

'It would be helpful if we knew just what the women at the market were telling her right before she died,' Rubiah reflected.

'I heard that's what Rahman was doing there yesterday, or the day before, I can't remember.'

'Yes, but did he find out anything? You know, there's gossip and then there's meaningful gossip. I don't know if men really know the differences there.'

'Rahman might,' Maryam defended him. He was, after all, her son-in-law. 'But then again …'

'He might not,' Rubiah finished for her. 'But whether or not he can doesn't make it likely that they'll speak to him as honestly as they'd speak to us.'

'So you think we ought to go back and talk to them some more.'

'Of course. We're market women, they're market women …'

'Good point. We'll go tomorrow.'

The next afternoon found them at the same small market Rahman had just explored. They sat down with Khadijah after being referred to her and convinced her to take a few minutes off and share some coffee with them. In order to sweeten the deal, they bought a large quantity of keropok, enough to hand out to family and friends for weeks to come.

They sat at the only coffee shop close to the market, with the same man who'd served Rahman. He felt as though he was becoming part of this investigation, though all he did was serve coffee and fried bananas and stay quiet, all the better to listen.

'You know,' Khadijah opened, 'the police were already here, asking questions. I think they wanted to find out why this woman – Yati was her name? – was killed. And I gave them my answer, "I don't know." It's still my answer.'

'But you were talking to her right before she was killed, weren't you?'

'Yes, there was a bunch of us.' Khadijah drank her coffee and reached for a banana. 'She was collecting little anecdotes her husband could use in dikir barat. Nothing serious. You know, it's entertainment, no one's supposed to be angry or embarrassed. We weren't gossiping about deep, dark secrets. We never met her before, why would anyone tell her things which could cause trouble? Come on.' She took a sip of coffee. 'If you think she got killed because we told her something Zulkifli couldn't bear to have known, you're wrong. First of all, I don't know anything like that. If I did, which I don't, I wouldn't start babbling it to someone I just met. No one would. And thirdly, is it thirdly, is that what I'm up to? Thirdly, Yati never asked about Zulkifli or about real secrets. If we'd offered them, she wouldn't be able to use them. She wanted light stuff – stories people could laugh at.' She finished her coffee and raised her cup for a refill. Nothing tastes better than food someone else is buying.

Maryam saw the truth in this. 'Why do you think she was killed?'

Khadijah shook her head. 'I've been thinking a lot about this, since it happened right in front of me. Horrible. I didn't even realize what was happening until it was too late to do anything. I feel so sorry for her.

'You're going to laugh at me if I tell you what I think. But, anyway, here it is. I think Zulkifli made a mistake. I don't think he meant to kill this woman, I think it might have been one of us he wanted to kill, and in the moment, and with his vision, which I hear wasn't that good, he killed this poor girl. Alright now, go ahead and laugh.'

'I'm not laughing,' Rubiah stated. 'I'm listening. It makes sense. But who do you think he might have been after?'

'Not me. I haven't had much to do with him; nobody in my family has. We don't have any lawsuits threatened, *Alhamdulillah*. But a few of the girls have husbands who've had run-ins with Zulkifli in the past, and one that has a problem with him now. If I had to guess, I'd say he was after her. But who knows?'

'Who is she?' Maryam leaned in closer to get the name.

'Well, I guess since you're working for the police, I have to tell you.' She narrowed her eyes. 'It's Afzan. She's a young girl, pretty new to the market. She used to help her mother here, but her mother died about a year and a half ago, poor thing. Lungs, you know. Just couldn't cure them. People said it was tuberculosis and maybe it was. She got medicine at the clinic, but it didn't really work. Very sad. She'd been selling here a long time.

'Anyway, when she died, Afzan took over the business. Very competent, works very hard,' she said approvingly. 'Nice girl, too. I like her. She's kind of quiet, but she'll grow into it.' Into what, Maryam wasn't sure, but didn't want to interrupt the flow. 'I heard she and her husband are having trouble with Zulkifli. Well, not anymore they aren't, and I'll bet they're relieved about it, too. Not to kill him or anything.' She thought about what she said and tried her best to clarify. 'I'm not saying they would do anything about it, you know.'

'Understood,' Rubiah said.

'It's about Zulkifli's fishing boat. Her husband thought Zulkifli cheated him on his share, and I'd believe it. Cheap? You'd be amazed. Everyone who crews his boats says the same thing. I think if there were enough work on other boats no one would work for him. But you've got no choice, you have to work somewhere. So, where was I? Yes, the boat. This argument starts, and then Zulkifli cheats him again, so now there are two day's shares he's short on. He's getting angry, well of course you would. I heard he went to talk to Zulkifli's oldest son, he knows him because they went to school together here in Tapak Gajah.

'The son, Razaleigh, he sympathizes. He says he'll talk to his father, but of course, nothing happens. No one could pry any money out of him. You know what, though, I hear after the funeral, Razaleigh pulls her husband aside and pays him everything his father owed. It'll be different now working for that family now that the boys are in charge. They know what their father was, and I don't think they'll be like him.

'Was Afzan happy? You can imagine. The whole thing just went away.'

'Did Zulkifli pressure them?' Maryam asked.

'You mean did he want to sleep with Afzan if they wanted to get their full share?' she said tartly. 'I think that's what you're asking, and the answer is no. He's way past all of that. He wouldn't know what … Never mind. Anyway, no. Nothing like that.'

'Well, thank goodness for that. Did he do that earlier in his … career?'

Khadijah looked keenly at Maryam. 'That's what I hear, though I don't know it has anything to do with him getting killed. Though you're the experts, not me.' She drank some more coffee and contemplated the beach and the sea. 'He used to be a lot worse, Zulkifli. He was slowing down. Not just in making everyone unhappy, I mean in general. Not that I spent a lot of time watching him, you understand. Just that I noticed it.'

She returned their gaze. 'You might ask about that. I mean, ask his wife. She may not have noticed. She's an odd one, she is. Doesn't care about anyone. Zulkifli could have died at her feet and she'd step over him. I don't know that she'd bother to kill him, mind you. Might be too much trouble for her to take. If he were sick, she might not even know. She wouldn't care, that's for sure, but she might not even notice what was going on. What a couple.'

'So, you think he had some disease?' Rubiah asked.

'He could have. I'm no doctor. I'm just telling you what I saw, and that's a man getting old fast. Faster than usual, and that usually means illness. But again, what do I know? And I didn't even like him, but I noticed it. I didn't feel sorry for him though, like you usually would if you think someone's getting really sick. Whatever he had, he deserved it, you know?'

'You've been really helpful,' Maryam said, meaning it. 'You've made things clear to us.'

Khadijah rose from her stool and took another fried banana for the road. 'I hope so. Don't spend too much time on Zulkifli. He wasn't worth it alive and he certainly isn't worth it dead.'

She said her goodbyes and sauntered back to her keropok.

Chapter XIII

Yi was thinking about college. He was in high school now and wondering what he would do next. Teach? Maybe. Join the police force like Rahman? That seemed far more interesting. Of course, there were alternatives like doctor or lawyer, but Yi wasn't sure he was cut out for that much studying. He was smart, but also what his parents might call unmotivated. Maryam had spoken to him about his future and received monosyllabic answers. Eventually, fed up with Yi's silence, she asked his sisters to talk to him. She wanted to be present, of course, but no one could get information out of Yi more efficiently than Ashikin and Aliza. They'd had extensive practice.

Cornered one evening after dinner, Yi surfaced from television watching to see his mother, father and both sisters surrounding him in the living room. He knew their presence meant he was in for either a lecture or questioning, and he didn't think he'd done anything wrong. Therefore, lecture. He sat up straight, fatalistic about what was happening, and faced Ashikin with a solemn face.

'Since you're all here, I guess I'm in trouble.'

'No trouble, Yi. We just wanted to talk to you about your future.'

'All of you?' His eyes swept around the room. 'Where are Rahman and Daud?' The males in the room might be natural allies.

'They're babysitting,' Ashikin answered shortly. 'It's just us.'

Yi sighed. 'What do you want me to do?'

'It's not what I want, Yi,' Ashikin said quietly. 'It's what you want.'

'I want to watch TV,' Yi said hopefully, and then realized immediately it was the wrong thing to say.

'Not that,' Aliza said, annoyed. 'This is serious. This is about the rest of your life.'

'Oh,'

'Yes, oh.' Aliza was on the offensive. 'What have you been thinking about doing after high school? You'll be a grown man soon.' Aliza did not believe this for a moment, but Yi needed to hear it. 'We don't want you drifting out of high school and doing nothing. We all need to plan if you need to study somewhere or train or whatever. Azmi joined the army. I went to teacher's college. Ashikin started working with Mak. And you?'

'I don't know.'

'That's what I thought,' Ashikin took over. 'Now it's time to know. What have you thought about? And if you haven't thought of anything,' she said, forestalling his obvious comment, 'start right this minute so you have something to say.' She stared at him sternly, and he began thinking quickly.

'Well,' he started to buy some time, 'I have been thinking a little. I thought maybe the police. I might like that. I don't think the army, though I guess, maybe ...'

'The army is not for you,' Aliza cut him off. 'You wouldn't make it past two weeks.'

'I might,' said Yi, stung. 'But I don't really want to.'

'Good. The army is out,' Ashikin said briskly. 'Let's think of things you want. You said police, right? Anything else?'

'Teach?' he bleated.

Aliza snorted. 'Teach? Yi, think about it.'

'I think I could do it. But I'm not sure I could keep all those kids quiet.'

'First thing you'd have to do! Do you want to go to University? University of Malaya, Universiti Sains Malaysia? You could go to Kuala Lumpur or Penang.'

Yi was uncomfortable. 'I think I want to stay in Kelantan.'

'Fine,' said Ashikin. 'Now we're getting somewhere.' Maryam and Mamat were pleased; here they all were in a family conference. And Yi was thinking about his future.

'Do you want to open a business?' Aliza continued. 'Like Pak Long Malek with a batik factory or something like that? A lot of people make very good money doing that. Make keropok, or budu or something.'

Yi appeared thoughtful. 'Maybe.'

'You know Rosnah's family has a keropok factory. You could talk to them about it. Or Pak Long Malek if you want to run a batik factory. You make it, I'll sell it,' Ashikin assured him.

Yi brightened, talking about it. 'You know,' he said, animated for the first time ever discussing his future, 'I might like having a batik factory. I always liked working with Pak Long Malek, and I might have a talent for it.' Maryam was amazed to hear it. 'Do you think if I spoke to him, Mak, he might let me start with him? Maybe I could start during school vacation?'

They all stared at Yi. What had happened to galvanize him like that to choose a career and seem happy about it?

He examined their faces. 'What? Why are you all so shocked? I have things I'm interested in,' he said indignantly. 'I like working with with my uncle, and I think I could be really good at it. Why don't you think so?'

'We do,' Ashikin agreed. 'It's just that you never said anything about it before.'

'Because I never thought about it,' he admitted. 'But now that we're talking about it, it seems a natural thing for me to do. I mean, it's in the family. I know I can do it.'

'If you're working with Pak Long Malek after you graduate,' Maryam began to think, 'maybe you can stay with him in Kedai Buluh,' the town where he lived, farther down the road toward to beach. 'That way you're right there in the morning when you've got to start work.' In the good feeling of the moment she did not want to comment on Yi's current inability to get up in time in the morning. Why bring up unhappy subjects?

Yi's eyes grew large. 'Do you think he'd want me to stay there?'

'Of course,' Mamat laughed. 'He'll be so happy! And so will your Auntie! You're family, Yi. And your cousins will be happy to have you there.'

Yi smiled goofily, as only Yi could, at his surrounding family, congratulating himself on having sorted out the rest of his life.

'Unless,' Ashikin interjected, 'you're interested in a keropok factory, or budu. Then you can go stay with Azmi and learn the business.'

'I think I'll like batik better,' Yi said simply. 'You know, it's just more …'

'Clean,' finished Aliza. 'You don't like the smell of fish.'

Yi shrugged. 'I'm just saying I'd like batik better. I like the idea of making batik and then giving it to you to sell,' he said to Ashikin. 'Then we're working together. We're a team.'

'We've always been a team,' Ashikin smiled.

Maryam fought back tears of happiness.

Chapter XIV

'Well, think of it. Yi, all grown up.'

'I can't believe it. My little boy, thinking about what he'll do after high school. And it's almost here! Well, he can hardly do better than working with Malek. He'll teach him everything.'

'Of course he will! And you won't have to worry about him, being with your brother. How perfect is it? How lucky!'

Maryam nodded happily. 'It's such a worry off my mind. Now Yi has a plan, and it's a good one. I'm very glad.'

She certainly was, Rubiah noted. Her face was bright, and she carried herself with an enthusiasm for life which she could not find for a long time after their case with Omar. None of them slept that well after that – they had inadvertently peeked into hell and seen things no human being ought to see. Rubiah wished she could scrub her mind of the images of Omar and his silent, unmoving wife, a woman who longed to pass into the next world but was held here because her husband could not let her go. And Omar, a character conjured up by the devil himself, although when Rubiah said this she was roundly shushed by her whole family. But she knew it to be true, even if they did not care to acknowledge it.

Now, they were finally coming out of it. Sharifah Aini had

been born, Azman had been born and Rubiah's daughter Puteh had married. Now, Yi was thinking about his future. Life really had moved on.

'That Khadijah,' Maryam was saying, 'she's really something, isn't she? Do you think she's right?'

Rubiah remained blank, not being ready to switch gears so abruptly. 'Khadijah?'

'You know, the market woman in Tapak Gajah that we just spoke to,' Maryam said impatiently. 'She said Zulkifli appeared ill, that he cheated this other woman's husband of his share in the boat. You remember!'

'Right, Khadijah.'

'What was the market woman's name she was talking about? The one with the husband?'

Rubiah stared at her.

'Afzan, that's it. Don't you think we should talk to her? It seems to me her husband might be a perfect candidate for Zulkifli's murderer. Or maybe she was, if she's tall enough. You have to be able to strangle him right there and then, with no fighting about it. Are you listening to me?'

'Yes!' Rubiah said a bit louder than she'd meant to. 'I'm listening. I'm thinking, also.'

'Alright then, tell me about it. What are you thinking?'

Rubiah regarded her crossly. 'Just thinking about whether they could be the murderers. The two of them. Or maybe,' she slid her eyes sideways, 'Afzan is who Zulkifli was trying to kill. We should meet her and see if she's the same general size as Yati. Would that be something if it were true?'

'Something horrible, yes.'

'Well, now that I have Khadijah firmly in my mind, I remember her suggestion that Zulkifli was actually trying to kill someone else, not Yati. It was just her bad luck to be standing there are the wrong time.'

Maryam nodded encouragingly.

'We should think about who Yati might have resembled, to see who it might be Zulkifli was really after (assuming this is all true, naturally) and then we can build a case around that.' Rubiah considered the problem again, knowing if she didn't do it fast enough Maryam would interrupt her and break her thread of thought. 'Let's go to the market in Tapak Gajah, and see the sellers there, and who favours Yati. But first we should visit Amin, and get a picture of her, so we can compare it with the women in the market.'

'Good idea. Let's get going.

And so, they went. They found Amin at his house in Kubang Kerian. He had a new wooden house which felt empty, though there was furniture in it. His oldest daughter was doing her best to make it a home, and take over for her mother, but it was not quite coming together. She politely invited them to sit on the porch, called her father out, and provided them with tea and snacks. She was so innocent, and so anxious to please. Maryam's heart went out to her, she was too young to shoulder such responsibility.

'Che Amin,' Maryam began. 'We are so sorry …'

'Yes,' he said briefly, and waved them away. 'Yes, I know.' He stared into his teacup. 'There isn't much to say.' He sat quietly.

'How are you and the children doing?' she asked with a

glance towards the door where the daughter had disappeared.

'About how you'd think,' he said sadly. 'My eldest is trying her best, but she's still a kid. She can't be a mother to the younger kids. She's got school …' He ran his hands through his hair and regarded Maryam and Rubiah. 'I've been thinking of sending them to my wife's sister's house. She's got two children around the same age, and then they'd be kids with a mother to care for them. Not like here. I don't know if I can manage …'

'Does her sister want to take them?' Rubiah asked, ever practical.

He nodded. 'She asked me at the funeral. She's been here a lot. She says she's worried about them and they need a family. They need to be cared for. I think she thinks I can't do it, and maybe she's right. Anyway, I thought they might be relieved right now just to be children, without feeling they have to take care of me. They're worried about it, especially the eldest. She feels so responsible. What do you think?' He waited for their advice.

Maryam had not anticipated being asked for her opinion on this, but she could plainly see that Amin needed help. 'You don't need to make permanent decisions right now. I don't think you should, after the shock.' Rubiah nodded her agreement. 'Why not let the kids stay with their aunt for now? Is she nearby?'

'Down this path.'

'So they can go to school.'

He nodded.

'Let her help. You might want to stay there yourself,' Maryam said.

He nodded without thinking about what she'd said. 'It would

probably be better for them. She's always been very close to them.' He seemed lost.

'Che Amin, do you have a picture of your wife? We'll need to borrow it, just for a little while.'

'I have one. Why though?'

'I just want to be able to show it to people in Tapak Gajah,' Maryam said, answering by saying nothing.

'But everyone knows who killed her.'

'But no one knows why,' Maryam reminded him. 'And of course, we'd like to …'. She wasn't sure exactly what they would like to, but she was hoping not to be forced to specify anything further.

He got up without asking anything more. Maryam felt he didn't want to know anything more.

He came back in a moment with a snapshot of his wife, smiling with her children. She was pretty and was happy and full of energy. To think she was cut down so soon for what Maryam suspected was no reason at all. 'May I take it?' she asked.

'Yes, go ahead,' he replied, not really seeing her.

'Che Amin,' she began with a sideways glance at Rubiah, 'did you have any discussions with Zulkifli when you were in Tapak Gajah that day?'

'Sort of,' he said, examining his teacup. 'Everyone warned me away from him, so I thought I'd take their advice. He came over to talk to me, hinting he had some stories I'd want to know. Well, the last thing I want is stories that might upset my audience, so I didn't follow up on it. The guy at the coffee shop told me there was bad blood between Zulkifli and just about everyone, but he didn't really go into detail.

'Zulkifli struck me as a bit strange, very lonely. Maybe he wanted to be, I don't know.'

'Did he appear sick?' Maryam asked.

'I don't think so, but then I don't know what he usually looked like so maybe he wasn't healthy. He was dressed like a beggar. Honestly, all these wealthy men who pick their clothes out of the garbage, I just don't understand it. He was one of those. And he kept talking to me sideways, as if always hinting there was something else he could say, but wouldn't. I don't have a lot of patience for that.'

He tapped his cup and lost most of the animation which had carried him through his explanation.

Maryam thought it would be best for the children to be with their aunt's family right now. Though they too would be in mourning, she was sure the adults there would be functioning, and could care for children as they should be cared for. In this house, right now, they were on their own, and it wasn't fair to them.

As they rose to leave, Maryam leaned in to speak to Amin again. 'Please let them go today. It would be best for them. And you might want to go somewhere as well. You also need someone to watch over you.'

He smiled thinly and nodded. Maryam felt he'd make sure the children were alright, but she wasn't sure he'd do anything about himself, poor thing. As they went down the stairs, they saw two of Amin's children playing quietly in the yard, shell shocked, and a woman who resembled the photograph coming into the yard to greet them. It made both women feel better to think their aunt was coming to their rescue.

Chapter XV

Rubiah kept the photograph with her as they walked through the afternoon market at Tapak Gajah. She stole stealthy glances at it while comparing it with women selling fruits and vegetables, hoping to remain inconspicuous, though she felt she was anything but. Not much of a detective if everyone sees what you're doing, she thought, but it was hard to judge too quickly. She had an idea of Yati's build from her sister, and so could identify possible candidates. However, depending on how bad Zulkifli's eyesight really was, it really could have been anyone.

Afzan could have been mistaken for her from afar. Her face was nothing like Yati's, but they were of an age and height, and maybe from the back … ? Still, there were two or three other women who might be considered. Rubiah found Maryam, also gawking at the women there while trying to be casual. Heaven only knows what people were making of them, staring at people like that. She pulled Maryam aside to speak to her away from the crowd.

'We should talk to Zulkifli's wife to find out how blind he really was. If he really couldn't see, he could have mistaken anyone for … whoever it was he was thought he saw. It's so vague. I don't know myself what I mean to prove by this.'

'We're here for a reason, Yah. It can't be just a random killing, like Zulkifli went into the market with a parang and killed whomever happened to be in front of him. I can't believe that.'

'I can.'

'I know. But it doesn't make it true.'

'It might,' said Rubiah stubbornly.

Maryam sighed, and squinted at her cousin. 'I see. With you, *empat gasal, lima genap,* four is odd and five is even. You'll disagree with everything I say.'

Rubiah shrugged. She felt like arguing over anything Maryam suggested. Just because. 'Anyway,' she said, to get off this particular topic, which she wasn't enjoying, 'I still think we should talk to Zulkifli's wife again. I'd like to know whether he was really sick, and how bad his eyesight was. That would make quite a difference in what we'd think he'd do.'

'Do you think she would have noticed?'

'No,' Rubiah was blunt. 'But if she thinks hard maybe she'll come up with a clue. Besides, I'm in the mood for someone who really doesn't care.'

Maryam said nothing, because there was nothing Rubiah wouldn't quarrel with. They walked in silence to see Halimah, Zulkifli's wife, who was, luckily, at home. She invited them in without any great excitement, sat them on the sofa, provided tea and waited for them to explain themselves.

Rubiah began. 'We wanted to talk to you about how Che Zulkifli was in the time before he passed. Was he ill, for example? Was he having problems with his eyesight?'

She raised her eyebrows, but otherwise just observed them. They sat in silence for a few moments, while the two women began to feel awkward. Halimah, however, seemed to be comfortable with it.

'Let me think,' she finally said. 'Ill. Yes, he might have been. I thought he was kind of yellow for a few months. You know, sallow. Might have been a liver problem: it sometimes turns you that colour. He went to a doctor in Bacok; I'm sure I can find the name, and then you can talk to him. That way you'll get all the information you need.'

'He never discussed it with you?' Rubiah found this hard to believe.

'With me? No. Why? I know you think I'm cold and heartless. That's alright. Everyone does. But we had no reason to discuss ailments with each other. That simply wasn't our relationship. And if I thought he wasn't well, what would there have been for me to do? Suddenly decide we had a close relationship and I should take care of him? No. So, think what you want,' she said tiredly, not defiantly.

'Might he have mentioned it to anyone else?'

'His doctor, I imagine. If you're asking me if he had a mistress, then I don't know. Maybe, though I doubt it. Not because he'd have moral qualms – he's had them in the past, I think. I don't know for sure, but I suspected he might when he was younger. But now, he'd hardly need one. He wasn't active that way.'

'Due to illness?' Rubiah pursued.

Halimah shrugged. 'Maybe, if he was ill, which I'm not sure about. But sex was no longer important to him. Too much trouble,

I suppose.' She gave a small laugh. 'Well, men change, you know.' She clearly expected them to agree, but they sat stonily and said nothing. She shrugged again, this time more delicately.

'How was his eyesight?'

'His eyesight? What a strange question. It was getting worse of course: he was getting older. He had glasses now, and he never had before. He couldn't read without them.'

'Could he recognize people?'

'I guess so. You should really ask his doctor.'

Maryam surmised she was miffed because they hadn't joined in with anecdotes about how their own husbands were no longer interested in sex, but that was something they had no intention of discussing with her. Besides, Maryam thought loyally, that kind of thing did not apply to Mamat, or Dollah, probably, and she would not pretend it did even to get Halimah talking. This strange woman inviting confidences made her uneasy, and she was glad to escape to the outside again.

'Let's go straight to the doctor,' Maryam suggested, walking in the direction of the Bacok road, where they might find a taxi. 'She is so odd. I really don't like talking to her.'

'She was annoyed there at the end,' Rubiah commented.

'I know. But I'm not telling her any stories …'

'Certainly not.'

'So strange of her to ask for them.'

'Exactly.' Rubiah, too, seemed quite put out by the whole visit. They arrived at the doctor's office in high dudgeon, so much so they had to wait outside for a few minutes to calm down.

'The nerve …'

'How can she even imply ... ?'

'Never has anyone asked such a question!'

'We've got to get over it,' Maryam advised, though she herself was rather far from it. 'Otherwise we'll go in and ruin our discussion with him.'

She stood for a moment, just trying to calm herself. 'That ... well, I won't say it. But you know what I'm thinking.'

Rubiah did, and wholeheartedly agreed. 'Are we ready?'

'We are.'

They introduced themselves to the nurse at the desk and took seats in the small waiting room. Clearly, not up to Dr. Bates' standard in Kota Bharu, but after all, this was Bacok and far from the bright lights of the capital. They waited, slightly impatient but determined not to let it show, until they were called in to a smaller doctor's office, where they were greeted by a surprisingly young man in a white coat.

'Dr. Mustafa,' he said standing up politely and smiling. 'And you are?'

They introduced themselves and explained their errand.

'Ah,' he said. 'Che Zulkifli. Yes, a shame about his death. *Semoga dia tenang disana*: may he rest in peace. I'm sorry to hear it. His wife asked you to come here to inquire about his health?' He seemed to consider it. 'An odd request, don't you think? But you are helping the police, yes?'

'Yes,' Maryam answered emphatically. 'You can call the Kota Bharu Police Headquarters if you like.'

'No need.' He played with a pencil on his desk. 'I don't doubt you. It wasn't good news. Zulkifli had cancer. In his liver. He'd been to Kota Bharu for tests but wasn't interested in any treatment really. For that, he'd have to go to Kuala Lumpur, and he wasn't willing to do that. Didn't want to leave his family, I guess.'

Maryam was convinced that would not be the reason but said nothing.

'It was, of course, fatal. Not right away, I didn't think, but not that long from now either. I estimated something like six months or so. He wasn't really symptomatic yet, he was slowing down but not yet in too much pain. I had him on some painkillers. It was going to deteriorate soon, you know. These were his last few months of really living.

'He seemed to take it well, I thought. Stoically. Like many older Malay men, you see. They don't like to show too much emotion. Well, none of us do, do we? My job, as I saw it, was to keep him as comfortable as possible for as long as possible. There wasn't too much more I could do for him, unfortunately. I wish there were.'

'How was his eyesight?' Rubiah asked, leaning forward.

'His eyesight?'

'Yes. Could he see well?'

The doctor was puzzled. 'It wasn't part of his illness.'

'I understand.'

'I don't think he could see that well. He had cataracts, you see. Not too bad; I would say average perhaps for his age. Maybe a little worse than most. There would be no surgery planned of course: why? If he didn't want treatment for the cancer, certainly he didn't want surgery for more minor things.'

'Why didn't he want any treatment?'

The doctor thought for a moment. 'The treatment for cancer is difficult. Some people say it's worse than the disease. The chemotherapy would be done in Kuala Lumpur – we don't have the equipment here in Kelantan. I can understand why he wouldn't want to spend so much time so far from home, getting sicker with chemo. Especially with the kind of cancer he had, where the recovery rate is so low. I sympathize with the decision to stay home and live your life as well as you can for as long as possible.'

'Of course,' Rubiah agreed. 'So he was at peace with it.'

'It seemed to me he was, though perhaps I didn't see all of what he felt. It's a lot to handle, I would think. I believe we all fear death.'

'Thank you for your help,' Maryam said, as they rose to leave. 'You've really made a difference for us.'

'I'm glad to hear it,' he said. 'Please come back if you have other questions. Poor Che Zulkifli. Well, we do what we can.'

They smiled and left. As soon as they closed the door behind them, the nurse called in the next patient. He was a very busy doctor.

'So young,' Maryam said as they left. 'Or are we just getting older so everyone else is a kid? He's not much older than Yi.'

'I wonder if he's married,' Rubiah was always scouring the area for single men. She had unmarried nieces any one of whom would be an excellent match for a young, successful doctor. And not too far away, either. Perhaps she should bring one of them for a mild, non-existent ailment to meet him. If he was single, after all.

Maryam was depressed. '*Kubur kata mari, rumah kata nanti*: the grave calls you to come, the house tells you to wait. But the house didn't say anything to him. All he heard was the grave.'

Chapter XVI

'Cancer!' Aliza said. 'Well, that certainly makes a difference.'

'Yes, it makes whoever killed him hate him even more, if they knew. He was dying anyway, what good would killing him do?' Rahman replied.

'If you really hated him, you'd just let him go,' Aliza said. 'Dying from liver cancer? That's got to be one of the most miserable deaths possible, don't you think? In a way, whoever killed him did him a favour, sparing him that.'

'Unless …'

'Unless what?'

'Unless they didn't know he was sick. Maybe they might not have known he would die soon anyway. And if they wanted to make sure he was dead quickly, they'd kill him. They'd be so angry to find out it was in vain, you see.'

'His family?' Aliza was aghast. 'Cold, yes, I've heard all of you talk about it. But killing your own father? That's way beyond cold, Man. That's … well, that's just beyond. I don't even know what to call it.'

'What if,' Rahman leaned back in his chair, shifting the sleeping Sharifah Aini to a more comfortable spot against his shoulder, 'someone was worried about him changing his will again. His wife said he threatened to change it all the time and had written several wills. Maybe one of his sons feared he'd write him out and needed him dead before he could do that.'

'Aren't there less drastic ways to keep him from doing that?'

'I don't know. He seems like quite a difficult man to deal with.'

'Do you think the only person who noticed he was sick was that woman in the market?'

'She probably talked about it with her friends. I'll bet most of them knew.'

Aliza looked sage. 'If you want to know what's happening, ask a mak cik. That's what everyone always says. We should talk to her again.'

'I think she's tired of us. I definitely got that feeling.'

'Maybe if Mak and Mak Cik Rubiah and I went, it might go better. I can take Sharifah Aini! Who doesn't love a cute baby? Of course, she'll talk to us if she sees her.'

Rahman laughed. 'I'll drive you. I don't want Sharifah Aini in a taxi. She's too little.'

This seemed a bit of a non-sequitur to Aliza, but she thought better of commenting upon it. She'd prefer Rahman to be there anyway, and the more people to hold the baby the better. This would be one of her first trips away from the houses of her family and into the wide world. Aliza had to plan what the baby would wear.

***

Sharifah Aini was absolutely adorable. She wore a little white cotton dress with strawberries on it and a matching hat to keep out the sun. In honour of the occasion, she wore all four of her gold bracelets, on both wrists and both ankles, to keep her *semangat*, her life energy from slipping away. Each had a tiny bell on it, so she tinkled sweetly whenever she moved, which was constantly. Her grandmother and great-aunt fussed over her, her mother admired her, and her father itched to get out of the car and carry her, even though Aliza insisted they pack the stroller.

They garnered quite a bit of attention as they walked through the market, with Sharifah Aini grabbing most of the spotlight. It was a novel experience for most of the people there to see a policeman as a real person, with a family and a baby. They all knew they had them, but they'd never actually seen them, and were all the more friendly because of it. When they came to Khadijah's pile of keropok bags, she smiled happily and cooed over the baby.

'I didn't know you had such a little baby!' She rose to see her more closely. 'And this is your wife. And mother-in-law. The whole family!' She patted the baby's cheek and was rewarded with a wide, toothless smile. 'And what are you doing here today?' she asked.

'We had a few more questions, Kakak,' said Maryam. 'And we wondered if you could take a few minutes to talk with us …'

'Yes, let's get out of the sun,' she invited them. 'This little one mustn't get burned.' Aliza had been right: everyone would talk with them if they had a baby with them. They went to the coffee shop where they were greeted as old customers, and Aliza sat under the miniscule awning with Sharifah Aini.

'So, what can I help you with?' Khadijah asked when kopi peng had been served all around. Maryam had never really considered iced coffee before, but discovered a taste for it, especially in the heat of the sun. It might become her new favourite daytime drink.

'Kakak,' Rubiah began, 'you mentioned you thought Zulkifli was ill.'

'He was.'

'Did anyone else ever mention it?'

'Well, naturally, we women in the market all saw it and we mentioned it to each other, but I never heard anyone else say anything.'

'Not even your husbands?' Rubiah asked.

Khadijah laughed. 'My husband wouldn't want to hear anything about Zulkifli, and if I'd said I thought he was ill, he'd say "Good for him." He wasn't popular, you know, and I don't think many people talked about him. He wasn't worth their time.'

They all nodded. 'So, you don't think it was general knowledge he wasn't well.'

She shrugged. 'I'd never heard anyone say anything. Not too many people paid a lot of attention to him. They didn't want to be noticed by him, because they didn't want to get involved with him, with his threats and all. It would only be a problem. So they ignored him whenever possible. And they didn't talk about him much because they didn't care. The farther they could stay away from him, the better.'

'And you said his eyesight wasn't that good,' Maryam reminded her.

'It wasn't.' She stared longingly at a small box of Rothman's cigarettes on the back shelf. Rahman took the hint and bought them, handing her the box. She took a cigarette and offered them around, then lit her own. 'I noticed, you see, he would squint when he'd come to the market. Stare at things longer than anyone should. I could tell sometimes he didn't recognize people he knew until they were right up close to him. Mind you, I had better things to do that notice what Zulkifli was doing. It's just that I paid attention and knew what was going on.' She said it as a statement of fact, not touting her own abilities.

'He could have easily mistaken Yati for someone else.'

'Probably. Maybe if he were right up next to her, he'd know her, but then again, she'd never been here before, so he probably didn't know who she was. But he wouldn't know she wasn't whoever he thought she was, if you get what I mean.'

Maryam nodded. 'But ill as he was, what would be the point of killing him?'

Khadijah assessed whether Maryam was pretending to be naïve or was just thick. 'Kakak, it seems to me, and I'm no detective,' she added pointedly, 'that whoever killed him might not have known he was ill. Or if he did, he wanted him dead right away anyway. Why that is, I don't know, but I imagine these things have to do with money or sex, or both. Actually,' she relaxed in her seat to begin philosophizing, 'it's both the same thing, in a way, isn't it? For older people, it's money, for younger ones, sex. But no one's killing Zulkifli because of sex, are they?' She lit another cigarette and considered her rapt audience. 'So, if I were a detective,' there was an unmissable dig there, 'I would think it's money, and I'd have an excellent chance of being right, don't you think?' She appealed to Maryam for her opinion.

'It doesn't seem as if Zulkifli was competing with anyone for a particular woman,' Maryam began.

Khadijah snorted. 'Any woman,' she corrected her. 'He was past that, I told you. Not that I checked myself, you know. But you can tell, if you care to think about it.'

'And you cared to think about it,' Rahman interrupted.

She gave him a withering glance. 'Only since you've been asking me. Otherwise it didn't actually come up much. But you've been asking a lot.' She blew smoke out of her mouth and took another drag. 'I feel like I'm really helping you. Now, do you have any other questions? Because I need to get back to work. Goodbye, little girl.' She shook Sharifah Aini's toe and set her bracelets to jingling.

'See?' Rubiah said to the assembled family. 'If you want to know something, ask a market woman. They notice everything.'

Maryam nodded wisely. 'They know a lot more about Zulkifli than his own family does. And they haven't even paid that much attention. I don't believe she thinks much of us right now. Not that we couldn't have said the same thing to her, about sex and money, but we weren't there to talk to her, we wanted to hear what she had to say.'

'We don't have to justify ourselves,' Rubiah reminded her. Plainly, they both felt they did and had been shown up to some degree. It was a feeling they did not enjoy.

'But why,' Aliza asked slowly and softly, 'would he want to kill any of the other women in the market? I hear there were tensions, of course, but worth him killing? It seems that he was threatening them more than them threatening him. What would any of them have known that he would have felt compelled to do something so drastic?'

'I think Afzan would be the next person to speak to,' Rubiah said, gathering up her handbag. 'She seems the most likely person Zulkifli was after, and anyway, I'd like to know more about the argument with her husband.'

They all nodded in agreement, and Rahman went off to find her, leaving everyone else under whatever shade there was. There was no point in all of them traipsing around in the sun, especially with the baby's delicate skin.

Afzan came back with Rahman, frightened, twisting her hands together and murmuring about how she didn't know anything. Maryam and Rubiah tried to set her at ease, stressing that she was speaking to other Kelantanese women and not the police officially, and offering her iced coffee and snacks. She reached for a home-rolled cigarette, for which Rahman gallantly substituted a Rothman's, which seemed to be hard currency in Tapak Gajah. She accepted the cigarette and the coffee, looked pleadingly at the two mak cik, and awaited her fate.

'Cik Afzan,' Aliza started, as the one closest in age to her and least likely to be intimidating. Besides, she had the baby on her lap, so how fearsome could she be? Afzan smiled at the child with relief and began playing with her. 'We are investigating the two murders which happened here,' – Afzan nodded, signalling she remembered them – 'and we have some questions to ask you about Che Zulkifli.'

A cloud passed over Afzan's face at the mention of his name. 'He was a horrible man,' she said immediately after hearing his name. 'I'm not sad he's gone. I'm relieved. Is that a terrible thing to say? It's the truth.'

'I hear he was difficult,' Aliza said diplomatically. 'What happened between you?'

'It was between my husband and Zulkifli, not me. My husband, Ibrahim, works on one of the fishing boats. Zulkifli owned a share. He was always there when the boats came in and the fish and money were distributed. So cheap! It was hard to believe. He cheated my husband out of part of his share. We don't have that much, you see, so stealing the wages he earned is serious for us. It doesn't matter to Zulkifli, this was less than nothing. *Bagai duri sebatang terbuang:* like a single thorn thrown away. But to us it was something. And, it wasn't fair! He did this twice.

'Ibrahim went to complain to Razaleigh, that's Zulkifli's son. Well, Razaleigh was sympathetic, he knew it was wrong. He said he'd speak to his father, but if he did, nothing happened. Of course it didn't. But he's a good man, Razaleigh. After the funeral, do you know he paid Ibrahim for the money he was owed? Right away! He's fair, Razaleigh is. He's taking over the shares of the boat from his father, and Ibrahim's very happy about that. All the men are. They know they'll be treated well, and they have respect for Razaleigh. He works hard and he treats people as they should be treated. Yes, I'm happy he'll be in charge.'

'Did Ibrahim have any arguments with Zulkifli?'

She considered this, clearly calculating whether the answer might land her husband into trouble.

'Don't worry, Cik Afzan,' Aliza reassured her, 'you won't make difficulties for your husband, just answer honestly. That's all we ask.'

'Well, of course they had arguments; Ibrahim went to talk to him about what he owed them, and they also had a fight right there on the beach when Zulkifli didn't pay him his share. Everyone saw it and heard it. Ibrahim was very angry. Who wouldn't be?'

Aliza agreed, anyone would resent what Zulkifli had done.

'Ibrahim didn't kill him though,' Afzan said with confidence. 'His ship had just come in and they were pulling it up on the beach. He didn't even hear about it until he came to the market afterward and saw all the commotion.'

That was great news for Afzan, but Maryam was a bit disappointed. 'When did he get there?'

'The Bacok police were already there when his crew came up. The Kota Bharu people hadn't come yet.'

'He must have been relieved to see you were alright.'

She nodded. 'Yes, he was. He feared the worst when he saw the police and everyone chattering, but he saw me and felt better.'

'Why would he think you might have been hurt?'

Afzan was mystified. 'Don't you always worry about your family when you see something like that? Of course, that's the first thing he searched for.'

'Naturally,' Maryam said firmly. 'He'd try to find you right away. Did he ever talk about suing Zulkifli for his share?'

'With what, Mak Cik?' she said, almost angry. 'Zulkifli could afford that kind of thing, going to court and lawyers and all that. How would we do it? What he took from Ibrahim wouldn't pay the lawyer's fees. He knew that, and he used it against us. He took that small bit of our money, believing we couldn't do anything to get it back. *Dia makan nangka, kita kena getah:* he eats the jackfruit, we get sticky fingers. It's completely unfair, but he was a miserable person. A sad excuse for a man,' she said bitterly. 'I'm glad he's dead,' she repeated. 'I'm glad I'll never have to see him again.'

Aliza leaned in, with the baby on her lap. 'Cik Afzan, was there anything that Zulkifli had against you personally? Not against your husband, but you.'

'No,' she said shortly, and a trifle too quickly, Aliza thought. Afzan sat quiet with her lips shut tight, as if to keep any other words inside. She'd been so talkative answering the rest of the questions, and suddenly, monosyllables were all she would allow.

'Are you sure?' Aliza pursued, 'because I wonder whether …'

'I'm sure,' she interrupted, but said nothing more.

She wasn't going to say anything more, though all their curiosity was piqued by the sudden and complete change. Maryam decided they'd heard all they were likely to today, though it might merit another try later.

They thanked her profusely, but the good feeling was gone. She seemed a bit frightened and no longer friendly. She left with the barest terms of courtesy she could get away with without being obviously rude.

'What happened there?' Rubiah asked as they left the market.

'She's hiding something, but it's going to be difficult to get out of her. She must think it's dangerous.'

Maryam nodded, settling Sharifah Aini in the backseat of

the car with them. The excitement of the day had gotten to her, and she was already asleep. Maryam envied her, wishing she too could just pass out in the back and take a rest. But she had a job to do and could not have the privileges awarded a baby. She sighed and began the post-mortem they had after all of their interviews. 'It can't be Ibrahim,' she began, 'though it would have been interesting if he was still a possibility. But,' here she paused for dramatic effect, 'I think we're getting closer to finding out whether Zulkifli mistook Yati for Afzan.'

'They could be identical if you couldn't see very well,' Rubiah agreed.

'I think Afzan knows why he wanted to kill her,' Aliza added. 'She just doesn't want to say.'

Chapter XVII

Maryam adored her older brother, Malek. She thought he was the smartest, handsomest, most charming man around, and if asked, she did not hesitate to say so. Mamat was amused at her hero worship, which turned her from the terror of the main market into a twelve-year-old girl around her brother. Malek's wife, Zafira, was a woman of extensive patience and a good sense of humour, which she needed to endure Maryam's adulation of her husband. This occasionally led to Maryam's comments about how lucky she was, espoused to such a perfect man. Zafira was not provoked by this, but she and Mamat often shared a meaningful eye roll at the time. Luckily for them, they had never been caught at this – Maryam would not have taken well to have eyes rolled at her expense. Malek clearly idolized his little sister, though he was far less voluble about it. All in all, there was a good deal of admiration going around.

Malek stopped by in the late afternoon, when he knew Maryam would be home from the market and it would be possible to catch her alone. He called from the bottom of the steps and Maryam came as close to running out to meet him as she ever would.

'Abang Lek! What brings you here? Come up and relax. You'll be having dinner with us, of course. Is Zafira with you? The children?'

'No,' he said, coming into the living room. 'They're at home. They send their love, of course.'

Maryam went into the kitchen to make tea, and Malek followed her. 'What's going on with Yi?' he asked, sitting down on the kitchen steps. 'Has he really decided to go into the batik business?'

'He says that's what he's interested in,' Maryam confirmed. 'He wants to work with you.'

Malek nodded. 'I heard.'

'That was fast. From whom?'

'Daud. He was over to pick up some fabric and he told me it had been discussed.'

Maryam nodded.

'I'm very happy about it,' Malek continued. 'it will be wonderful to have Yi working with me. I've wanted to spend more time with him, but somehow there's always something else. This will be perfect.'

'I'm so happy,' Maryam beamed. 'I had no idea Yi had any kind of thoughts about his future, though you know, he isn't far from graduating high school. It's time to think about it.'

'He doesn't want to go to university or anything like that? Go to Kuala Lumpur or Penang?'

Maryam shook her head. 'He wants to stay close to home. Besides,' she added honestly, 'I don't think he has the grades for university. And even if he could get in, I don't think he has the interest to study. It's never been anything he liked.'

'No, he was never a student. Not like Aliza. So why force it? I think he'll do very well making batik. He might even enjoy it.'

'Let's hope. I want him to make a go of something. Really work at it. He hasn't done much of that.'

Malek laughed. 'He's still so young.'

Yi walked in the front door, heralded by an explosion of honking by the geese guarding the stairs, and the plunk of his schoolbooks hitting the floor. 'Pak Long Lek! You're here!'

'I am,' Malek agreed, stroking his luxuriant moustache.

'Did you hear? I want to work with you making batik. That's going to be my career,' Yi said proudly. 'We talked about it, and I really want to do it.'

'It's wonderful,' Malek answered with enthusiasm. 'I'm very excited for you to start. Will you stay with us, then?'

Yi nodded violently. 'I think so. I'll need to be there really early every day, so it makes sense for me to stay there.'

Malek nodded in return, less violently. 'Perfect. We'll get started as soon as school's over. When is that? A couple of months?'

'Yes.'

'I can't believe Yi's graduating high school,' Maryam interjected. 'The baby of the family is all grown up! It makes me want to cry.'

'Don't,' Yi ordered her. 'There's no need for tears, Mak. I'm not going anywhere.'

'All my children are grown,' Maryam said, almost mournfully.

'You still have your grandchildren,' Yi said calmly. 'And

you're having more every day.'

Malek laughed. 'You do seem to be having grandchildren often.'

'I'm lucky that way. But still, my youngest, graduating …'

'When are we going to eat?' asked Yi.

***

'Yi's all settled now,' Maryam said wistfully to Mamat after the dinner plates had been washed and Malek had returned home. 'No more children at home for us.'

'We can bring Nuraini to stay if you like,' Mamat suggested. 'Though I don't know whether it would be a good idea to take her away from her family, even though it's so nearby.'

'I think her parents will be better at teaching her how to act than we will,' she said firmly. 'I don't want her running wild …'

'Running wild? With her grandparents?'

'You know what I mean. She has to learn to get along with her brothers and be nice to them. She won't do that if she's living here. It'll make things worse as far as that goes.'

'Everyone blames Nuraini,' Mamat grumbled. 'And she's just a little girl. A sweet girl.'

'A sweet girl,' Maryam agreed, 'with a princess problem. Really, it's got to be fixed before she gets too old. I think Ashikin is best suited to get it under control.'

'Under control,' Mamat repeated, burying himself in his newspaper. 'Under control indeed.'

'What does that mean?'

'She doesn't need control. She needs good, loving care. Anyway, I can't talk about this. I'm reading the newspaper.' He immediately illustrated the behaviour though Maryam suspected he was just pretending to read to end the conversation. Fair enough, she'd end it. She never meant to have Nuraini live with them; she doubted Ashikin would permit it and would be no doubt hurt to hear her parents even thought to bring it up. It was best to let it go.

The next morning, Osman was greeted at his office by Razaleigh, Zulkifli's oldest son. He was already waiting for Osman before he arrived, and Osman as a rule arrived quite early. He arose when the police chief entered, and politely asked to speak with him.

Osman ushered him into his private office and closed the door behind them. He sat behind his desk and Razaleigh took the chair facing him. He cleared his throat anxiously, and Osman decided to help him say what he wanted.

'It's nice to see you come in,' he began. 'How can I help you?'

'I would like to ask that the investigation be done by the police. The investigation of my father's death, that is.'

Osman was mystified. 'It is, Che Razaleigh. We're already hard at work on it.'

'I meant only policemen. Only official policemen.'

'What are you saying?'

'I don't want those two ladies,' he amended that, it sounded so rude, 'Mak Cik Maryam and Mak Cik Rubiah investigating. This is not a party, it's a crime. I don't want it treated as a family outing.'

'What do you mean?'

Razaleigh tried again. 'They come to Tapak Gajah and sit with the market women, listening to gossip and drinking coffee.' Osman thought this sounded a lot like general police work but said nothing. 'They came to the market a few days ago with a daughter, a baby, the policeman son-in-law, a whole party. Chattering with the market women, making a spectacle of it. What will everyone think,' he asked, 'when those who claim to be part of the police investigation are showing up with the whole family to sit around and laugh with the lowest people in the kampong? How is that helpful? It makes my father's murder into entertainment.'

Osman was deeply uncomfortable and squirmed in his seat. Described in that way it certainly did sound unprofessional, though he had complete faith in Rahman, and had never known Maryam and Rubiah to take their investigating less than seriously.

'Are you sure they weren't just interviewing witnesses in the most convenient place? It might be difficult to bring all the market women into the police station all the way from Bacok.'

'And for that, did they need to bring a baby? The wife? Who else needs to come to this travelling circus? Who will take it seriously? I heard they were talking away with some of the worst busybodies I know, who will tell tall tales about everyone involved, and even people who might never have been any part of this. How does this get us to identifying the murderer?'

'Police work often takes far different forms than you imagine,' Osman intoned. 'It is the people no one notices who see the details of what occurred. I'm thinking of the market women who witnessed both killings. Where else will we find witnesses?

You may not like it, but they're the people who can tell us what transpired.'

'There were respectable people there,' Razaleigh began to raise his voice. 'Solid citizens, as they say. Men whose word you can depend on, not someone just making up stories.'

'I'm sure they've spoken to everyone who was there,' Osman assured him. 'And that would include those you call solid citizens and those you don't like. We must follow the threads of the investigation wherever they lead.' Osman particularly liked this last comment. It sounded very scholarly.

Razaleigh was clearly losing his patience. 'Is it too much to ask that people act professional when they come to work? Babies have no place at serious interviews.'

Osman thought he might have been right but was not in the mood to admit it. 'Sometimes you need to put people at ease, depending on who you'll be interviewing. I'm sorry if you don't like my officers and our civilian consultants,' nice turn of phrase again, 'but unless they have treated you unfairly or disrespectfully, I must ask you allow us to conduct our investigation as we think best.' He stood up to indicate the interview was over.

Razaleigh stayed seated. 'I want my father's memory respected. I don't want it turned into market drivel.'

'Che Razaleigh, as soon as he was murdered in the market it was unavoidable that it would be talked about there. Come now. What is the problem with the market anyway? I don't understand why that of all things upsets you so.'

'I don't like those people talking about it.'

'Market people?'

'Yes. I want the police investigation to be discreet.'

'Murder is not discreet, Che Razaleigh.'

'Still.'

'There is no "still". We must investigate as we see appropriate.' He changed direction. 'Were you close to your father, Che Razaleigh?'

'Are you now interviewing me?'

'You're here,' Osman informed him. 'We like to conduct our interviews wherever and whenever we can. So naturally, since we're already talking, it seems only right we take advantage of the situation …'

'I didn't come to be interviewed!'

'Of course not, but here we both are. We should put this time to good use. So, tell me, Che Razaleigh,' Osman sat down again, no longer dismissing him. He leaned back and waited.

'Well, not really. It hurts me to say it but it's the truth. My father, as you've no doubt heard, was a difficult man. It was hard to get close to him.'

'You worked for him,' Osman stated.

'Yes, in the keropok factory.'

'Which you will inherit.'

'With my brother, yes.'

'Did your father always intend to leave it to you?'

Razaleigh sighed. 'My father was constantly threatening to disinherit either one, or both of us, all the time. So now, we are inheriting. But he always kept it over our heads.'

Tea arrived with Din, and Razaleigh offered a cigarette to not only Osman, but to Din as well, who was delighted to be included. It was a nice gesture to a young man, and Osman had trouble reconciling a man who would be so unthinkingly polite and thoughtful to the one complaining about the lower orders being consulted.

'Don't think I don't know it puts me under suspicion,' Razaleigh continued, 'that my father kept threatening to leave us nothing. Like I'd kill him to make sure I got the factory and all before he could cut us off again. But you might as well know the truth. It would be worse if I didn't tell you. So, I know what I'm saying sounds bad, but there it is.' He shrugged and smoked his cigarette.

'Did you know he was ill?' Osman asked.

'Ill?' Razaleigh was startled.

'Liver cancer.'

Now Razaleigh was shocked. 'I didn't … are you sure?'

'We've spoken with his doctor in Bacok.'

'No, I didn't. *Astigfirullah!*'

'Surprising, isn't it?'

'Why didn't he tell us?' Razaleigh seemed genuinely shaken.

Osman shook his head. 'I don't know. Not that it changes anything. He's still passed.'

'Well, of course,' Razaleigh now appeared confused. 'Yes, of course he's passed, but he should have told us.'

'It doesn't appear he told anyone much of anything.'

'That's true.' Razaleigh still seemed upset.

'It didn't seem your parents talked much.'

'Not at all,' he said, distracted. 'They hardly ever spoke. I suppose that's why he never mentioned anything.'

'Was there someone he did confide in? Do you know?'

'I don't know. He didn't seem to have friends. A solitary man, you might say. And certainly not close to his family, but still, something like this, you'd think …' he trailed off, still taking it in. 'I wonder if my mother knew. I'd think not. Not that she'd care if she did – you've met her. But then, just keeping it to yourself and not telling anyone. A terrible secret to keep bottled up. I wish he told me.'

'And if he had?'

'I don't know. I wish I did. Would I have been sympathetic? Or would I have ignored it? I don't know. He was not an easy man to like, you see. And my family leans more to painful frankness than any other emotional reaction. So, would I have said nothing, or would I have been helpful?' He sighed. 'I'd like myself better if I could say with any confidence I'd be someone for him to lean on, but I don't know.'

'You're frighteningly honest,' Osman told him. 'Most people would say they'd have done all manner of things for him if only they'd known. I like it that you only say what you actually know to be true.'

'You like it now. I don't think you'd like it if you had to live with it every day. Then, you might get really tired of it.'

'Is your wife tired of it?' Osman was truly interested.

'No, she's just like me,' he said sadly. 'We're cousins, and our family is blunt, sometimes frighteningly so. In truth, she's more like that than I am. It doesn't make for a particularly tender marriage, but at least you know just where you stand. Anyway, I make her comfortable, financially, I mean. Maybe that helps.'

He stared at the floor, wondering why he'd confided this much to Osman without really having been asked.

'Are you still angry about the questions asked in the market?' Osman asked him

He smiled thinly. 'I've already forgotten. You don't want to do psychological analysis on me, so I think I'll leave now. Thank you for your time.' He rose, shook hands and left, Osman staring after him, thinking.

If he lied, it was a masterful job of it. He admitted the suspicions against him, thereby disarming Osman. He became friendly and almost too honest, but it was hard not to believe him, which neutralized his near confession. All in all, an excellent performance. Osman felt he was taken in even while hearing it, though he was attentive to signs of guilt. Razaleigh was a first-class liar if he was inventing all this, and Osman wanted to believe him even as he felt that would be impossible.

Chapter XVIII

Rahman was driving back to Tapak Gajah with Maryam and Rubiah. Again. For the hundredth time. He'd memorized the route there from the traffic circle in Kota Bharu to the Pasir Puteh Road along the coast. He was so tired of it. When this case was over, he'd never visit Tapak Gajah again, although it wouldn't be that difficult, as he'd spent all his life up to now not visiting it, and he'd surely never miss it. He wearily got out of the car, holding open the doors for Maryam and Rubiah, as they stared up at Zulkifli's compound. Osman had asked that Razaleigh's wife be interviewed, to see if she had considered leaving, or spoken about it to anyone. Osman thought he saw a frightened man and wanted to know whether his wife might be the cause of it.

They walked over to the house, slowly, no longer eager to meet with possible witnesses. It just seemed sad right now, or maybe they'd all caught Rahman's mood, and found it hard to work up any enthusiasm.

They'd called before they'd come, as Zulkifli's home had a telephone, one of the few in the village. Razaleigh's wife, Fatimah, was waiting for them on the porch. 'Come in, out of the sun,' she called to them. They ascended the stairs feeling thoroughly unmotivated.

Cold drinks and hot fried bananas were served, which perked them up a bit: it was very hot indeed, and a cold drink was always welcomed. Fatimah invited them onto a comfortable sofa, and an armchair for Rahman, and they began to feel perhaps this would not be as difficult as they imagined. Fatimah appeared pleasant, at least, and Rubiah decided to lead the conversation, hoping Fatimah would follow her.

'We've spoken to your husband, Cik Fatimah,' she began, and Fatimah cut her off immediately.

'I know. He told me he'd spoken to you and then gone to the police chief in Kota Bharu. Why? I can't imagine. I don't think he had much to say, and there's really no point in going to complain about how the interviews are conducted. It's your business, you can talk to people however you like. It just makes him a fool.' She pursed her lips in disapproval. 'I told him not to go, but he's very headstrong.'

Rubiah was struck silent. She didn't predict this straightforward conversation, but this family was odd that way. How did they find a wife for their son who was just like them? Rubiah didn't think there were others around so outspoken. Especially young women. It just went to show: *enggang sama enggang, pipit sama pipit*. Hornbills go with hornbills; finches go with finches. Each with its own kind.

Fatimah continued, intent upon her explanation. 'Razaleigh thinks he knows how everything should be, and he doesn't mind telling people how to do their own jobs. It isn't going to make him popular, is it? You know,' she leaned forward, as though sharing a secret, 'he's now a partner in a fishing boat, and he owns the keropok factory with his brother. He can't lecture the sailors about how to fish. They'll never listen to him, and why should they? He's never fished in his life. I just hope he realizes that it's important for him to … well, to keep his mouth shut and let the men get on with it. Otherwise, he's going to end up like his father and everyone will hate him.'

'I thought the men were quite fond of him,' Maryam put her two cents in before she was cut off.

'Now, maybe,' Fatimah tossed her head. 'But in the future will they if they think he's trying to order them about? *Itek diajar berenang*: teaching ducks to swim, that's what they'll take it as.' She shook her head as if already imagining this disaster.

'He might not …' Maryam sought to defend him, even for a moment.

'And he might,' his wife contradicted her. She then waved her hand over the refreshments and bade them eat. She took a sip herself to encourage them, for it would be rude for them to eat or drink before the hostess.

'Was he always planning to take over from his father?' Rubiah asked, keeping her expression as bland as possible.

'Well, who could tell? His father was always going back and forth on that. Telling them about how much he wanted them to follow him one day and disinheriting them the next. You could never count on him being in the same mood for more than a few minutes at a time. A very argumentative man, as I'm sure you've already heard. Thank God, the sons aren't really like that. They aren't seeking out lawsuits wherever they go. Otherwise, it would be impossible to live with them. Take my mother-in-law, Cik Halimah. I don't know how she managed. Maybe by ignoring him altogether. It's the only way, right? Though she took it to an extreme. But maybe she felt she was forced, who knows?'

'Did she ever talk to you about it?'

'Me? No, she wouldn't talk to me. She hardly spoke to anyone. But when she did speak, watch out! She didn't sugarcoat anything. Not her. Razaleigh, he isn't as bad as his father. But I'm afraid maybe he might be.'

Maryam tried desperately to interrupt. 'What would you have done if he didn't inherit the factory and the boat and the rest? If Che Zulkifli really did leave them out of the will?'

Fatimah stared at her, disbelieving. 'That wouldn't have happened,' she said with finality. 'A will like that, it would be thrown out of court. Just like that! They'd never let him cut out his own sons. The shariah court, why, they would never allow it. It's unthinkable.'

Fatimah had clearly done her homework and must have spent a good deal of time studying this. Maryam didn't think she would have been too shy to inform her husband about her research, either.

'Che Razaleigh would have known about that as well,' she commented, steeling herself for a torrent of words, which did not fail to arrive.

'Well, of course he did! We discussed it. That's when I told him not to worry about his father's threats. It would never stand up. I had my brother check with a religious teacher, so we knew what to expect. As I said, you never knew where you stood with

Che Zulkifli, and I didn't want to have my husband, and myself, you know, always worried about what might happen. This way we'd already asked the question, and we knew.' She was very pleased with herself.

'You've been anxious about it,' Maryam said, her face creased with concern.

Fatimah regarded her for a moment before responding. 'Well, of course. You know, that's our livelihood, and when someone is threatening to take it away, naturally you want to find out what the legal, um, legal possibilities are. Razaleigh and his brother Jusoh have worked in the factory for, well, I don't know how long. And worked hard. And for his father, his own father, to then say he's going to take it all away from them ... You can't just do nothing, can you?'

'What can you do?' Maryam asked.

'What do you mean? We can check to see if he can do such a thing, and that's been done.'

'Anything else?'

'Are you asking if we killed him? No, we didn't. Don't be stupid, of course not. He's their father, that would never happen.' Maryam nodded. 'That you would even think that!'

'I didn't think it,' Maryam said calmly. 'It would never cross my mind.'

'Then what did you mean?'

'Just a question, nothing more.'

'Well, I thought you were accusing us of something.'

'No.' Maryam took a dainty sip of tea to show her appreciation of her hostess' generosity. She wished Fatimah would relax, and not work herself into a tantrum. She felt it was the next step in the conversation. 'How many children do you have?' she asked politely.

'Two.'

'Boys, girls?'

'Two boys,' she answered grudgingly.

'Just like their father! Two brothers. How nice for you. How old are they?' She steered her slowly but firmly to less sensitive subjects.

'They're eight and ten. And quite a handful!'

'Boys certainly can be. I have two boys myself, but of course, much older.' She smiled at Fatimah. 'Tell me, what is Razaleigh's brother like? Razaleigh is the older brother, isn't he?'

'Yes, Razaleigh's the oldest,' she said. Maryam's short detour to more innocent subjects seemed to have worked, and Fatimah had regained her composure. 'Jusoh just worships him. He follows him around, he does whatever Razaleigh asks. He hasn't really grown into his position. As the boss, you know. He tends to be a follower rather than a leader,' she continued loftily. 'I imagine as he matures he'll become more assertive. In the meantime, he's second to his *abang*, his older brother. I suppose that's as it should be,' she finished, as though she'd given infinite consideration to how Jusoh should act, and the respect he should accord Razaleigh.

'Are they together much?' Rubiah asked.

'Oh always! You know, Jusoh just follows him around. And they work together, so it only makes sense, doesn't it?'

'Do you see much of Jusoh?'

She made a face. 'I see him all the time as well. Whenever I see my husband, I see Jusoh there, right next to him. No privacy at all. Alhamdulillah, he sleeps at his own house, or he'd sleep right at the end of the bed! But I suppose he's devoted to his older brother, so he wants to be with him all the time and learn from him. It provides him an education.'

Maryam tied to reconcile the picture of this business mentoring relationship with her description of Razaleigh moments ago as someone who could easily lose the respect of the sailors fishing in his boats. He'd morphed from a bit of a boor to a business tycoon with a flair for teaching in the blink of an eye. 'I thought you said he had to learn how to act around his employees,' Maryam said nicely. 'I'm wondering if he …'

'No need to wonder,' Fatimah snapped. 'Do you think you've caught me out? You haven't.' She narrowed her eyes. 'He's a good businessman and an excellent example for his younger brother. He will learn about the businesses he knows less about, like fishing. I think you're trying to get me tangled up in my own words so that I'd say something incriminating. I haven't done anything to incriminate myself about. So, there's nothing to find out.'

'No one would dare accuse you of anything,' Rahman spoke up. 'Perhaps we have asked our questions in too pointed a way and given you the false impression we thought you were guilty of anything. No indeed, we don't. We just wanted to get some background on the family, and you've been most helpful. We are all grateful, aren't we?' The two women nodded enthusiastically. 'Thank you for assisting the police as we investigate the death of your father-in-law. Your help is appreciated, and we'll call if we have any further questions.'

Rahman led them out of the house with all due thanks and expostulations about how much they'd enjoyed meeting her. For the moment, she was silenced, and stood at the top of the stairs waving to them as they left.

'The family seems to run to type,' Rahman commented as he opened the car. He'd be relieved to get away from Tapak Gajah this afternoon. He'd thought briefly about talking to some other people since he was already there but decided he could not face any more information on this case at the moment. 'I've had enough of them for now.'

'Shall we say hello to Minah?' Maryam asked, or rather couched a command as a question. 'Why don't we stop there on the way home?'

'She could easily convince them to kill their own father,' Rubiah suggested. 'Can you imagine? I can see how they would be browbeaten into it.'

'Don't make this all someone else's fault,' Maryam reminded her. 'Whoever killed Zulkifli did it by himself and bears the blame for it. No matter who said what to him.'

'Do you think it was his own family?' she asked Maryam as they drove away with the air conditioning on. Rubiah had never gotten over the recurring miracle of cool air on demand.

'Who knows?' answered Maryam moodily. 'There are still a few people we've got to speak to. Ibrahim, for instance.' She gazed out the window. They didn't have to go far to get to Minah's house, but it was nice to do it in style.

When they were courteously escorted out of the car by Rahman, Minah was already standing on her porch grinning. 'Ah, finally you come to see me,' she called out in a voice easily heard throughout the kampong. 'Come right up, don't stand around in the yard with the chickens!'

Minah was a cousin, and therefore knew just what to do to put family at ease. Cold drinks, hot drinks, cakes, curry puffs, an assortment of cut fruit – so much food the table could hardly hold it. And of course, a fresh carton of cigarettes just waiting for them. It was a lavish spread, and they were very impressed, particularly as it was done on the spur of the moment. Just that she had all this lying around in the kitchen was reason enough to be dazzled.

'Alamak, is there any fruit left in the whole village?' Rubiah exclaimed. 'You're too generous, you don't need to make this kind of effort just for us.'

'Nonsense,' Minah waved away any compliments or polite protestations of their unworthiness. 'I'd do more, but it might fall off the table!'

'It's falling off the table already! Really, Minah, you needn't go to this kind of trouble. But we're very grateful.'

'Talk!' Minah ordered. The women in the family shared a predilection for taking command. Rahman was anxious to see how three generals interacted. It promised to be excellent viewing.

'You've certainly caused quite a stir in Tapak Gajah. I hear Halimah is fit to be tied about you asking questions. And Razaleigh has complained about you talking to the market women. Fool that he is,' she dismissed him. 'Market women like us know the most about what's going on, right? Your best witnesses.' She opened the pack of cigarettes and passed it around while urging fruit and cakes on them at the same time. The fruit in particular was cool and tempting, but it was nice to relax with a cigarette and a drink with a relative.

'Absolutely,' Rubiah agreed. 'Who else noticed Zulkifli was ill? Not his family! Cik Khadijah in the market noticed by just a quick glance as he walked by, but his family? No one knew. How is that, do you think?'

'That family is another story,' Minah told them. 'You've met them. They're like … from outer space. I've never seen people so cold. They don't care what they say. Especially the women: Cik Halimah and Cik Fatimah. It's always an experience talking to them. Cik Halimah ignores whatever she doesn't like, and not like other people would ignore it. She can't see it at all; it doesn't exist for her. I don't know how she does it. Not that I want to copy it. She was married to Zulkifli for I don't know how long, but she was able to act as though he simply wasn't there. Not even noticing he had cancer. And not embarrassed about it! She's told people who she's seen at the market she didn't notice. Just like that! Can you imagine?'

Maryam nodded. 'I was really amazed. I even wondered if his sons killed him.'

'No!' Minah breathed. 'Can it be?'

'I'm not saying it's true,' Maryam reminded her. There was no need to tell her not to speak about it. After all, it was Minah's investigation in a way and she'd never jeopardize it. 'I'm saying I thought about it. I don't think there's anything they wouldn't do if they thought it would help them. Where did they find this Fatimah? She's just like them.'

'A cousin,' Minah said, reaching for a cold drink. 'Had to be a relative, that sort of thinking would only run in the family. Another family might have taught her some manners.'

'I wouldn't want to be them,' Rubiah added. 'They can't have many friends.'

'They don't want them. They just want to say whatever pops into their heads. Even if it's not nice – especially if it's not nice. Halimah's said it's because they're honest. I think it's because they're rude.'

Maryam noticed the polite 'cik' had now been dropped. Well, it had to happen. This was not a woman about whom you had warm and friendly feelings. 'Did you ever have any problems with them?'

'Me? No, because I don't have to deal with them. I don't work in their factory; my husband doesn't work on their boats. They wouldn't consider us their equals, but they feel we're at least a step above labourers. Alhamdulillah, we have a little respect from them.' She thought for a moment. 'Though Nasir once had a disagreement with Zulkifli. Some time ago. I'm not sure I even remember what it's about,' she finished blandly.

Rubiah considered her for several moments, which seemed even longer. 'Well, I remember sort of,' she admitted, blushing. 'Nasir considered buying a share in a fishing boat, and Zulkifli blocked it. From meanness only, you understand. He threatened some of the other partners with a lawsuit if they took Nasir in, on the basis of Zulkifli losing some of his investment. Or something like that anyway.' She stared at her cigarette. 'Nasir hates him. So do I, I'll tell you that right now. But that was years ago. And Nasir wasn't at the market.'

'Where was he?' Maryam asked. Best to get the uncomfortable questions out of the way as quickly as she could.

'He was sitting on the porch here with his friends. Don't take my word. Ask the neighbours and the men drinking coffee with him. I'll give you the names.'

Rahman nodded. 'Later,' he said. 'There's no rush, Mak Cik Nah.'

'Let's get back to real suspects,' Rubiah said heartily. 'Do you think his sons would kill him? I mean, if they thought he'd disinherit them,' Rubiah explained. 'Or would they hire someone to kill him? I'm just thinking if he constantly threatened them with taking them out of his will, did they feel it was time to get rid of him and get on with their lives? I know it's a terrible thing to think about, but could it be true? I wondered when we were talking to Fatimah. Would she stop at killing someone if she thought her money was at stake? I don't know.'

Rahman nodded slowly. 'I'd thought of that, but I didn't want to say anything because it sounded so wrong.'

Minah thought about it. 'She'd do it herself if she had to. Was she at the market?'

'I don't think so.'

'Too bad. Then you wouldn't have to go any further.'

'Do you think she'd get her husband to do it?' Rahman leaned forward to ask.

'I don't know about that,' Minah said.

'Someone would have said he was there, don't you think?' Rubiah said slowly.

'Why?' Maryam asked. 'No one saw anything, as far as I could gather. Which means they don't want to name the person they saw. And people like Razaleigh, you remember what Afzan said.'

'Razaleigh? I don't think it could be Razaleigh,' Minah interjected. 'He's the best of them. More likely his younger brother, Jusoh. He'd be easier to push around.'

'We haven't met him,' Maryam admitted.

'You must,' Minah told them. 'You'll enjoy it.'

'He's not married, is he?' Rubiah asked.

Minah shook her head. 'He should be, you know. He's old enough. But no one seems to have done anything about it. Strange, isn't it?'

'What's wrong with him?' Rubiah asked.

'What's wrong with all of them? He's a bit weird. Maybe that's too strong a word. He's just a little eccentric, but then so are a lot of people, right? Not so eccentric that he couldn't make a good match, with his prospects. That's up to his mother. She's the one who ought to be working on it and she isn't. That would be an interesting question to ask. Let's see how honest she is then! I'd love to be there during that conversation,' Minah said gleefully. 'It's a shame I can't. But you must promise me you'll let me know what she says right away!'

'You'll be our first stop,' Rubiah promised. 'Though, as a mother, I can't understand why she isn't on that. What mother would let that slide?'

'She didn't let it slide for Razaleigh,' Maryam added. 'So why for the younger one?'

'Who knows with them? But it's a good question to ask.'

'What does it have to do with the murder?' Rahman asked.

They all turned to stare at him. 'It's background,' Maryam informed him.

'It will give us some insight on how the family works,' Rubiah offered.

'Sometimes you have to go at things from the side rather than the front,' Minah said.

Rahman knew he'd asked the wrong question.

Chapter XIX

All the babies were at Maryam's house playing on the porch. Azmi's daughter, Ashikin's two boys and Sharifah Aini. There was a lot of noise and a good deal of crawling about, which kept all the parents on their toes. Zakaria, who was already two and walking, was the boss, and told the babies what to do. They completely ignored him, which didn't seem to bother him at all – his fun was in issuing the orders rather than making sure they were followed. Yi and Nuraini were sitting on the top step to see no one came tumbling down. Maryam and Mamat were blissful watching all of them roll around, all their beloved grandchildren together. Maryam sighed with contentment.

'Look at them all,' she said to Mamat. 'Would you have believed, all those years ago … ?'

'Of course, I knew it the moment I saw you.'

'That we'd have these beautiful grandchildren?'

'That we'd have a happy life together.' He smiled. 'I was right. As usual.'

Maryam laughed out loud. 'You were right about that at least. As usual, I'm not sure.'

'Look at them,' Ashikin nudged her sister. 'They're so content.'

Aliza tore herself from observing the babies' every move. 'I hope I'm like that at their age. Happy with one another the way they are.'

'We both will be,' Ashikin told her airily, and Aliza absolutely believed it. Ashikin always knew things.

Today Sharifah Aini was not dressed in the height of baby fashion, as her mother often preferred. She was dressed for comfort alone, as were they all, in diapers and t-shirts. They remained under the eaves of the roof, out of the sun, squealing like puppies, with Mamat's singing doves in elaborate cages hung above them. It was a lovely scene; the whole family gathered happily together, the giggles of the babies and singing of the birds, occasionally punctuated by the honk of a goose scratching for food in the yard. How could life be improved upon?

The intermittent honk of one goose suddenly became the determined blast of them all as they flocked to one end of the yard in open alarm. Minah arrived with her husband Nasir, coming by taxi from Bacok, acting a bit flustered. But flustered or not, Maryam noticed Minah was wearing a good half forearm worth of bangles, and at least three necklaces of different lengths, so whatever brought her to Kampong Penambang did not rush her from the house before she could dress.

Minah smoothed her hair and put on her best visitor's smile. 'Hello!' she greeted them, to be answered by a chorus of, 'Come out of the sun! Come on up and sit down! How marvellous to see you here!'

'See all these children!' she exclaimed as she picked her way up the stairs and onto the porch, sitting down next to Maryam.

'How wonderful to have them all here!'

Aliza and Ashikin went immediately to the kitchen, and dispatched Yi and Nuraini to bring back some cold drinks and fried bananas but only if they were freshly made and still hot. Tea and keropok were presented in moments, and they sat down to hear her news. They were happy to see Minah, as they always were, but Maryam knew this was not a lazy Sunday afternoon visit to pass the time. The babies were corralled where their parents could guard them, and they waited to hear what Minah had to say.

She took a small sip of her tea and Maryam urged her to have some keropok. 'You've come such a long way. You need to relax and have a little to eat. We'll have cold drinks in a minute. But here, catch your breath.'

Nasir was already sitting with Mamat, Rahman and Daud, a bit removed from the women, but close enough to both hear and participate in the conversation.

'Well,' Minah began. 'After our last visit, I was thinking about Jusoh and Halimah and that whole family, like we said. And what do you think? It was as though I conjured them up with my thoughts alone! Suddenly, who turns up at my door but Halimah and her horrible daughter-in-law Fatimah. Never before have they come to my house, not that I was hoping for it. I was happy enough not to deal with them, but they were there at the steps so I had to ask them to come in, didn't I? Alamak, I didn't see that coming at all.

'They came in and sat down and I could tell they were examining everything in my house and calculating how much it cost. You know that silver tray that my mother left me?' The women all nodded. It was lovely. 'They couldn't take their eyes off it. Thank goodness it's as big as it is, or I'd be afraid she'd try to sneak it out of my house!

'She said to me, "Minah, why is your cousin snooping around here? I don't understand." And I said, "She's working for the police. She and my cousin Rubiah have done this before; the police set a very high store by them for how they've solved crimes. You should be honoured they've asked them to come in on this." And Halimah said, "The police brought them in? No, you did. Now I think you should bring them out." I laughed at her. I said, "Me? You overestimate me. No, if you don't want the police investigating, you'd better talk to them. Although I hear your son already tried that and they weren't convinced."

'Well, she was getting furious. She doesn't want anyone investigating this, for either Zulkifli or that poor woman who was killed. However, it isn't up to her, is it?'

'I don't think so,' Rubiah answered.

'Exactly. But she's hiding something, there's no doubt about it. "I'm leaving this to you," said the queen as she got up to leave. "But I'm expecting you …" "Don't expect anything from me," I told her, "because I'm not doing anything. The police will investigate as they like, and if they have faith in my cousins, as they obviously do, then they can call them in as they please. They don't need your permission." Her face was red! And her assistant daughter-in-law was getting red as well.'

Maryam wondered whether Minah had been quite so outspoken with Halimah in front of her; Minah was very polite by nature and it would take quite an effort for her to speak to someone like that, especially a guest in her own home. Still, Halimah was really goading her and perhaps Minah had taken as much as she cared to.

'She glared daggers at me! But I know what she is. Unfortunately, she showed everything about herself, not that she cares, mind you. *Kaki untut dipakaikan gelang:* putting a bracelet on a diseased leg, drawing attention to something best left alone. But I won't be intimidated,' Minah declared in ringing tones. 'I don't care who she thinks she is.'

Maryam was congratulatory, it was an admirable sentiment. She was concerned, however, since she didn't want her cousin in any danger, and even if this strange family had done nothing to harm anyone, she didn't like them paying more than passing attention to Minah. Or to any of them.

Yi and Nuraini arrived back, with Nuraini staggering under two bottles of Green Spot. Maryam put out the cold drinks, but fretted – what would she do when Yi went to Malek's house? Would she have to run all her own errands? Go to get Rubiah on her own, go to the shop at the end of the road for cold drinks when people came to visit? She hadn't done that since Azmi was old enough to be sent. Surely, she was too settled to be running all over Kampong Penambang on these small but necessary trips. Another thing to worry about, but not now, when her cousin was here, and she must be mindful of what Minah needed. Later, she'd consider this and discuss it with Rubiah.

'You must be careful, Nah,' she advised her, seriously. 'These are odd people, and who knows what they might do.'

'Or did,' added Minah.

'Exactly. I don't like them coming over and bullying you like that. Not,' she amended, 'that you can be so easily bullied, but that they would even try. I think Rahman should go over there and have a talk with them. Let them know the police are watching them.'

'Do you really think that's necessary?' asked Minah, a bit troubled. 'Don't you think it was all big talk on Halimah's part?'

'I do, of course. But she can't just walk into people's houses like that and think she can order them about, can she? She's got a very high opinion of herself, I'd say.'

Minah was calmer again. 'Indeed, she does. It would do her good to be taken down a peg, don't you think?'

'Yes,' Maryam said flatly. Rahman, sitting only a few feet away, came forward to join their conversation.

'Well, she certainly thinks she runs Tapak Gajah,' Rahman commented.

'She always did,' Minah allowed, flicking her cigarette ash into a waiting ashtray.

'No matter what she thinks, she doesn't get to try to intimidate you. I think that's illegal.'

'It should be, even if it isn't,' Aliza added.

'Right,' Minah concurred.

'Well, Mak Cik, I think tomorrow I'll go over with another policeman and we'll talk to her.'

'But then she'll know I told you!' Suddenly, Minah seemed anxious.

'Is that a problem?' Maryam asked.

'I guess not,' Minah said doubtfully. 'I mean, what does it matter if she knows I told you?' But her eyes belied her words.

'She knows you're related to me,' Rahman said quietly. 'Perhaps it's a good thing she knows you can talk to your family at any time and they'll respond. After all,' he continued, 'Razaleigh has already complained about nothing. He can't really come back again without looking foolish.'

'That wouldn't stop him,' Minah said distractedly. 'It wouldn't stop any of them.'

'Probably not,' Rahman agreed. 'But it won't help their case, will it? Do you want me to post a guard at your house for a day? So she knows we're paying attention?'

'You should think about it, Nah,' Maryam urged her. 'It would be a sign that you aren't alone.'

'We were never alone,' Nasir joined in. 'I think it might be a good idea. Let her see the police are taking this very seriously.'

Rahman agreed. 'I'll have someone out as soon as you get home.'

Which was how Din found himself sitting in front of Minah's house, watching the sun go down and seeing the lights come on in the houses. He insisted on sitting outside on the porch, to remain visible to anyone who passed by, and ensure the talk in the kampong was about Minah's police guard and why he was posted there. Minah had sent out dinner and cold drinks, then dessert and hot drinks, and then snacks with more tea, until Din feared if anything were to happen, he'd be unable to move. He tried to appear as tough and fearsome as possible, keeping a kerosene lantern lit next to him, so he would be visible to anyone so much as glancing in his general direction.

Razaleigh walked by together with his brother Jusoh, examining Din as they passed. A few minutes later, they were back again, this time stopping in front of the porch to talk.

'What are you doing here?'

'I'm guarding the house. I was sent by the Kota Bharu Police Department to make sure there were no attempts to intimidate the family.'

'Has anyone attempted it?'

Din was sure Razaleigh knew. 'There have been attempts. There will not be any going forward.'

'Who tried?'

'I can't answer that,' Din said officiously. 'That's police business.'

'I see,' said Razaleigh. He moved his toe in the dirt and appraised it. 'I don't suppose you'd want to defend anyone else.'

'I don't get what you mean.'

'Well, what if other people were being intimidated?'

'You should report that to the Kota Bharu Police Headquarters. I'm unaware of any other attempts at intimidation, but certainly if you know of any …'

'I do! I've been intimidated myself.'

'Have you?' Din asked drily, trying to mask the depth of his disbelief.

'Yes, it was very frightening.'

'As I said, the Kota Bharu Police Headquarters is the place to report it.'

'What if something happens to me tonight?'

'Che Razaleigh,' Din said impatiently, 'Why is this just starting now? Where were you when you first had the experience? I believe you are trying to distract me from my duty here.'

'But I'm scared too!'

'Of whom?'

This led Razaleigh to hesitate for a moment. Din could almost see the wheels turning in his head. Accuse Minah and it might not be believed. Accuse someone else and they'd be shocked, seeing no one else had spoken to him. But what about …

'Khadijah! The woman from the market! She tried to make me stop talking to the police. She said she'd kill me like she killed my father.' Razaleigh was shocked to hear himself say that but it was already out, and he'd have to stand by it. He gazed up at Din, who gazed back at him with absolute scepticism.

'Before you continue this, Che Razaleigh, remember lying to the police is a crime. We're conducting an investigation here, so if you're giving us false information to waste our time, you could end up in court, maybe in jail. I find your accusation difficult to believe, so I'm going to help you out.

'I'll pretend I didn't hear what you just said, and you can walk away and there will be no problem. If you want to insist on it, I will investigate it, but if it turns out to be false, you'll be in serious trouble. Do you want my advice?' He waited for a second to see if there'd be an answer, though he doubted he'd get one. 'Go home, now. Leave this alone.' He stood up at the top of the stairs and stared down at Razaleigh, who seemed nervous, now that he felt he was committed.

'But you must …'

'Take my advice, Che Razaleigh, or you will be unhappy. What would you like to do?'

'I stand by it!' Razaleigh stuck his chin out stubbornly.

'So,' Din began slowly, so Razaleigh would understand his every word. 'You're accusing Cik Khadijah of not only threatening you, but of killing your father in the market. Where witnesses have placed her talking to Cik Yati when she was unfortunately killed. You are testifying that you saw her kill your father, though you weren't at the market, as far as I understand. Have I described it correctly?'

'Well,' Razaleigh searched around for something to say. 'She said she killed my father.'

'Are you sure? Because this is important. It would contradict all evidence to the contrary, including witness accounts and the height we've calculated the killer must have been, but of course if you heard the confession, we'll need to take it into consideration.'

Razaleigh seemed to retreat now that it was all spelled out for him, but Din continued on the offensive. 'Where did she say this to you? When? Were there any witnesses? You're accusing someone of murder here.'

'But she threatened me.'

'Exactly! That's what I'm trying to understand. Who are the witnesses? We'll want to talk to them immediately. I can't leave my post, naturally, but I can call in reinforcements from Bacok to make sure we move on this right away. Sit down here on the porch.' He pointed to a spot near him. 'Stay here, I'll do what's necessary.'

'I think I'd better go home first,' Razaleigh whined.

'No, stay here. You could be in danger if someone's said they'd kill you like they killed your father. We won't let that go.' He ducked into the house for a moment, and the re-emerged, to find Razaleigh twisting his hands and was apparently near to tears.

'Don't worry. Minah's son is going for the police. They'll be here soon and then we can find out what's happened. Were there any witnesses?'

'N-no.'

'Where did she say this to you?'

'At the market.'

'Today?'

'Yes, I think so.'

'Yes or no.'

'Today. Listen, I ...'

Din held up his hand. 'Let's continue. She said this to you at the market but there were no witnesses. Surely someone at least saw you talking together even if they didn't hear exactly what was said.'

'No, no one ...'

'Did anyone see you at the market? Did you speak to anyone? Are there any witnesses who can place you there?'

'I didn't see anyone.'

'No one saw you at all? How is that possible?'

'I just didn't see anyone.'

'What were you there to buy?'

'Fish.'

'Good. Which fish seller did you buy from?'

'I can't remember.'

'Che Razaleigh, I have police coming here late in the evening because of your accusation. You need to be more specific than what you've said so far.'

Razaleigh hung his head miserably. Din, usually the most empathetic of men, forced himself to stay stern. This man had just baselessly accused Cik Khadijah of killing his father and threatening him: one accusation patently impossible, the other highly improbable. What kind of a man did that? Razaleigh seemed more suspicious by the moment.

'You will, of course, be questioned, Che Razaleigh,' Din used his most magisterial voice. 'I remind you once again, misleading the police is a crime.' He paused. 'I think you've already got one lie in there, since Cik Khadijah could not have killed your father. I want you to think hard about your second accusation.'

'I ... she said it to me.'

'This afternoon, at the market.'

Razaleigh nodded.

'You were frightened.'

'Yes.'

'But you did not report it until, by chance, you saw me here.'

Razaleigh was not a stupid man. He saw exactly where this was headed and the trouble he'd be in, but he was stubborn, and did not have much experience backing down. He twisted his hands worriedly.

'Well?'

'That's right. I just reported it now. Because when I saw you, I realized I could get help. So I told you.'

'Right,' Din nodded, and made doodles in his notebook as

if he were taking notes, so as not to miss one syllable of this conversation. He met Razaleigh's eyes and capitulated to his pity.

'Don't you want to go home now, Che Razaleigh, and forget what you've tried to do here? It would be far better for you. Once the Bacok police get here, you'll be committed to this and you know it isn't true.'

Razaleigh opened and closed his mouth but made no sound. Din viewed him with a kindly expression.

'Alright,' he choked out. 'Maybe you're right.'

'Maybe,' Din agreed, feeling a bit put out by the conditional. There was no doubt he was right.

'I'll be leaving.' Razaleigh turned abruptly and trotted away, not breaking into a run until he'd turned a corner and Din could no longer see him.

Minah came out onto the porch with more food and a magazine. 'Is he gone?' she asked.

Din nodded. 'That whole family is crazy.' He immediately thought better of the remark. After all, he was a police officer and should not be commenting on possible suspects to members of the public, even if they were part of Rahman's family. 'I didn't mean it,' he said to Minah. 'I shouldn't say things like that. I'm sorry.'

'Don't worry about it. No problem,' Minah assured him, arranging the food for him. 'He took it back.'

'Yes, in the end.'

'So, no one needs to go to Bacok.'

'No, not necessary, Alhamdulillah. What a trip at this time of night.'

'Just as well. I'm glad he managed to recant, as they say. That family has a lot of trouble with that. They just keep insisting …'

Din nodded. 'Very proud. Too proud, maybe.'

Minah scoffed impatiently. '*Kasehankan raja berusung pitying* a prince carried in a litter. He isn't there because he can't walk!' she told him. 'Don't waste any sympathy on him.'

'No, I wasn't …' Din decided to drop it. 'Anyway, I don't think they'll be back tonight.'

'Not now. They've already tried all they can do.'

'I'll be here all night, Mak Cik, so don't worry.' Din settled himself in for a long night, but one in which he felt he was fulfilling his destiny and taking care of the people who needed him.

Chapter XX

'Are they trying to act guilty?' Maryam asked, in all seriousness, sitting in the 'interrogation room' at Kota Bharu Police Headquarters. She and Rubiah had been summoned for a high-level meeting on the case, attended by Osman, Rahman and Din. Din was sitting up very straight and tall, thrilled to be included. He knew he'd arrived when he was invited to sit down with Maryam and Rubiah. It wasn't just police, it was their consultants as well. Rubiah give him further consideration as a possible husband for her several nieces. He had a good job, after all, and Rahman and Osman thought well of him. And he was a handsome boy in a way – he'd mature and fill out in a couple of years and then he'd be a great catch, with a good job and some maturity. Perhaps it made sense to try to reel him in while no one else noticed him. She'd discuss it with Maryam later. Right now, she had to pay attention.

'I mean, they keep threatening people, skulking around, visiting my cousin. What else could they do?'

'True,' Rahman agreed. 'But could it be they have so few manners they don't even realize what they're doing?'

'You don't need manners to know not to lie to the police,

especially when you've already been warned. This is beyond rudeness or over-honesty. This is actual stupidity,' Maryam said, and they all had to agree.

'There's no use talking to them and asking about it, not after Razaleigh's performance with Din,' Osman said, playing with a pencil on the table. 'I don't think we'd get any sense out of them. There isn't one of them whose word I'd trust.'

'Do you think,' Rubiah said slowly, 'there could be anything to his accusation of Khadijah? Could she have killed his father?'

'He was killed in front of the whole market,' Maryam reminded her. 'People agreed she was speaking to Yati and the other women. How could she have done it?'

'I guess not. It's just … it's just that it seems almost too pat. Razaleigh makes an absurd accusation so we don't even consider her. Maybe he accused her in order to take her off the list.'

'She was never on the list,' Rahman stated. 'Are you saying the two of them are working together? I just don't see them as a team of any kind.'

Maryam considered it. Ordinarily, she would have dismissed this suggestion out of hand as impossible, but she had long since learned never to ignore any of Rubiah's ideas, no matter how farfetched they seemed at first. She was having trouble with this one, but if Rubiah put it forward, it deserved consideration.

'Do you think he'd actually protect her?' Maryam asked her. 'Do they even really know each other?'

'I don't know,' Rubiah admitted. 'I just have a strange feeling about Razaleigh coming up to Din, apropos of nothing, and accusing her, even after Din warned him. And in the end, he withdrew it, but now we just think it's ridiculous. Therefore, we won't even add her to a list of suspects. And if someone else brings up her name, we're likely to reject it as well. I don't know if it means anything, I just know it bothers me.'

'If it bothers you,' Maryam supported her, 'then we must investigate it. You and I will take care of that, alright?'

Rubiah nodded, relieved. At least no one was mocking her premonitions, and even if they turned out to be wrong, didn't every detective pay attention to hunches? She'd be no different than that English lady whose name she could never remember, who'd written reams of mysteries where hunches were prominently featured. She was well within the norm for practicing sleuths.

Osman continued. 'Though I hate to say this, I think we've got to seriously consider Zulkifli's family. They had a wonderful motive, they were certainly capable, and although no one actually places them at the market at that time, there's so much covering up going on I'm not sure that matters. Since no one saw anything, it could still be anyone, couldn't it?'

'And Ibrahim,' Maryam chimed in. 'Afzan's husband, who'd had the argument with Zulkifli. Afzan told us that Razaleigh paid him all him all he was owed at the funeral, and I was wondering if indeed, he was being paid for a job well done. Of course, he's got witnesses that he was at the boat at the time, so I suppose that's a problem.'

'He'd be a perfect suspect,' Rubiah mused. 'Really, it's a shame he'd been seen at the beach.'

Din cleared his throat and prepared to say his piece. Everyone turned to him, making him nervous, but all the more determined to speak. 'I think we should examine Jusoh, Razaleigh's younger brother. Everyone says he follows Razaleigh around and does whatever he tells him. They haven't arranged a marriage for him, and I think that's odd, because he's more than old enough and yet no one even speaks about it. Which makes me think,' he said modestly, thankful that his voice didn't squeak although he was way past puberty, 'there's something wrong with him. Mentally, I mean. And that could lead him to kill, though no one in that family would ever mention it.'

'That's true,' Osman murmured, while Rahman nodded thoughtfully and both women made very positive noises. Everyone wanted to encourage Din, and Osman was particularly proud of how he'd handled himself.

'So there we go,' Osman enumerated. 'We've got Razaleigh, Jusoh, Ibrahim. We haven't discussed Ali and Yusuf again. It seems forever since we talked to them, but it actually hasn't been very long.'

'Yusuf seems too lazy to actually kill someone,' Rahman offered. 'Even if he thought about doing it, it would take a lot of effort.'

'Ali would do it,' Maryam said. 'We should add him to the list.'

'What about Halimah? And we should find out why Zulkifli might want to kill Afzan, if we think it was a case of mistaken identity,' Rubiah said definitively.

'Yes,' Maryam agreed. 'All of these. Din? Are you keeping notes?'

Luckily for Din, he had been. He gave a heartfelt inward sigh of relief. Imagine! His first inclusion in the big leagues and if he made a mistake? But, he hadn't. He bent again over his notebook to read back to everyone what they had decided.

'Good,' Osman finished. 'Now, we need to go back to everyone and examine their alibis.'

'They don't have any,' Rubiah corrected him. 'Except for the people at the boats. The rest were either at the market or could have been.'

'Then we've got to straighten it out. This has gone on long enough, and I'm tired of people simply not talking and thinking we'll go away.'

***

Naturally, Maryam and Rubiah drew Khadijah as their subject, since as fellow mak cik and market women, it was assumed they would have an unspoken bond which would work to make their interviews easier. Maryam and Rubiah were not sure this was true, but it did sound as if it ought to be, and they were content enough with their task. The alternatives were not all that attractive: anyone in Zulkifli's family was bound to be difficult, and Ali would also argue for the sake of it. No, after due consideration they knew they'd drawn the long straw.

Khadijah was exactly where they'd left her, leaning back behind her stock of keropok, which was really very high quality – both had served it at home and garnered positive feedback from a panel of experts including Yi, Mamat and Abdullah. She seemed to be waiting for them.

'I thought you'd be back,' she said, wrapping several bags of keropok for them to buy. 'This case is going on forever, isn't it?'

'We hope not,' Rubiah said, dragging over an unoccupied plastic chair and sitting down on it. Her knees were not what they once were, and although she could still sit on her haunches, it wasn't a posture she'd choose if it could be avoided. Maryam was a little envious but remained standing. Her knees weren't that great either. 'We were hoping you might be able to help us.'

'Alright,' she said, counting out their change. She certainly appeared to be calm and unruffled, not at all like a witness who'd hidden important information and possibly killed Zulkifli. 'What's bothering you?'

'Well first, how well do you know Razaleigh?'

'Razaleigh?'

'Yes, Zulkifli's son.'

'I know who he is, but I don't know why you'd ask me. The answer is not well at all. I see him at the market occasionally when he's shopping, although why he's shopping is a mystery to me. He has a wife you know, who'd be a far better shopper than he'll ever be. But he does come to the market, though not necessarily to me. He doesn't like keropok, I guess.'

'Do you speak to his family much?'

'Are you serious? You've met them. Do you think they're the kind of people I'm going to sit down with? Like they'd let me into their house, not that I'd want to go. Why would you even think I'd know them well?'

'It's possible. It's a small town.'

'Yes, it is that. But even so, I don't talk to them much.'

'Even Zulkifli.'

'Even Zulkifli,' she agreed, perplexed. 'I don't know what you're after, but if you thought perhaps Halimah and I were secret best friends, you're wrong. I can't imagine where'd you get an idea like that.'

'Well, you know …'

'No, I don't,' she answered, annoyed. 'Why are you wasting my time with questions about Razaleigh? I don't have anything to do with him. I don't know him well at all. I don't think I've ever had a conversation with him. Does that answer you?'

'Yes,' said Rubiah, embarrassed. This had been her idea, and it had not only led nowhere, it had antagonized someone who'd actually given them good information. She now believed Razaleigh had pulled Khadijah's name out of the air and tried to place the blame on her, but still, it rankled. She didn't like unexplained coincidence. 'It's just that he mentioned your name and said he'd had a conversation with you …' Rubiah wasn't at all sure she was doing the right thing in telling Khadijah what had happened, but she felt she needed to make amends. Maryam shot her a warning stare, asking her to be quiet. She pretended not to see it.

'A conversation? No, we've never had a conversation. Are you sure you understood him correctly?'

Rubiah nodded, becoming more miserable. She was a terrible failure as a detective and might actually have made things worse. She could tell Maryam was angry at her, though she resolutely refused to meet her eyes. Her famed hunches had failed her this time, and probably ruined everything, although she couldn't have said what 'everything' actually was. But it was bad.

Khadijah regarded them both, then settled on Rubiah. 'What's the matter?'

'I'm fine.'

'No, you aren't. You're upset about something. Are you unhappy that I've never had a conversation with Razaleigh? That's kind of strange, you know.'

'I'm just trying to understand …'

'Rubiah!' Maryam interrupted. 'What are you saying?'

'I don't care. I had such a strong feeling and now it seems I was completely wrong. And yet, I can't believe it.'

'Can't believe you were wrong? Well, I like that.'

Rubiah tossed her head impatiently. 'No, I mean I was so sure about it, I need to know why it wasn't true. What did I miss?'

'What are you talking about?' Khadijah seemed interested. 'What was your feeling?'

'My feeling was that Razaleigh wanted to mention you in something really ridiculous so we'd pay no attention to it at all, and then that would protect you …'

'Rubiah! Enough!'

'No,' she barked, determined to get through this. 'It would protect you from anyone accusing you at all because we'd already discounted it.'

'I'm not sure I'm following, but are you saying you think in some way Razaleigh was protecting me?'

Rubiah nodded.

'Why would he do that?'

'I don't know.'

'Are you sure it was me you were having your feeling about?'

'What?'

'Could he be protecting someone else? Just not me. Someone he'd have a reason to protect.'

'Who?' Maryam asked.

'I don't know,' said Khadijah. 'It's just I doubt he cares about what happens to me, so perhaps your feeling is that he's protecting someone. But not me.'

'Thank you,' said Rubiah unhappily. She rose to leave, feeling an abject failure, and certain to be admonished for some time to come.

Chapter XXI

It was even worse than she'd imagined. Maryam had never been so disappointed, so angry at her. She upbraided her as soon as they got out of the taxi in Kampong Penambang, for she had no intention of saying what she said in front of anyone else, Alhamdulillah. Rubiah was ashamed, because she knew she deserved it, and she'd known she'd deserved it even as she was doing it but couldn't help herself. She had no defence, no excuse. It was an impossible situation, and all she could do was listen, and actually agree, which infuriated Maryam all the more.

'If you agree with me,' she hissed, 'then why did you do it? You knew it was wrong! You knew you were putting our whole investigation in danger.'

'I know.'

'Then why?'

'I just thought … I hoped Khadijah might know something and tell me. She seems so perceptive.'

'Are you crazy?'

'Maybe. Well, not now. Maybe then.'

'That's not so long ago.'

'I know.'

Maryam stamped her foot in frustration. 'Stop it! You can't even defend yourself!'

Rubiah was about to say 'I know' again but caught herself. It would only make things worse.

'I can't even tell anyone!' Maryam was now walking around in circles trying to calm herself down. 'If I mention it to anyone, they'll never let you talk to a witness again. I have to protect you, and you know, right now I really don't feel like it.'

Again, the urge to mutter 'I know' was strong but was again disciplined. Why could she not control herself with Khadijah as she was controlling herself now? She might have saved herself a world of trouble.

'Alright,' Maryam said with a steely glance. 'Let's just hope Khadijah doesn't talk about it with anyone. We will never mention this again. I will tell Osman it doesn't seem your hunch was correct. You can never do anything like this again. *Sebab mulut badan binasa*: because of the mouth, the body is destroyed. Keep quiet!'

Rubiah nodded silently, hanging her head.

'I'll see you tomorrow. I need to go home and rest.' Maryam turned on her heel and began walking home, while Rubiah watched her with tears starting up in her eyes. How had she made such a mistake?

***

'How was it?' Abdullah asked as she came in the door, dragging her feet. 'You're exhausted.'

'It was a difficult day.'

'What happened?'

She waved him away. 'I'll tell you later,' though she wasn't sure she ever would. 'I just want to rest now.'

Abdullah was concerned but remained practical. 'What about dinner? Should I go out and get something?'

She nodded and headed toward the back of the house where she could bathe. Usually she'd object to the suggestion that they eat take-out dinner, she prided herself on her cooking and saw no reason to spend money on food she often found inferior to her own. For her to merely nod and agree was a troubling development. Abdullah watched her take a towel and an old sarong and prepare to wash at the well. She was defeated, not at all the way she usually was when returning from detecting, when she was often triumphant. He stood for a moment longer and then went out to the small local market to pick up something to eat.

Maryam meanwhile returned to an empty house – Mamat and Yi had gone to Aliza's for dinner and left a note for her to join them there. She was relieved to find she had no need to explain herself and her foul mood; indeed, she could go outside to bathe and bash things to her heart's content, which in fact she did. She lined the rubber tubs she used for washing clothes up against the well, so when she kicked them she wouldn't have to chase after them. It was an excellent system, and she actually felt better after a few good, solid kicks. She then settled down to bathe, change and have a calming cigarette before going out.

She was stunned at Rubiah's lack of professionalism. Her

belief in her own hunches had gone too far: every time she had a feeling, which was very often, she took it too seriously for her own good. Maryam remembered many sprints back to Kampong Penambang from either the ferry or the market when Rubiah was sure a catastrophe had taken place in their absence. Upon arrival, nothing had happened. This was the same kind of thing, Maryam reflected, but even worse. Her predictions would have to be tamped down – they could not continue to take off after each one as if it were absolute truth. This is where it led. The family would often laugh about Rubiah's forebodings, but now they needed to stop treating them as a loveable quirk. They could be dangerous if they were blindly followed. She hoped Rubiah came to the same realization, but even if she didn't, Maryam would no longer treat them as less than possible perils. She smoothed back her hair and headed to Aliza's house, hoping she could spend a pleasant evening and not think about the afternoon's debacle.

It was the first time Maryam could remember being angry in this way with her cousin. Their relationship was always solid, immutable. They'd been together their whole lives. Maryam could not understand what came over Rubiah. Did she feel she needed another friend and chose Khadijah to be that? It couldn't be. Now that she'd told Khadijah about her 'feelings', would Khadijah take advantage of that knowledge, and feed them information she knew would conform to Rubiah's inclinations? She felt as though the whole investigation was now contaminated, and that any answers they received would have to be filtered through the possibility they were crafted especially for Rubiah. And would the guilty party know? Could they use it to shine suspicion on someone else? If Khadijah were involved in any way, Maryam did not know how to go back and make it right. And she did not want to tell Osman, or anyone else, but wasn't at all sure she could reasonably withhold such information.

She arrived at Aliza's house quiet and preoccupied but did not confide what Rubiah had said. Everyone noted her distracted air but thought better of pursuing it once she told them she was only tired. They didn't believe it, nor did they feel it would do any good to annoy her. Aliza asked about the case, which was usually Maryam's cue to go into detail with relish, but tonight she merely waved it away with an anodyne comment which gave away nothing.

She could not abide by her own decision never to mention it again. The next morning, she opened her booth in the market – this was her fortress, the place where she felt completely in charge. She sat on her pile of cotton batik and brooded, unable to formulate a plan for going forward. Her reverie was interrupted by Rubiah appearing with coffee and cakes, more than abashed, but determined to face Maryam and get the worst over with.

'I should never have said it.' She put the coffee on the ledge and placed a tray of cakes next to it. The cakes were carefully chosen to be all of Maryam's favourites, but Maryam had little stomach for them this morning.

'You don't have to apologize,' she said morosely. 'I still don't understand why you did it.'

'I'm not sure myself,' Rubiah admitted. 'Maybe,' she hesitated, as if unable to find the words to explain it even to herself. 'Maybe … I just felt it so strongly. Felt that we were being led away from

Khadijah so I couldn't accept that she didn't know Razaleigh and there wasn't any reason for him to move suspicion away from her. I mean, really, we never suspected her anyway, so why do it? You see …'

'Don't you think it possible that it was just what it seemed? He wanted to guide us towards Khadijah, to incriminate her to keep us away from someone else. His brother, for instance. Or his mother, for all that. I wouldn't put it past her.'

'I wouldn't put anything past her. She'd kill him with as much thought as she'd kill an insect.'

'Maybe it's that. He's not protecting her; it isn't as complicated as you thought. You've given him too much credit.' Maryam was cheering up rapidly and turned to the cakes at her elbow. Small rice balls with molasses syrup inside and coconut flakes without, called *onde-onde,* were her absolute favourites. They were very small, and you could eat quite a few before they caught up with you. She delicately popped one in her mouth.

'He probably thinks his mother did it,' she said with some satisfaction. 'Or his brother. Then tried to say it was someone else. You thought he was more diabolical than he was. Or shall I say he was not cunning at all, but you mistook what was obvious for something devious.' She took a sip of coffee. She was so much happier having hit upon an explanation than she had been faced with the incomprehensible.

Rubiah concurred. 'I did think he was being crafty. How could I not?' she appealed to Maryam's intelligence. 'How could I think he was just doing what any three-year-old would do? I thought he was smarter than that.' Rubiah picked up a cake and chewed it thoughtfully. She too was cheering up. Maybe it wasn't quite the disaster it initially appeared, and Khadijah would write it off as eccentricity rather than bone headedness, which is what Rubiah now considered it. They both ate contentedly together, relieved their argument had dissolved into nothing, and their relationship back to normal. It had been a very difficult night, and neither was willing to repeat it.

They were silent together for several minutes, serene and composed; the worst was over.

'I wonder what happened with everyone else,' Maryam finally said. 'I thought I'd see Osman sidling in, but he hasn't shown up.'

Rubiah nodded. She didn't have much to add. The market was beginning to fill up, and Rubiah gathered her cups to bring upstairs. She might well have customers already eating her cakes and waiting for coffee. She disappeared into the middle of the market, leaving Maryam to search the crowd for songket buyers. She didn't see any.

A woman walked towards her whom she recognized but could not place. Young and slight, with a head cloth wrapped like a turban around her head, as so many women in the market wore. Maryam squinted, hoping that might bring the woman into focus, but even then, she couldn't place her until she came right up to her. It was Afzan from the Tapak Gajah market.

'Cik Afzan, what are you doing so far from home?' Maryam greeted her, moving over slightly to indicate Afzan to sit down. 'Such a long trip from Bacok. Would you like something to drink?'

Afzan shook her head. 'No, thank you. Mak Cik, I'm frightened,' she said quickly, dispensing with any chitchat to begin. She sat quickly and kept turning her head to keep aware of all that went on around the market.

'Don't worry,' Maryam tried to soothe her. 'We're safe here.' She hoped she was right.

'I came here to see you, Mak Cik, because things are going on in Tapak Gajah. My husband hadn't come home yet from fishing, and I was alone in the house, and I heard someone come in. I went into the living room ... people don't just walk into your house, do they? A thief, I thought, but what they thought they could steal I have no idea. We don't have much.' Maryam fought back the instinct to hurry her along. 'I couldn't find anyone in the living room, so I went down the stairs, and saw a shadow under the house. I ran down the ladder and saw someone running from under the house. I chased him, why I can't say since I'm not so brave and I didn't know what I wanted to do when I got hold of him. But I caught him, on the beach. And it was Jusoh, Zulkifli's son.'

'Did you talk to him?' Maryam led her through her story.

She nodded. 'I did. I asked him what he was doing, and he denied he was ever in my house. "I saw you!" I told him. How can he try to lie about that? It doesn't make sense. He started yelling at me, he said I'd better stop talking to the police or he'd hurt me. Or kill Ibrahim. He said he could do it on the boat, he could throw him over into the sea. It was his boat.

'It isn't really his boat,' Afzan continued, calmer now that she was discussing economics rather than crime. 'The family owns a share of the boat, but not all of it. I don't even know if it's the largest share. I mean,' she thought hard about it, 'I suppose he could get onto the boat if he wanted to but throwing Ibrahim overboard would be a whole different job, especially if Ibrahim were warned, and I warned him. I told him if Jusoh is on the boat, stay away from him, and if he comes near you, you throw him over first. Ibrahim's much stronger than Jusoh will ever be,' she said with some satisfaction. 'I'd like to see them in a fight.'

'Why would he do this?' Maryam asked. At this point it still didn't make sense to her.

'He doesn't want me speaking to the police. But Mak Cik, I don't really know anything, so I don't know what he's afraid of.'

'You don't know anything?'

She shook her head. 'Afzan, no one can protect you if you don't tell the truth.'

Afzan was stricken. 'I don't know what you mean.'

'Why would Zulkifli want to kill you?'

'What?'

'You heard me.' Maryam was losing patience with this game. She kept glancing at the staircase, willing Rubiah to come down and join her.

'He didn't …'

'I think he did. We think he killed Cik Yati by mistake, thinking she was you. He couldn't see that well, that's what we've been told. So, in a blurry sort of way you resembled Yati. Otherwise, why would he kill a woman he'd never seen before in his life? No, I think it was you he was after. Can you tell me why?'

She began to stammer a reply, and Maryam reached out and put a motherly hand on her shoulder. 'Cik Afzan, calm yourself. Take your time and talk to me slowly so I can understand you.'

Her tone turned stern. 'And don't lie to me. I can't bear it anymore. Everyone's been hiding some truth or other and it's wasting my time.' She fixed a cold eye on Afzan and waited for her to speak.

'I, well, I think,' here she stopped. Maryam was becoming impatient, and Afzan could see that.

'You came here to see me,' Maryam reminded her. 'Now, if you have something to tell me, tell me. Otherwise …'

'Yes, you're right, Mak Cik,' Afzan agreed. 'It's like this. Zulkifli thought he was my father.'

'Was he?'

'My mother said no.'

'I'd listen to your mother, then.'

'I do. I didn't even mention it to my father. I don't know if he knows what Zulkifli thinks, but if I know anything about Zulkifli, he's already told him.'

'Maybe not.'

'What does it matter? I told him I'm not his daughter, and he laughed at me and said someday I'd be happy to be related to him. This was a few years ago. I ignored it. My mother said it was absolutely impossible and I believed her. So, I didn't think about it. Whenever he saw me, he'd smile at me as if we had something we shared, which we didn't.

'Then, a little while ago, he spoke to me at the market. I told him again, "I'm not your daughter." He said that he hoped I believed it, because I wouldn't be inheriting anything from him. I told him I didn't want anything, and he said, "Now you don't. But just wait till the will's being read. You'll decide then you'd like some money." I won't, you know. Not from him.'

'Good idea,' Maryam approved. 'It wouldn't be worth it.'

'I know. I told Ibrahim, and he didn't believe it either. But I can't figure out why he'd say that and then tell me he won't give me any money. Something must have changed in the meantime, and now he's afraid I'll use it to take some of his money. I don't know why he ever told me!' She continued to answer her own question. 'I think he wants to think I'm his daughter, or somebody is. There was talk about another girl, Che Hamid's daughter being Zulkifli's, but I don't think that's true either. I think it's the opposite problem,' she announced. 'I've been thinking about it. I don't know if his sons are even his sons. That's why he's claiming other people's children for his own. But this inheritance, I don't understand that at all.'

'There's a lot going on,' Maryam commented.

'That whole family is obsessed with money. All they think about is this inheritance. Razaleigh is the best of them,' she opined, 'but even he worries about what he's going to get. It has nothing to do with me, you know. I don't want it, and I wouldn't take it anyway, especially if it made me say I was his daughter. I'm not.

'Anyway, the really strange thing is I don't think he'd ever mention me in the will, so what is he so worried about?'

'I imagine he was concerned that you'd contest the will and ask for your portion of the inheritance.'

Afzan shuddered. 'Never! Publicly announce this lie? Humiliate my family? I would never do that. I don't want his money and I don't want his family. All I want is for them to leave me alone, and not try to break into my house.'

'Why do you think Jusoh was in your house?'

'Jusoh is a little bit crazy, I'd say. A bit off. That's why he isn't married, and only follows Razaleigh around. I doubt he could manage by himself. If he got the idea into his head that I would try to get any of his family's money, he'd go off the deep end. He probably feels he's protecting their wealth. From me! If it wasn't so ridiculous it would be insulting.'

Maryam noticed she wasn't frightened anymore. She was angry, and it carried her along. 'Have you told the police about Jusoh coming into your house?'

Afzan shook her head.

'You really should, you know. The police can help you in ways I can't. If you don't want to tell them all the background, at least tell them he's coming to frighten you. If they don't know they can't help.'

'I hate to bring it up.' The light had gone out of her eyes as quickly as it had come in. She became listless again, and Maryam doubted she'd go to talk to the police.

'Do you want me to go with you?' she asked. She hated to leave the market in the middle of the day, and possibly lose business, but she felt obligated to get all the information out, and this seemed important. She sighed heavily and began to close up while Afzan stood next to her chattering, giving her thanks and explaining why it was so important Maryam accompany her. Maryam tuned out her words as noise, figuring she'd hear them again at the police station.

She gave her a polite smile, a little tight at the corners because she really was annoyed about leaving. Afzan was a grown woman and fully capable of doing this on her own. It was difficult being called upon to help at all times, when people who could be stronger decided not to bother, but to lean on Maryam instead. This was the conundrum of competence, and Maryam lectured herself that if she'd agreed to go with Afzan, she should do it happily.

They left the market and began walking to the roundabout and then to the police headquarters on Jalan Ibrahim. The traffic was heavy, and the air felt dirty, even with their headscarves held over their faces. It was hot and humid, standard for Kelantan, and yet this afternoon Maryam found it more oppressive than usual. Perhaps it was the noise of the traffic, or the exhaust and smell of diesel fuel which surrounded them; the sidewalks were crowded as they always were at this time, but Maryam felt choked by the crowd and the air and the noise. She stopped for a moment and leaned against the fence bordering the sidewalk, and Afzan stopped next to her. 'Bacok is never like this, Mak Cik,' she told her. 'It's so busy here! I don't know how you live with it.'

At this moment, Maryam didn't know herself, and felt like she might burst through the air to find something to breathe. How had she never noticed this before? Staying still was not an attractive option, and the only way to get through this cacophony was to keep walking and get into the police station, where air conditioning and refreshing tea would lift her spirits and allow her to breathe once more. They walked with determination, eager to arrive as quickly as possible, and Maryam threw herself into the building gasping for air and desperate for a cool atmosphere. Rahman saw her come in, and immediately rose to meet her.

'What's the matter?' he asked anxiously.

'The air is terrible! I never noticed it was so bad. I can hardly breathe.' She lurched to a chair and sat down, waving the end of her headscarf in her face to create a breeze. Rahman turned the air conditioning up higher, which would give Maryam some comfort but threatened to freeze the rest of the police force. 'Din, go get some kopi peng,' he ordered, but Din knew his job and was out the door before Rahman had finished the sentence. The promise of a cold drink kept Maryam going, and between deep breaths of air cold enough for snow, she told Rahman of Afzan's plight.

'Did you ever talk to this Jusoh? Well, he broke into Cik Afzan's house. She'll tell you all about it.' She gulped air for a few seconds and then willed herself to continue. 'She thinks he's worried about his inheritance; he's afraid she'll claim some. Oh, right. Zulkifli told her a few years ago she was his daughter.' She had a feeling she was telling this completely out of order but was very anxious to get it told so she could relax, which she was finding near impossible. 'Then not too long ago he told her she wouldn't receive anything from him when he died. And apparently, he might have mentioned this to Jusoh, or Razaleigh did, and he's taking care of it, so he thinks.' She stopped talking and tried to still her heart, which seemed to be pounding out of her chest. She waved an undirected hand at Afzan. 'You tell him.'

She could hear her speaking, but it began to fade into a buzz, and her world seemed to shrink to a small area in which she was breathing deeply, but not feeling as if she was getting any of the air where it needed to go. She assumed Rahman was listening to Afzan and that she was for all intents and purposes invisible, until Rahman's face swam into her vision looking concerned, and his voice seemed to come from far away, asking if she was alright. She didn't know whether she'd answered or not and didn't care. It was too complicated. She needed all her energy to concentrate on breathing, which wasn't going too well, but she kept trying. The next thing she noticed was a mask being placed over her face, and someone talking, holding her hand. Or was it her wrist? Keep breathing, she told herself. You have one job right now. Do it well.

She did not notice her surroundings. The police station, with Rahman and Afzan and Din seemed to fade into the distance, and she found herself not bothered by it, though she knew under usual circumstances she'd be terribly upset by her inability to interact with the world. Right now, however, it seemed irrelevant. She listened only to her lungs, working hard but still ... She was dizzy now, but thankfully lying down. She didn't know how that happened but was grateful for it, nonetheless. And then she stopped paying attention altogether.

Chapter XXII

It seemed as though she was swimming up from an inestimable depth, dark and thick, where anything she saw was blurred and ran like watercolours in the rain. She wasn't trying very hard to focus, either, because it was too hard, and she was too tired. She heard things, but they were muted, hard to trace, impossible to understand. The world was a far-away place, and she couldn't muster the energy to return to it.

She opened her eyes once and thought she saw Mamat from a distance but couldn't be sure. She closed them again, promising herself she'd see it at a later date. Her lethargy was a palpable thing, something she held in her hands and could not release. It was best not to wrestle with it, but to succumb.

She tried to think about things, but the thoughts eluded her, and she couldn't chase them. She was left with incomplete thoughts which swam through her mind, leaving little trace. It was pleasant enough, in an entirely disconnected way, and she did not try to pull them together into a coherent whole, even if that would have been possible.

Maryam felt she had lived in this world between living and dying for years, just drifting without understanding. But she began to surface, to understand snippets of conversation she heard, occasionally opening her eyes and seeing light. She closed them quickly again. It hurt move her eyes and things seemed unformed. She decided she might try again when it began to form an image.

'She's opened her eyes!' Rubiah called out to Mamat, who was sitting next to the bed. 'Did you see it?'

'No, are you sure?'

'I'm sure. I think she's coming around.'

Rubiah was slightly ahead of herself, and Maryam did not in fact come around for another night and afternoon, but then she opened her eyes to see shapes: Rubiah and Mamat in the forefront, and her children behind them. She tried to offer a pleasant smile, for she was not ready to speak, but when she asked them later how she looked, no one remembered a smile. Perhaps she tried and failed. 'Are you alright?' Mamat asked anxiously. She tried nodding. 'I think she's alright,' Mamat reported. 'I think she can hear me. Yam! Can you see me?'

Maryam wished he'd stop asking questions she couldn't answer, but she wasn't annoyed, just wistful. It would be nice to talk, but she wasn't ready for it. She wasn't sure where she was, either, and hoped to establish that before getting into a conversation. Things didn't feel familiar, but that could have been for so many reasons. She relaxed her head again into the pillow and closed her eyes.

'She's going back to sleep,' Mamat said, disappointed. He'd hoped she'd be back to normal but realized that was unlikely. The fact that she'd regained consciousness was cause enough for celebration.

'We've got to let her rest,' Ashikin advised the gathered family. 'Even if she wakes up, she isn't going to be able to talk to us for a few days. You remember what the doctor said.'

Mamat remembered perfectly, even as he wished he didn't. A heart attack, the doctor said. Was she stressed? he'd asked. Was she working too hard? The answer to both questions was yes.

'Well,' the doctor said kindly, 'she's reaching an age when she might have to take things a bit easier. We can't rush around like that, getting into danger, forever.' He'd been told about her detective work. Rubiah was glad Maryam wasn't able to hear what the doctor said: she'd be furious. It was just as well they were getting the information without her.

'But why?' Mamat pressed him. 'I mean, she was just working in the market, and walking to the police station. She wasn't in any danger. I would have thought …' he trailed off, not sure what he would have thought about anything. A heart attack! He'd never considered Maryam would have any weaknesses at all. He vowed to keep her happy and relaxed from now on.

'It doesn't necessarily happen at the time of stress itself. The stress builds up. There are various experiences, they all add up. I hear she was with a witness at the police station when she had the incident.'

'Yes, she was.' Maryam had pitched forward in the police station, and Rahman grabbed her to make sure she didn't end up on the floor. He cried to the others there to call an ambulance, which, it being the police station, came immediately, and she was taken to the hospital. Their witness was passed to Din and another officer, while Rahman went to gather the family, stopping first at the market for Rubiah and then at the coffee shop for Mamat. Rahman was terrified and had been since Maryam started gasping for air. This was not black magic, or an attack by a cornered murderer; no, this was just her body giving out after one too many threats. He sat outside the hospital room, trying to be cognizant of her children's' need to be near her. Aliza had been there for two days, leaving Sharifah Aini with his sister. Yi sat forlorn, feeling forgotten, unsure of what to do.

Rahman had no idea what happened with Afzan and what she'd told Din. He hadn't called into work and doubted anyone would want to bother him right now. He was grateful for it. He knew Osman only stayed away so as not to intrude but would be there when Maryam felt better. Of course she would. She'd had worse shocks and worse illnesses. At least this was one where medicine could be effective, and they wouldn't have to gather amulets.

Aliza motioned him to join her in the hallway. 'I never expected this,' she said, as she had every hour since this happened. 'I always thought she was so strong. I thought stress would never get to her.'

'She and Rubiah aren't getting younger.'

'You'd better not let her hear that. You'd have no hair left.'

'Probably,' he agreed.

'I wonder if we should stay at Mak and Ayah's house for a while, so I can take care of her ...'

'Won't you be at work during the day?'

She nodded, distracted. 'But someone needs to take care of her. Ayah can't do it on his own. Maybe Mak Cik Rubiah? But she has her own business. So, I was thinking I would take a leave of absence so I could stay home with her. We can't let her be home with Ayah alone and hope for the best.'

'What about Ashikin?'

As though conjured by the sound of her name, Ashikin appeared next to them. 'Are you talking about taking care of Mak when she gets home?' she asked with her usual mind-reading abilities.

'Yes,' Aliza answered. 'How do you always know what I'm thinking?'

'I grew up with you,' she said carelessly. 'Of course I know what you're thinking.'

'I grew up with you and I haven't a clue,' Aliza admitted.

'You don't pay attention.'

Aliza tossed her head to signify irritation, but Ashikin ignored her.

'We need a plan,' Ashikin effortlessly took over the conversation. 'Ayah will try his best, but he can't manage it. We need a woman to help her.'

'Right.'

'And she'll want the store open as well.'

'Right.'

'So, this is what I was thinking. Daud's parents won't mind if I don't work in the store till Mak is back on her feet. I'll go to Mak's house every morning, Mak Cik Rubiah can make dinner and they can all eat together, and Mak Cik Rubiah can help her get ready for bed. You can arrange your schedule so you teach in the mornings and come home by lunch time. When you come home,

I'll go in to the market. That way we have everything covered. I'm mornings, you're afternoons and Mak Cik Rubiah is evenings.'

'It sounds quite military,' Rahman said admiringly. The Kota Bharu police department could have done no better: few places in the world could out-organize Ashikin.

'We can bring the kids with us if they don't take up too much time. Mak would love to see them.'

'She would.'

'So, we're agreed?'

Aliza nodded again. She recognized her destiny was to follow, at least with her older sister.

'I'll tell Mak Cik Rubiah,' Ashikin said lighting a cigarette. Gazing speculatively at Aliza, she offered one to her. Aliza was thrilled. She was actually accepted as a grown up.

'No thanks,' she said airily. 'Not now.'

Rubiah joined them in the hallway, which was taking on the appearance of a conference room for captains of Kelantanese industry. 'You've organized the schedule,' Rubiah stated.

Ashikin offered her a cigarette, which she accepted. She squinted at Aliza. 'I've already offered her one, but she didn't want it,' she told Rubiah. 'You're on for evenings and dinner. I'll be there mornings for breakfast till lunch. Then I open the shop. Aliza comes home for lunch and stays till dinner: then you come over.'

'Sounds excellent.'

'Has anyone mentioned when she might go home?'

Rubiah shook her head. 'Not yet. But she needs to relax! No more running around to Tapak Gajah and worrying about

Zulkifli's wretched family. The police can take care of that.'

'They can,' Rahman put in, though Rubiah didn't seem to hear him.

'Minah should be showing up any time now,' Rubiah continued. 'I'm going to tell her Maryam can't do this anymore.'

'Maybe I can finish it up for her,' Aliza said, newly emboldened by being offered a cigarette. Strange how empowering that was.

'We'll see,' Rubiah said.

'I'd appreciate your help,' Rahman said, eager to accumulate brownie points. Aliza smiled at him, understanding his support.

'What happened with Afzan, anyway?' Rubiah asked him.

'I don't know. I have to ask Din and I just haven't done it yet.'

'Maybe you should,' she said meaningfully. He soon left for the station.

Chapter XXIII

The station was still agog over the recent emergency: Maryam's heart attack, Afzan's subsequent hysterics, Din's unforeseen heroism. Hero though he might have been, as soon as Rahman walked into the office, Din ran to get some kopi peng and curry puffs, in order to make him comfortable while he listened to the tale.

The uproar over Maryam's illness had not faded one bit when Rahman left with the ambulance. Afzan, who'd been watching with increasing alarm, began to cry and shake, and would not be calmed. Din tried to ply her with tea, which had no effect at all, and one of the men called Osman out to see if he could manage her. He tried, but could not, and her cries became louder and more insistent. Osman wasn't sure why she was keening as she was but found it unbearable. Din finally took charge and held her firmly by the shoulders.

'Stop!' he ordered her, giving her a good shake. 'I don't know what's the matter and I can't help you until I do. Stop crying. Alamak! I can't stand it anymore!'

Horrified at being scolded with such force, she stopped crying and stared at him open mouthed. 'That's better,' he said with relief. 'I really don't know how much longer I could take that. Your voice is very piercing, did you know that?'

The rest of the office tried to hide their smiles, but Din was right. Their eardrums still rang in the silence.

'Sit down,' he ordered her, and she sat. 'Now, have some tea. Slowly, so it doesn't make you choke.' She obediently drank her tea, her eyes on Din without blinking. 'Now, tell me, what's the matter? Why did you go to see Mak Cik Maryam? I hope she's alright,' he said as an aside, and Afzan nodded her agreement.

'I went to see her,' she began shakily, while Din nodded his encouragement. Osman observed, mesmerized by Din's quiet masterfulness. He regarded Din as a reliable gofer, extra hand, enthusiastic underling, but Din had clearly been learning his chosen profession.

'I'm afraid,' she gulped. 'Jusoh broke into my house. That's Razaleigh's younger brother. He's not all there in the head, you understand. I heard a noise in the living room and went in. I saw him running down the ladder and I chased him. I don't know why, like I told Mak Cik. I don't know what I thought I'd do with him if I caught him, but I did. He denied being in my house, which was clearly a lie. Then he told me he'd kill me if I spoke to the police.'

'Why?'

'He threatened to throw my husband overboard on the boat if I didn't. He's crazy.'

'But why doesn't he want you talking to the police? What do you know?'

Afzan sighed. It was the second time in as many hours she'd been told to get to the point. It was difficult telling this story but drawing it out wouldn't help. 'Zulkifli told me a few years ago he was my father. I didn't believe him then, and I don't believe him now. I asked my mother about and she said absolutely not. So, I don't think so.

'I told him I didn't believe it, and he just said he was. After that I avoided him, which really wasn't difficult. Our paths don't cross unless he comes to buy vegetables, and it's easy for me to stay out of his way. We wondered if that's why he'd cheated Ibrahim, my husband, out of some of his share on the boat. In a strange sort of way, to keep in contact. Maybe it doesn't make sense, but I always wondered about it any time anything happened involving Zulkifli.

'So, a little while ago, he stopped at the market and told me to forget about it, because he wouldn't be leaving me any money. I told him that was fine, I didn't want any money from him, and besides, there was no reason for him to do that because I wasn't any relation to him. He said that as soon as his will was read I'd want some, and I could forget about it now, because there was no proof I was his daughter. 'Of course there isn't,' I told him, 'because I'm not!' He didn't make a lot of sense. So that's where it was left. I shouldn't try to get any money when he died. I wouldn't so it didn't matter to me.

'And then Jusoh tries to kill me. Or says he will. What else could that be except he fears I'll tell you this story, and he's afraid I'll go after his money. I swear by all that's holy I don't want his money and I won't try to get any. But now I'm scared. What if he tries again? He could succeed, you know. And I want you to help me!'

She began to cry, but this time without any wailing. Din passed her a box of tissues and waited, making sure her cup of tea was topped up and a curry puff waiting for her. Sometimes grief left you hungry.

She blew her nose and dabbed at her eyes. 'Thank you. I'm sorry I'm crying like this. I'm very frightened.'

'Of course you are,' Din agreed. 'And rightly so.' He looked hopefully at Osman, asking him to take over this interrogation cum therapy.

Osman joined Afzan, pulling up a chair next to her. 'We'll give you guard, Kakak, who will stand in from of your house from the afternoon until morning.' Din had a feeling who that guard might be and resigned himself to not sleeping until this case was over. 'Let that family see the police take this very seriously indeed. They won't be walking around Tapak Gajah free to terrorize their fellow citizens. We won't allow that.'

Osman turned to his men and planned their arrest of both Razaleigh and Jusoh. Osman had had enough of their threats and would no longer hope they would behave themselves. Afzan examined her hands.

'Din, will you take Cik Afzan back to her house? And stay there?'

He nodded and escorted her to the police car. As soon as he eased it into traffic, Afzan began to speak. 'I'm not sure I really need a guard,' she began.

'If someone has threatened to kill you, then you do, Kakak. We can't allow that kind of threat to be made and not react to it. What kind of a signal would that send to them?'

'Well, he did attack me.'

'Yes, he did.' Din took the Pasir Puteh road towards Bacok.

'But I don't know if I want a guard.'

'Why not?'

'What will people say? What will Ibrahim say? He'll probably go over and beat up Jusoh.'

'He won't need to, because you've got a police guard.'

'I don't know if he'll see it that way,' she said. 'He'll think he needs to prove a point.'

'That could get him into a lot of unnecessary trouble.' Din was worried. 'It's bad enough this guy broke into your house. You don't have to make it worse, so he can claim to be the victim. Really, you've done the right thing and we should go forward with our plan.'

She seemed unconvinced but stayed quiet.

Din then picked up the story to tell Rahman. 'We get to their house, and she's right, her husband goes mad hearing what happened. He wants to leave immediately to get Jusoh outside and beat some sense into him. I don't know how much beating would be necessary to get that done, but let's just say a lot. I talked him out of it for now, but I wouldn't put any money on it staying that way.'

'Where are the brothers?'

'In jail. That's why I'm back here, because we don't need a guard anymore. They won't be going over there.'

'What about the mother? And the daughter-in-law? Do you think they might try something?'

The men in the station all looked at one another. 'I never really thought about it,' Osman said. 'I thought it was very possible the mother told her sons what to do, but she didn't do it herself.'

'What a family,' said Rahman, not for the first time. 'But even though the ladies didn't kill Zulkifli in the market, couldn't they have been responsible for telling Jusoh what to do? And now that Jusoh and his brother are out of the picture for the time being, might they not take matters into their own hands?'

'Do you think they could really manage it?' asked Din.

'I don't think they could beat anyone up, no. But use a knife? Why not? Even though at this point it doesn't matter anymore, because we know all about them, and trying to kill Afzan won't save them and their money.'

'They might not see it that way,' Osman folded his arms and leaned against the desk. 'They could believe it would end the whole discussion and leave them with the money. Though from what Afzan says, she doesn't want it anyway.'

'Her husband might.'

'He might, but then she'd have to say publicly she was Zulkifli's child. Think of her family, think of her father. That can't be anything you'd undertake lightly.'

'True.' Rahman was lost in thought. 'Have we seen the will?'

'I was just thinking the same thing,' Osman smiled. 'Let's get it.'

Rahman grabbed Din on the way out. After all, he'd been invaluable in this case, and deserved to be included. He shone with delight.

Back in Tapak Gajah, they received a frosty reception from Halimah, who met them in her living room but turned her face from them. 'You've arrested my sons on the word of some illiterate market girl,' she told them, spitting the words between her clenched teeth. 'You're punishing them while they mourn for their own father. I'd hate to see what your family life is like. Or is this what it's like in Perak?'

Osman was stunned at this attack, although later, when he thought about it, he shouldn't have been. They'd use anything they could against you and not give it a second thought.

Rahman took over the conversation when Osman sat silent. 'That's unfair and untrue, Mak Cik. I hope someday you'll see that and apologize. Your son broke into someone's house and threatened to kill them.'

Halimah sniffed, making it clear that she'd never see that it was unfair and untrue, and absolutely never would she apologize. 'Jusoh, I imagine that's whom you're talking about. I don't know that he broke in anywhere. He says he didn't. You've already arrested him, so you aren't here to ask my opinion or my permission? So why are you here?'

'We'd like to see the will.'

'Zulkifli's will?'

Who else's? 'Yes.'

'I don't have to show it to you.'

'Not entirely true,' Rahman felt as though he was beginning to talk like a lawyer himself. 'But if you'd prefer not to, just let me know who your lawyer is, and we'll contact him.'

'Zulkifli wrote his own. He didn't need a lawyer.'

Rahman felt immediately this was likely to be trouble. No lawyer, anyone in the family could amend the will if they thought it was not in line with their own opinion. 'May we see it?'

Halimah sighed as though she'd never been as annoyed as she was by the police, and that might have been true. 'It isn't any of your affair.' She said it slowly, as if teaching it to a particularly slow student.

'I'm afraid it is,' Osman said sadly. 'There's been a murder.'

'What has this got to do with it?'

'Another motive.'

'There was never a motive to begin with. This has nothing to do with it.'

'I need to see it anyway.' Osman's voice was getting less quiet.

'I don't know where it is.'

'Mak Cik, do not make me take you into the station. Please give it to me now.'

'What if I can't find it? Then we'll just go to shariah court and have it divided among the family as it specifies in Islamic law. Surely that can't be illegal.'

'No, it isn't. But surely in the days since your husband's unfortunate death you already found it to start dividing the inheritance …'

'Surely not! Do you think we thought of nothing but money?'

This was exactly what Osman thought, but there was no polite way to say it. He stood up. 'We'll check the legal records, of course, to see if anything has been submitted, and speak to the shariah court as well. I will note you were uncooperative, not that I think that will bother you at all.'

Walking down the steps, Osman said loudly to Rahman, 'I doubt the shariah court will allow any disposition of the assets while a murder is being investigated. That way, at least, we'll make sure nothing gets done until we're finished.'

Rahman turned discreetly back to see if anyone was listening, and of course Halimah was. She appeared exasperated but determined.

Chapter XXIV

'What does it matter if they can't probate the will?' Rahman asked in the car. 'They all have everything they want anyway. It's all in the family and they want to keep it that way.'

'Very true. It might make them think about it, though.'

'If there was a will leaving anything to anyone else, they'll have long since found it and destroyed it. We'll never find it now.'

'Oh definitely. If there was such a will, it was burned five minutes after Zulkifli was killed. Or five minutes before. No, that's not it. I'm just wondering, and of course, I could be wrong,' Osman said modestly. Rahman waited while the obligatory self-deprecation was proffered. 'What if they were cutting Jusoh's share? Thinking that Razaleigh could take care of him. Maybe Halimah was afraid to put all that money in his hands if he wasn't that smart. What do you think?'

'I wouldn't give him a lot of money. God only knows what he'd do with it.'

'Exactly. It's just a thought, you know. I was just wondering about it last night and I have no proof at all. It's just a theory. But what if they're trying to do that and Jusoh feels betrayed? Do you think he might talk?'

'He might. He isn't that bright,' Rahman repeated. 'There's a lot people will say when that's the case. *Rapuh mulut:* a babbler. He might well tell any secrets he knows.'

'That's what we're counting on. Let's go talk to him.'

Thankfully, they did not have far to go, since Jusoh was in custody in their own jail. Din, as was his nature, had provided their prisoners with lavish breakfasts and a choice of tea or coffee. Better breakfasts and more cheerfully served than those they would have gotten at home, Osman said. More people might volunteer to be put up in the Kota Bharu Police Headquarters with Din as the innkeeper.

When they called Jusoh out to talk, he was at least well fed, and carried with him his bag of *teh tarik*, pulled tea, that Din had fetched for him from a seller on the street. Osman shook his head at Din's munificence. If he ever decided to leave policing, he had a wonderful career before him as a caterer.

'Jusoh,' Osman began, after signalling Din to go out and get teh tarik for himself and Rahman. Shouldn't they be treated as well as any prisoner? 'We were just out to Tapak Gajah to see your mother. She told us she couldn't find your father's will.'

Jusoh regarded them over the top of his plastic bag.

'Do you know what was in it?'

Jusoh shrugged. 'I don't pay that much attention to things like that,' he told them. 'I'm not interested.'

'Would you be interested if it meant you would get less of an inheritance than, say, Razaleigh?'

'Why would that happen? We're brothers.'

'Exactly.' Osman sat back and started on his own teh tarik.

'So?'

'As brothers, you ought to have the same inheritance. Yet if yours were less, that wouldn't be fair, now would it?'

Jusoh seemed confused. 'I don't see why that would happen.'

'It could. If your mother, for example, didn't think you could handle the money. I'm just thinking out loud here, but then she could give it to Razaleigh to take care of you. As I'm sure he would, I don't doubt it.'

'I can handle money.'

Osman nodded. 'Does your mother think you can?'

Jusoh stared at him, confused. 'I guess so.' He sounded less than convinced.

'Did your father?'

'Maybe.' He sounded even less convinced.

'Well then, maybe I'm just seeing things that aren't there, right? You'll get the money coming to you with no problem.'

'Could she really take it from me?'

'Well now. I'm not saying take it from you. I'm only thinking, mind you, because I don't know, that she'd give it to Razaleigh to watch it for you, and to take care of you.'

'I don't need anyone to take care of me.'

'Of course not. I'm just thinking about it. I could be completely wrong, right, Rahman?'

'Absolutely. But you also could be right.'

Jusoh swivelled back and forth between them, the dawn of bafflement showing on his face. 'But …'

'Yes?' Rahman encouraged him.

'But they couldn't do that.'

Rahman shrugged, seemingly uninterested. 'You're right. I don't know why we were even thinking about something like that. A waste of time, right?' He glanced at Osman. 'Come on,' he said to Jusoh, 'you can finish your teh tarik in here. Do you want a curry puff? I'm sure we have them. Din always makes sure to provide them. Ah! Here they are! I'll take one for myself, too, if you don't mind.' He smiled enquiringly at Jusoh, who nodded uncomprehendingly. Was this policeman really asking his permission to take one of his own curry puffs? It certainly seemed like it.

'I'll leave you for a little while, so you can relax.'

And Rahman quietly closed the door behind him, leaving a furiously thinking but not entirely focused Jusoh to work out what had just been said.

'What do you think?' Osman asked in a low voice.

'He hasn't quite grasped it,' Rahman told him. 'But he will, just give him time.'

Osman nodded, and everyone in the large office got busy with paperwork keeping things quiet, and conducive to serious thought. Having calculated that even the slowest eater would have gone through three or four curry puffs, Rahman walked back into the room, to find Jusoh frowning at a nearly finished plastic bag of the teh tarik.

'Everything OK?' he asked cheerfully, collecting the empty plate and motioning Jusoh to stand up. 'Let's go back into the cells,' he invited him.

'Don't you want to talk to me?'

Rahman was momentarily nonplussed. 'About what?'

'About the murder.'

'Sure.' He sat down facing Jusoh and offered him a cigarette. They both lit up.

'You think they're going to cheat me out of my inheritance,' he said to Rahman.

'I didn't say that. I believe we said it was possible, and so it is. Let me get Osman.' He signalled to Osman from the door, and he joined them. 'We said it was possible Che Jusoh here would not get his full inheritance, didn't we? Not that we necessarily know anything about it, but just that it could happen.'

Osman nodded. 'It could. I'm not a lawyer, and I also don't know what your mother might be planning. But I'm sure whatever it is, it's for your best interests. She's your mother, after all. Who would take care of you better?'

Jusoh snorted. 'You don't know her.'

'What do you mean?' Osman asked innocently. He could well imagine.

'She's not worried about me,' Jusoh said sulkily, airing what was clearly a long-held grievance. 'She thinks I'm just a dolt. Someone to do the dirty work. She doesn't even think I'm smart enough to get married. Of course I am! Everyone gets married, why not me?'

'You're right,' Rahman cheered him on.

'But every time I suggest someone, she just pushes it away. "You, Jusoh?" she says. "How would you run your own household?" He imitated her voice, speaking in a falsetto. "You should just help your brother and let him take care of you. Never mind." And when I'd argue with her, she'd say "*Tak terpagut di ayam, tak tersudu di itek*: chickens won't peck at it, ducks won't put their bills to it. Completely worthless, that's what you are." That's my mother.'

'That's awful!' Rahman said, and he meant it. He could not imagine his own mother and doting grandmother even thinking anything like that. What would it be like to grow up knowing they thought that about you? Unthinkable.

'You ask me,' Jusoh continued, still sullenly thrusting out his lower lip, 'if my mother has my best interests at heart? I don't think so. So now I've been thinking, after all this is she going to leave me with nothing? No money, no way to marry, always living with my brother as the family servant, being ordered around by his wife? I won't stand for it.'

They both nodded. Rahman asked, 'What do you mean, "all this"?'

Jusoh waved his hand, scattering cigarette ash all over the floor. 'You know. My father dying and all.'

'I'm not sure I understand.'

Jusoh stamped his foot in frustration. 'My father dying. The money coming to us. My mother said he kept changing his will, and he was liable to leave us all out of it. Maybe leave it to Afzan, since he thought she was his daughter. Who knows?'

'He told you that?' Rahman was shocked.

Jusoh nodded. 'He told me. A little while ago. She's smarter than I am, he said. She could use the money and I'd just lose it. But then I think he changed his mind again and said maybe she wasn't his daughter after all. So, it didn't matter. But my mother said we needed to do something, quick, because he could die at any time. I didn't know he was sick but then she told me. She said he had cancer and he might die soon and right before people died they got sentimental and decided to take care of everything they'd ever done in their lives. I'm not sure what she means exactly, but she said he'd be throwing money around to try to buy his way into heaven's good graces, and we needed to make sure it stopped.'

'So you knew he was sick?'

'She told me. And Fatimah. She told me too, that we had to stop him from getting maudlin and make sure he took care of his family before he started giving money to all these other people who had no business getting it.' He paused for a moment. 'That's what she said.'

'Did she tell you to kill him?' Osman asked quietly.

Jusoh nodded. 'Always me. She'd never ask Razaleigh, he's too valuable. I'm not. Whenever there's a dirty job to do, it's mine. It isn't fair. Especially if I had to do it and then I don't get any money. Like I'm just a servant and they're the family.' He sounded very unhappy, and Rahman felt sorry for him. It wasn't fair. But he did kill his father.

Chapter XXV

Minah came to visit soon after Maryam came home. She entered the house both literally and figuratively wringing her hands, proclaiming her dismay at all that had transpired, and accepting responsibility for getting Maryam and Rubiah involved in the first place.

'If I'd known,' she wailed, but very quietly, so as not to disturb the patient, 'I never would have called you. As God is my witness … *belah dada melihat hati*: cleave my chest and see my heart!'

'It's all right,' Maryam said tiredly. 'You don't have to get so dramatic.'

'Dramatic? Of course not. You know I never would have asked you to investigate it if I'd thought it would come to this.'

'It might have come to this anyway. It isn't as if anyone attacked me.'

'But you were stressed. I'm so sorry!' Minah plumped herself on the couch next to Maryam and continued to acknowledge her own fault in Maryam's illness. After a few minutes of this, Aliza, who was on duty at the time, came over and tried to redirect the conversation.

'Mak Cik Minah, please don't tire her out. She's resting and still working out the case. But we don't want her upset, do we?'

Minah made a horrified moue to illustrate how little she wanted anything like that. 'Exactly,' Aliza said. 'What can I get everyone?'

Aliza left to get the tea tray together, while Minah sat and talked. 'I hear Jusoh has been arrested for murdering his father.'

Maryam nodded. 'I heard. It happened soon after I went into the hospital.'

'Can you imagine what kind of a family?'

Maryam nodded. She was still interested in the case, and very proprietary about it, but it was now combined with a bone tiredness she'd never felt before. And humiliation: she was deeply embarrassed about what had happened, passing out in the police station. She understood there was nothing she could do about it, but she was used to being in charge, and helplessness did not become her. It frightened her almost as much as the heart attack itself.

And although she knew she was in no position to work on it, she was upset to find herself on the periphery of the investigation as it went forward. Rubiah, too had withdrawn from it: taking care of Maryam was her first priority, and she had no time in which to work with the police. While Maryam regretted it, Rubiah was actually relieved by it, happy to be excused from participation. Aliza, moving straight from work to her mother's house every day, returning home to her husband and child only after Rubiah arrived, had little energy for anything other than her most pressing responsibilities, which did not include crime fighting. Rahman filled her in on what was happening in Tapak

Gajah, but she found she could not always keep the suspects straight, and after a few days stopped asking about it. Maybe later, after her mother recovered.

Naturally, the plan Ashikin put together worked perfectly. Daily handoffs were made at breakfast, lunch and dinner, while the business was opened every afternoon, Aliza taught every morning, and Rubiah worked all day and came over at night with dinner. Mamat knew for certain after two days of this that his daughters did not trust him to take care of Maryam without oversight, since he was never alone with her unless she'd already gone to sleep. It was touching to see how hard they all worked to serve her meals and give her medicines and make sure that he and Yi were fed and kept to a schedule. Deep down, he believed he could do it, and take care of his wife, but neither Ashikin nor Aliza would take the chance on allowing him to do it unsupervised. He and Yi became another responsibility for the women, which annoyed him, but he couldn't bring himself to chide them with all they did.

Aliza returned with tea and cakes, setting them down carefully on the coffee table before the two women and Mamat, who'd wandered in and sat down to talk. 'I hear the police are talking to Halimah; they say she told Jusoh what to do.'

Maryam agreed, it was what she'd heard as well. She chose her cake carefully, taking only one, and sipped her tea slowly. She was feeling old, but perhaps Minah's talk would invigorate her.

'Telling your son to kill his father,' Minah exclaimed. 'Alamak, Yam, I find it almost impossible to believe. Almost impossible,' she noted, 'but since it's Halimah, I'm sure she did it. Your Osman was out in the kampong yesterday, I saw him, but not to speak to.

Rahman was with him, but of course he was working. Aliza, did he say anything to you?'

'No. I've been so busy, you know, here and at work. By the time I get home, I just don't feel like talking business. Strange, isn't it?'

'Not strange at all,' her mother told her. 'This is too much work for all of you. Ayah can take care of me, you know. Each day I'm getting stronger, and I think we can manage.'

'And Yi can help, too,' Mamat offered.

Aliza refused to even acknowledge any of this had been said. Leave her mother to Yi? It sounded to her like a slow-motion disaster. 'It isn't too much work at all, and we're all happy to do it. Please,' she turned to her father, 'don't tell me that Yi could take care of Mak right now. The very thought of it makes me shiver.'

Minah laughed, and so did Maryam. 'You're right,' she said, smiling, really smiling, for what seemed like the first time since she'd gotten home. 'I'm thinking about Yi helping me wash my hair. I'd do better with the geese.'

'Oh yes,' Minah agreed. 'I can't even picture that. I don't want to.'

'Tell me,' Maryam said more eagerly than before. Talk about washing her hair seemed to imbue her with energy. 'What's the talk about Halimah and Fatimah? Any gossip?' She leaned forward, unable to explain to herself why she suddenly felt so interested. Maybe she should wash her hair more often. Or let Yi do it, God help us all.

'Well,' answered Minah, clearly delighted in Maryam's

change, 'as you can imagine, there's talk of nothing else. Of course, the two of them are boarded up in their house, plotting I don't doubt. But then, at the market, I saw the lady who comes to do their laundry, and she said they're beside themselves with fear, now that Jusoh's in jail. They trust Razaleigh to keep his mouth shut, and besides, Razaleigh didn't really do anything, but Jusoh, you never can tell. And the word is he killed his own father, after being pushed by his mother and sister-in-law. Not,' she leaned back again, and picked up a cake, 'that it's an excuse. Far from it. But can you picture your own mother telling you to kill your father so he wouldn't give money to anyone else?' She shook her head at the sheer unnaturalness of it.

'Afzan?' Maryam asked. 'You know, she'd come to see me when I had the heart attack.' She could say it now without bursting into tears. 'I was in the police station with her.'

Minah nodded. Of course she heard. Everybody knew. 'She amazed us all,' Minah announced. 'I thought she'd have no interest in Zulkifli and his money. That's what everybody said, anyway. You remember Khadijah? From the market? She knows a lot about her, and everyone else for that matter. She told everyone who'd listen the girl was just pulled into it by Zulkifli's fancies. Absolutely no possibility it was true. I think her father wanted to sink into the ground for shame, even though he didn't do anything. But he thought everyone was imagining it, and that was just as bad.' She shook her head in commiseration. '*Dari jauh orang angkat telunjok, kalau dekat diangkat mata.* From afar, people point, from close, they raise their eyebrows. To be shamed like that for nothing you've done. Because I'm sure it all isn't true.

I wonder though, whether Afzan would try to get some money out of it. But,' she said, perplexed, 'I can't help but think how Zulkifli would think this was true. I mean, he must know if it's impossible, you know. I don't know how to explain that.'

Maryam nodded along with her recitation. 'That's the strange thing, isn't it? He tells her he is; he tells her he isn't. He might not know if he actually is, but surely he'd know if he couldn't be.'

'There you have it,' Minah said emphatically. 'Mamat,' she turned to him. He'd been listening with full attention, but seemed startled to be called upon, 'what do you think? I mean, of course he'd remember …'

Mamat actually blushed. Maryam turned away to hide a smile. It wasn't often he'd get caught like that. 'Naturally he'd know if he couldn't be. You can't remember something like that if it never happened. Forgetting something that did happen, that might be another story. But this?'

'So, you think it was possible?' Minah had a prosecutorial gleam in her eye.

'No.' Mamat was clear. 'I don't think anything. He may have just been lying, you know, to upset his sons, and the girl as well. He doesn't sound particularly good natured. The whole thing seems mean, no matter what actually happened.'

'There's a man's opinion,' Minah stated definitively. 'I think he lied, as you say. To upset his sons and to get Afzan and Ibrahim tangled up in his lies. Maybe he wanted her mother, a long time ago and she wouldn't. That, I can absolutely believe. And years later, he drags out some story to embarrass her and make his sons crazy. That sounds just like him.'

'Sounds terrible. I'm glad I never met him,' Mamat said as he stood up. 'Excuse me, I've got to feed the birds. I'll be right back.'

'Did I drive him away?' Minah whispered as he left.

'Yes,' Maryam said bluntly. 'He never thought he'd be asked for an opinion. I wouldn't worry about it.'

'He'll get over it,' Aliza put in. Maryam and Minah had forgotten she was there. She was a married woman and mother now, so they didn't have to spare her maidenly modesty anymore, but Maryam still couldn't help thinking of her as a little girl, which irritated Aliza no end. After all, she'd finally been offered a cigarette by Ashikin, which meant entry into the sorority.

Minah welcomed her as a fully-grown woman as well. 'He will. Men, you know. They can get so uneasy when women bring up things.' She shrugged. 'What to do?'

'Zulkifli didn't know what he started with his story,' Aliza continued. 'That's what got him killed.'

Maryam started, and began to stand. Both Aliza and Minah rushed to her and sat her down again, one pulling, one pushing. 'Wait, wait!' she cried. 'I just thought …'

'What?' Aliza asked, relieved that Maryam was down on the sofa again.

'I just wondered, I mean, those two are still out. Someone ought to check on Afzan.'

They stared at her, not realizing the import of what she'd said.

'Fatimah and what's her name? Halimah,' she said impatiently. 'Jusoh's in prison, but his mother isn't, and neither is his sister-in-law. Don't you think they might try to kill Afzan? If they think she's decided to take some money, maybe fight the will. I don't know if it would work, but it might.'

Aliza stared at her. 'Do you think they'd actually try?'

'I don't know, that's what I'm telling you. But shouldn't the police keep an eye on them? Or do they think because they've got Jusoh, they don't need to worry anymore?'

Minah and Aliza looked at each other. 'I'll go over to the police here and call Rahman. At least let him know what you're thinking.'

Aliza left the house to get to the small police station in Kampong Penambang. There, she called Rahman and luckily found him at his desk and told him what her mother had suggested. He listened closely and left immediately, grabbing Din on the way out.

'My mother-in-law thinks Zulkifli's wife and daughter-in-law might try to kill Afzan,' he told Din as they drove to Tapak Gajah. 'I wonder though. If anything happens to her it can't be blamed on Jusoh anymore. Would they take that chance?' He swerved out of the way of a water buffalo considering whether to cross the road. It would not do to have a run in with the beast, who would probably win any contest. They screeched into the village and went straight to the market to find Afzan. Who was sitting quietly behind a heap of vegetables, calm and unruffled, while all around her the low buzz of the market went on as usual. Khadijah waved to them, and some of the other sellers smiled and asked about Sharifah Aini, and why she was not here.

Rahman scouted around quickly, aware that all eyes were on him, but he saw no sign of either of the women he sought. He bent over Afzan, who shrank back warily, and asked her if anyone had been unpleasant to her. Even as he said it, he felt he sounded like an idiot.

'Unpleasant?' Afzan asked him. 'What are you talking about?'

'I mean has anyone scolded you or tried to hurt you.'

'No. Who did you think would do that?'

'I thought maybe ...' Rahman suddenly thought better of announcing their suspicions to Afzan. Best to keep it to themselves. 'Oh, I don't know. Anyone.'

She shook her head. 'Are you afraid Cik Halimah will try to kill me? She might, you know. She's really unhappy about all of this, and she blames me.'

'But why?'

'Because she thinks I started it all, because Zulkifli said he was my father, because she has to be angry at someone.'

'He wasn't your father, though, was he?'

'I doubt it. But I'll tell you this, if he wants to include me in his will, I'm happy to take it.'

'He said that's what would happen, didn't he? That in the end, you'd want the money.'

'Don't talk down to me!' her temper flared. 'I'm tired of it. I didn't ask him to say it, he just did. And if now I want to take the money, why shouldn't I? We could use it; we could do a lot with it. Ibrahim and I might be able to buy a boat, or build a house, or something. Why should they keep all the money so they can stay rich, if I'm mentioned in the will? Or even if I'm not, they ought to think about putting me in. They're his official family, but sometimes it doesn't matter. He thought I was his daughter.'

'How does your father feel about this?'

She shrugged. 'I'm sure he doesn't like it one bit. Stirring up gossip, his good name dirtied. You can imagine what he's said. I'm not saying this is a fact to make everyone happy. I'm only saying if Zulkifli's giving, I'm taking,'

'To make up for the time he cheated your husband.'

'That, too.'

'Well, this isn't a police matter. Good luck to you getting hold of any money you can from the will. But you will be careful, won't you? You're dealing with people who won't hesitate to hurt you.' He prepared to leave.

'Thanks for the warning,' she said. He couldn't tell whether or not she was serious.

Chapter XXVI

'You should bring Din over for dinner sometime,' Rubiah said to Rahman during the evening handover. He'd come to see Aliza and escort her home.

'Din?' he said uncomprehendingly. 'Why?'

'He seems like a nice boy,' Rubiah said innocently. 'I'd think he'd like to meet your family.'

Rahman turned to Aliza silently asking what was up, and Aliza laughed. 'I think Mak Cik Rubiah wants to see if Din would be a good husband for her two nieces in Tumpat. She's been examining every young man she meets.'

'Din?' he asked again.

'Why not?' Rubiah asked defensively. 'He's a nice boy, good job. You think well of him. Why wouldn't he be a good husband?'

'No reason,' he floundered. 'I just don't know if he's even interested. If his family maybe has someone in mind.'

'Why don't you ask?' Rubiah suggested. 'That would be the quickest way to find out.'

'Do I have to?' he whispered to Aliza.

'Probably. Sorry,' she answered. 'He might be interested.'

Rahman sounded unhappy. 'I don't know about that. I don't

want him to think this is my idea.'

'Everyone has to get married,' Rubiah said sternly. 'It's not as if he wants to be a lifelong bachelor. Stop thinking this is something no one else has ever considered.' She sighed with exasperation and turned to Aliza. 'Maybe you can ask him then, whenever you see him. After all, he'll probably thank you. Remember how Azmi was when Ashikin set him up? And now look!'

Aliza agreed. First, because it would do no good not to, and second, because what Rubiah said was true, even if Rahman really didn't want to know about it.

Talk of marriage was also going on in Tapak Gajah. 'Maybe we should find a wife for Jusoh,' Fatimah suggested. 'It would make him more content, don't you think? He might be happier and more tractable.'

'I think he's getting less tractable every day,' his mother said waspishly. 'He used to take direction, and now it's like he fights all the time.'

'Jail might change him.'

'It might make him worse.'

'Mak, you should think about a wife for him.'

'A wife would wrap him around her finger. He'd be a *kerbau cucuk hidung:* a water buffalo with a ring through his nose.' She thought for a moment. 'He's not that bright.'

Fatimah shrugged daintily. 'He still might want a wife.'

'And when did you become so interested in what he wants? It was quite a different story you were telling not too long ago.'

Fatimah coloured. 'It was different. Now, I think we should make him content and let him live his life.'

'It's late for that. We're all in it too deep to just walk out. He's in jail for murder, you know. And he's probably telling everyone all about it.'

'You should never have encouraged him …'

'Me?' Halimah was enraged. 'I did what I did for all of us. Did you want to see him give everything away to Afzan because he thought he was her father? Which, by the way, I very much doubt. But he kept insisting right up until he decided to stop it, but you can't put those words back in your mouth. And though lately I heard he changed his mind, and told her she wouldn't be getting any money, did you want to fight her if she decided to take it?'

'We would win the fight. I don't think …'

'That's right.' She stood up and silently fumed for several moments, trying to calm her anger but not quite succeeding. 'You think we'd win the fight?' she turned on her daughter-in-law, who drew back. 'We wouldn't. Razaleigh would never be able to stand the talk in the town. He'd give her something to make it go away. And she'd be able to claim later she never said she was his daughter, she'd never admit it, and that Razaleigh gave her the money from guilt about what his father had said. You really don't think that's what would happen?'

Fatimah was resentful. Halimah had begun to notice this more lately. At first, she thought her daughter-in-law was a kindred spirit, and rejoiced to have her married to her son. She too was astoundingly blunt, even mannerless, which Halimah of all people admired. But lately, she also seemed to get pouty when she didn't get her way on the first try and lose interest in trying further. Halimah thought this was distinctly aggravating, as she thought Fatimah would be a fighter, as she was. When she didn't get her way one way, she'd try another; she wouldn't stick out her bottom lip and be snippy with everyone until they either figured out what she wanted and gave it to her, or decided it wasn't worth it and merely avoided her.

Her opinion of Fatimah was dropping quickly. Now was the time she needed an ally and helpmeet, not a petulant child who refused to take up her responsibilities. She moved immediately to get Fatimah out of her sulk and back to work on their most important problem.

'Listen to me,' she began firmly. 'Things are moving very quickly right now. Jusoh's in jail, he's probably going to tell the police everything he knows. He'll think he's been badly treated by us, and then …'

Fatimah was up on her feet. 'Us? Badly treated by us? You mean badly treated by you, Mak. You've been doing this all his life, not me. No, right now, I don't think there is an "us". There's a "you", and that's all.'

Halimah thought if she could be sure she'd get away with it, she'd strangle Fatimah right where she stood. Was this the extent of her gratitude? Halimah had handpicked her to join the family. While they were cousins, Fatimah's parents were far less better off than Razaleigh's, and by Halimah's reckoning, Fatimah had married up. Considerably up. Why, she was a wealthy young woman now! And she lived accordingly, with a nice house, all the clothing she wanted and a husband of whom she was fond. Or so his mother had thought. Right now, she had her doubts, but she could think about that some other time, when she had less pressing issues at hand.

All this was at risk now, and Fatimah did not seem to realize it. Halimah had never considered her stupid, but perhaps she hadn't noticed it. 'What are you saying? Do you want us all destroyed?'

'No, I don't.' Fatimah seemed strangely calm. 'I think I'll go home now. I don't think there's anything more for me to do here.' She turned around slowly, as if modelling the clothing she was wearing, and began to walk out of the house. Halimah reached out and grabbed a handful of her *baju kurung,* the long traditional blouse she wore. Fatimah tried to pull herself away, but Halimah held her fast.

'What is your plan, now?' she asked. 'Try to see Razaleigh at the police station?'

'No,' Fatimah answered, unsuccessfully pulling away. 'I just want to go home.'

'You don't think we should discuss what to do if Jusoh tells the police he killed his own father? You don't think that might seem bad?'

'It will,' Fatimah said, getting red in the face, continuing to yank her blouse away. She only succeeded in ripping it. 'He'll tell them you thought up this whole thing and ordered him to kill his father. I didn't. They're going to come for you, not for me.' She finally pulled free, tearing her blouse up the seam and nearly falling into the wall with her momentum. She righted herself and tried to smooth down her outfit, but it was to no avail. She was bedraggled, as if she'd been in a fight, which she had been. She stumbled down the stairs and out of the yard, intent on getting to her own house, visible from Minah's house where her husband and several of his friends sat on the porch talking. They fell silent, and their eyes followed her. When she could no longer be seen, Nasir stood up and announced, 'I don't know what that was, but I'm going to the police.' His friends nodded and walked over with him to get some help.

Osman was called immediately by the local police. This was, after all, his case, and they were anxious to keep it that way. However, since it involved a young woman, and not murder, a pair of policemen thought it might be safe enough for them to find out what had happened and if she was alright. Reaching her home, they waited politely at the foot of the stairs and called up to see if anyone was home. Fatimah came right down the stairs, having changed into a more presentable outfit, and announced: 'I want to speak to the police chief in Kota Bharu. I have information he'll want to hear.'

The police assured her he'd already been called and was on his way even as they spoke, which seemed to mollify her. She sat on the porch while they waited on the steps. She didn't offer them so much as a cup of tea. Naturally, she was not obligated to give them refreshments, but it could not be remembered when anyone had failed to do so. So, they sat silently, keeping out of the sun, watching for Osman's arrival.

Chapter XXVII

Osman went straight over to the house. He missed having Maryam with him, but that was out of the question now. She needed her rest.

Fatimah was unhappy: *masam muka macam nikah tak suka*: as sour faced as an unwilling bride. Osman wondered why she was always so out of sorts, as though she was never satisfied with anything she had. He thought she'd be hell to live with, but that was none of his affair: he was here in a completely professional capacity. He, too, sat on the steps, which was hosting quite a crowd, but none of them had been invited to come up. A first for him as well.

'Cik Fatimah, what's happened? Are you ill? Has something happened?'

'It has,' she replied emphatically. 'I wanted to tell you about Zulkifli's death. I have some very interesting information.' She gave the local police a commanding scowl, and they took themselves off with the occasional backward glance. Osman asked if he could come up to the porch to keep the conversation relatively confidential, and he also wanted to get out of the sun. He was less than pleased to not be invited. She agreed he could come up, but her expression remained disgruntled.

'It was Jusoh who killed him,' she began with no preface, diving right into the heart of the conversation. 'His mother told him to do it.'

'Why?'

'The money, of course! You know Zulkifli kept changing his will, not that it mattered.' Osman noted she denied him the polite 'Che before his name, as anyone else would have added referring to their father-in-law. He was liking her less every moment. 'She thought they'd be written out of it, but I don't think that would have made any difference. We could go to the religious court and have everything divided according to shariah law and we would get it. But she was nervous about it. She thought the boys would get most of it, which of course, they would, and she didn't care to be left with a smaller portion.

'He was sick, you know.' She gave him a hard stare. 'Cancer. She said she didn't know, but she did. Well, everyone guessed something was wrong, he was turning yellow and dry,' she shuddered. 'Horrible. And if he died soon and kept playing with the will, well, who knows what might have happened. So, she figured if he died sooner it would be to all our advantage. This was even before Afzan came into the picture. That would just have been another complication, because she'd probably ask for money. Razaleigh, he'd be likely to give her some just to avoid trouble. He could be weak that way.'

Osman wondered why these stories were so sordid, and where these people came from. Your average person didn't think like this, Alhamdulillah. If they did, the world would be unliveable.

Just listening to Fatimah made him want to go home and crawl under the bed. But he had his work to do, so he acted as though he heard things like this all the time, and it didn't bother him at all.

'You'd testify to this?'

She nodded. 'Of course.'

'Against Jusoh as well?'

She nodded again. 'Razaleigh will come home, won't he? He didn't kill anyone.'

'I can't say.' He certainly helped, Osman thought to himself. He might thank me to keep him away from this house, but who could tell? Maybe he enjoyed it.

A smile broke out on Fatimah's face. Self-satisfied, no, triumphant, preening. It clearly was not aimed at him, and Osman turned to see who might warrant a smile like that. It would be enough to drive anyone to slap it off her face, and Osman was glad not to be included in it.

Halimah stood at the bottom of the steps behind him. 'So, you went straight to the police.'

Fatimah tossed her head. 'I did. It was the right thing to do, wasn't it, Chief Osman?'

He didn't answer. It was the right thing to do, but the spirit in which she did it was all wrong. Nevertheless, he was clearly no more than a spectator here, with no ambition to be anything more.

'The right thing!' Halimah was enraged. 'You talk to me about the right thing?'

'Yes, I do. I'm doing it, and you? Not at all.'

Halimah advanced up the steps. 'You were a part of this. A large part. Did she tell you, Che Osman? Did she tell you how she worked on poor Jusoh until he was an *itek dengar gemuruh*: like a duck listening to thunder. Completely bewildered, he was.' She leaned closer to Osman, as though they were having a private conversation. He began wishing he'd brought backup. 'You understand, he isn't that bright. You must have noticed. Well, in such a case, surely it's easy to imagine, a boy like that, unable to reason clearly, with the sister-in-law he respects telling him what to do … At the start, I believe he fought against such a notion. If only he'd come to me! I would have brought him back to the right path. But I feel he was ashamed. Yes, ashamed of what she'd said and ashamed to tell me what was being planned. Poor boy. As a mother, you understand; you may have children yourself, right? You know how you feel when your dear child is being misused, by someone in your own house! *Musoh di dalam selimut*: an enemy under the blanket. Betrayed by your own family! Sacrificed! Yes, I believe he is being sacrificed by this woman here, who wanted my husband killed and brought his own son around to do it.' She dabbed at her eyes with a handkerchief, to soak up non-existent tears. Osman thought of one or two Malay proverbs which might also fit the situation and hoped she wouldn't drag them out as well.

'So you believe,' he began.

'Yes,' she said, grabbing the conversational reins, 'I believe, should I say I know? I know she's guilty of this crime. My Jusoh, my dear child, was just the instrument she used to get what she wanted. He thought of none of this. Well, let's be clear, he isn't capable. He could no more plan a crime than … well, anything. He's an innocent boy.' Osman noticed as her tirade went on that Jusoh got younger with each sentence. He'd be back in grade school in a few minutes. 'You should be taking this woman into custody. Let her feel the full weight of the law, of morality, of custom. Killing your own father! What boy would think of that? No one. But she didn't flinch.'

Actually, neither of them would flinch at anything, in Osman's opinion. 'Let's take this back to the station. I want to make sure it's all recorded as it should be.'

He walked down the steps and motioned them to follow. He wondered how to seat them in the car, afraid if he put them next to each other, only one would live to get out in Kota Bharu. His money would be on Halimah – he thought she might kill Fatimah with her bare hands. Once again, he wished for backup, but coming out here he thought it was just a discussion with Fatimah. He didn't realize he'd be in the middle of a verbal duel which bore all the signs of turning bloody, given the smallest chance. Perhaps he should leave policing, maybe get some land and grow rice and fruits. He snapped out of that immediately. He'd need to pay close attention to get them back to his office without harm. He even considered handcuffs, then remembered he had none with him.

Once in the car, he stopped at the small police hut nearby, and waved over one of the officers. 'Ride with us to Kota Bharu, will you? Sit between those two to make sure they don't kill each other.' The man was startled, but schooled in following direction, and obediently climbed into the back. Between Halimah and Fatimah, he sat frozen, while each of them glared at him in turn.

'Move over,' Halimah ordered him, pushing him away from her with her hip. 'It's way too close back here,' she grumbled, turning toward the window. Fatimah, not one to take second place if she could avoid it, pushed him back toward the middle. 'Stop crowding me,' she told him acidly. 'Move away.'

Osman saw his future when he and Azrina had more children. They'd drive back to Perak to visit their families, with Azman and his two as yet non-existent siblings in the back seat arguing. And he would, as he lost patience somewhere in southern Thailand or in the middle of the Malaysian jungle, stop the car, turn around, and threaten, 'If I have to stop once more, you're all going to get it, do you hear me? I don't want to hear any more arguing. I can't stand it.' And then he'd drive on, with at least fifteen minutes of peace before it started again. This drive was a preview, but worse, because none of those involved was a cute child.

Thankfully, they arrived in Kota Bharu with no injuries other than to self-importance, but in the case of these two, there seemed to plenty more to spare. He got them into the interrogation room, and before he realized it, tea and cakes were on the table, along with a pack of cigarettes. Din smiled, extremely pleased with himself, and Rahman entered to help in the interrogation. Though in this interview, Osman saw the problem as shutting them up rather than getting them to speak. All they had to do to get them talking was nothing at all.

Each retold her story with even more dramatic flourishes than they had in Tapak Gajah. It was the same story, differing only in the details of who was the evil mastermind behind it all. Of course, in Fatimah's telling, Halimah was the witch who set it all in motion. In Halimah's version, Fatimah was the snake who whispered in the ear of an innocent boy. The police believed they both were guilty, and they rejected the 'innocent boy' label for Jusoh, who was certainly old enough to know what he was doing.

'I wish Maryam and Rubiah were here,' Rahman whispered to Osman. 'I think they'd be able to get everything out of these two. You know, mak cik and all.'

'Is she well enough to get here? I mean, if we get her here and promise not to upset her?'

'I'm going to try. I just want to see mak cik to mak cik. Halimah wouldn't stand a chance to lie if my mother-in-law were here.'

'I'm putting them in the cells till you get back,' Osman told him. 'I'm afraid to have them running around loose.'

Rahman nodded and left quickly, before the argument over the cells began, as it inevitably would. Halimah burst into tears at the sight of her sons in custody, and then continued weeping at the thought of herself in the same jail. Fatimah gave her husband a tight smile but said nothing. It was difficult to get into trouble with silence.

'What are you doing here?' Jusoh asked his mother.

'If you knew what happened,' she said. 'That viper has tried to damn us all, but I defended us, and made the police see what had really happened.'

'What do you mean?' Razaleigh asked.

Din leaned against the wall, listening.

Chapter XXVIII

Rahman came into Maryam's house soon after Aliza arrived 'How's your mother?'

'As usual. Why are you here in the middle of the day? Is something wrong?'

'No, not at all. We have those two from Tapak Gajah in the station …'

'What two?'

'The mother and daughter-in-law.'

'Come over here,' Maryam called out from the living room. 'Where I can hear you.'

'We've brought them in, Mak,' Rahman informed her. 'The mother and daughter-in-law. For telling Jusoh to kill his father.'

Maryam nodded. 'What a family.'

'We're talking to them now. They're both informing on each other, claiming the other is guilty. I think both of them are.'

'Probably.'

'And we wanted to know if you and Mak Cik Rubiah wanted to come down to the station to talk to them, since you'll be able to tell if they're lying more easily than we can.'

'Help me up,' was her only comment. 'I have to comb my

hair.'

'Where are you going?' Mamat asked with alarm. 'You have to rest! I can't let you …'

'I've rested enough, and I can rest again when this is over. But I wouldn't miss this for the world! Aliza, can you help me with my hair? Yi!' she roared. 'Go get Mak Cik Rubiah right now.'

'But I …'

'Not now, Yi! Go and get her!'

With a glance at his father, he galloped out the door to get Rubiah. In the middle of homework! And then they were angry if it didn't get done.

When Rubiah came in, Maryam was ready to go. Mamat insisted upon accompanying her, and she leaned on his arm as he helped her down the steps, Rahman in front in case she slipped, Aliza behind in case she needed a push.

When she arrived at the police station, she was greeted by all the staff standing and welcoming her. It was as if the queen returned to her people, with a babble of excited voices, chairs being scraped to make it easier for her to sit down, and of course, Din serving a very respectable assortment of snacks. Rubiah took the opportunity to consider him as a prospective bridegroom and was pleased with what she saw. He might do nicely for her eldest niece. Din noticed she was examining him, but wasn't sure why, and therefore worried something was undone on his clothing or his hair uncombed. He smiled at her uncertainly, and she smiled back at him with approval. He was confounded.

Maryam and Rubiah, together with their entourage of Aliza and Mamat, sat at the table in the interrogation room drinking tea. 'So that's Din,' Rubiah whispered to Maryam. 'He'd be a good prospect, don't you think?'

'Excellent.'

Rubiah nodded. Now all she needed to do was get some details from Rahman and ask around. She sat there contentedly. Even if nothing else came out of this meeting, she'd accomplished a lot.

Soon, Halimah was brought in, slightly dishevelled after a few hours in the cells. Funny how that was – even the shortest time seemed to make people appear worse. Ungroomed, somehow. And it had not improved their moods at all.

'What are you two doing here?' Halimah asked as she set down. She quietly scorned the teacup pushed toward her. 'What am I doing here?' she demanded of Osman. 'You're here to be interviewed,' he told her. 'As we agreed.'

'Who agreed to having her here? I didn't.'

'She's working with the police. Please remember your manners.'

Osman thought she might explode. Her face was red, she was panting for breath and her eyes were on fire. He turned away, to avoid being caught in whatever she was planning.

'You told Che Osman that your daughter-in-law planned the killing,' Maryam began.

'I certainly did, because it's God's truth. My boys are good boys, even a little innocent, you might say. Naïve. Especially Jusoh. He's unused to the ways of the world, and that's the reason she could lead him on that way.' Maryam did not recognize Jusoh in that description but kept quiet. 'He respected her, and of course, he's very close to his brother. He'd do anything for Razaleigh, and so when she approached him to make sure their inheritance was safe, he couldn't hesitate. Not for an instant, really. If he thought it would benefit his brother, he'd do it.'

'How about if it would benefit you?'

'He might. He's a loving and affectionate boy.'

Maryam worked hard not to roll her eyes.

'And his father? Was he close to him?'

Halimah seemed pained. Sorrowful. 'No, and it's a pity. It was his father's fault. A very cold man not very interested in the boys once they were older. Jusoh wanted to be close to his father, what boy doesn't? But Zulkifli simply couldn't connect.'

'Close to you, though.'

She smirked, no doubt considering it a beatific smile. 'I'm his mother.'

'So you are. Now, if I understand what you're telling me, Jusoh was deceived and pressured into this plan to kill your husband before he could change the will once more.'

Halimah nodded.

'And you knew nothing about it.'

'How could I? Wouldn't I have stopped it right away if I thought it was going on?'

Maryam didn't answer this. 'You told me when we spoke at your house that you didn't know your husband was ill.'

'I didn't.'

'Your daughter-in-law tells me you all knew, and that was why you felt it imperative to act right away, before he died and left you all out of his will.'

'My daughter-in-law is trying to save her own skin, that's all. She's making things up to fit her own story, which is a tissue of lies. Yes, that's it. I have never lied to you. If anything, I'm too honest,' she said in the tone of someone freely confessing their flaws. 'But I don't mind that. I don't lie about anything, even if it's unpleasant.'

'You undoubtedly don't shy away from unpleasantness,' Maryam told her ambiguously. 'You positively enjoy it.'

Halimah wasn't sure whether she was being agreed with or not, so she gave a small smile which never reached her eyes.

'Let me sum up what you've told me: this was a scheme of Fatimah's who corrupted Jusoh as well as her husband and led them to kill their own father. The reason for this? To make sure he didn't change his will, and particularly to make sure he didn't include Afzan in it.

'Afzan!' Halimah spat. 'She has no business being involved in this.'

'I'm not sure what that means,' Maryam said, glancing at Rubiah as if asking for help. Rubiah shook her head, not really understanding that either.

'I mean this is not her family. She doesn't belong here. She has no claim on us.'

'Even if she's Che Zulkifli's daughter?'

'She isn't.'

'She agrees with you there. The whole story with Afzan really confuses me, since he began talking about her being his daughter, and she didn't believe him. I'm not sure she believes it now either, but then he told her in fact she was not his daughter and wouldn't be allocated any money from him when he died.

'I imagine dying was much on his mind lately, as his doctor said it could happen fairly soon. We do think it was Afzan he thought he was killing, but his eyesight was failing, and he killed the wrong woman, poor soul. How do you explain that?'

'I don't. I have no idea why he would do such a thing. Maybe his illness affected his brain.'

'Perhaps. Had he been talking to the boys about his impending death?'

'I don't think so.'

'So, he might have.'

'He was a private man.'

'Not that private. After all, he went talking to Afzan, then changing his story. He could never have said anything to her, and she would be none the wiser. It's almost like he wanted her to claim her portion, even if he didn't give it to her outright.'

'Never! He wouldn't do that! He knew his family. He wanted to provide for his sons, for me! Not for some, I don't know, market girl with nothing. And a husband who I hear he cheated out of his portion for work. How does that make you think he cared about her? Ridiculous. It isn't worth listening to.' She tossed her head to signify she wasn't listening. 'And anyway,' she said, narrowing her eyes, 'he wanted to kill her. So, tell me, how is he trying to help her? He wanted to get rid of her.'

'There's no need to get rid of her if there's no relationship there. To me, you see, his attempt to kill her just confirms that there was something he feared. He thought she could take a chunk of the inheritance, and he wanted to stop her.'

'Well, it's too bad he didn't. It would have saved us all …'

Maryam was starting to get angry – Mamat could see it in her face. He leaned over and whispered urgently, 'Yam! Remember you've been ill. You need to stay calm. Don't let this woman get you all riled up.'

Maryam turned and nodded. He was right.

'I'm going to ignore that,' she said, as primly as she could. 'I can't afford to get angry right now, and it's taking all my effort to keep from it. So, as I said, I will ignore that comment.'

She thought for a moment. 'Che Osman,' she said, 'perhaps we should bring in Cik Fatimah, and see what she has to say. She's had time to speak with her husband and brother-in-law now, and she may have thought about things a little differently.

Osman nodded, and Rahman went in to escort her into the room. She was a bit shaken and there was a stain on her expensive baju kurung. She kept staring down and brushing at it, as if it were the most important thing she had to do right now.

'Well, Cik Fatimah, it's nice to see you again,' Rubiah greeted her. In the interests of keeping Maryam calm, she decided to lead the discussion.

Fatimah shot her trademark pout at Rubiah and said nothing.

'I guess you know why you're here. Tell us what happened.'

'I've already told these people everything twice. They should be able to repeat it to you by now.'

'I'd like to hear it in your words.'

'I already told you! She did it! She instructed her sons to kill Zulkifli because she was afraid he'd change the will again. I'll tell you, if we went to shariah court, it wouldn't matter what was in the will. The sons would get most of the inheritance anyway, but no, she wanted to make sure she kept most of it. This whole problem,' she moved her hand in an arc illustrating the size of it, 'was because she wouldn't follow Islamic law. I've been thinking about it,' said the newly-minted religious scholar, 'and to me, that's the root of the problem. She wouldn't follow what Islam instructs.'

Her listeners were stunned by this startling argument. She regarded their faces and decided some more explanation was necessary. 'You see,' she said, leaning forward, 'she wanted to follow the will which left the most to her. That way, of course, she'd stay wealthy, and she'd continue doling out money to her sons as she saw fit. But if he died with another will, which left most to the boys, well then, she'd never be able to fight it, and might not be so grand anymore. So, as you can see, she needed to have the right will be the one used. I researched this.'

'It certainly sounds like it,' Maryam recovered her voice. This woman had lost her mind.

'And that's how I know she wasn't doing anything to help her sons. Just herself.' She glared at Halimah, who watched, unruffled. 'This was all her doing. Poor Jusoh.' She shook her head in apparent regret for him. 'Such a simple boy. Believed everything his mother told him, and what did it lead to? This. He's not the real culprit here,' she concluded. 'She is.' She leaned back and took a sip of tea and a small bite of curry puff.

'Che Osman, Che Rahman, can we talk to you in your office for a moment?' Maryam asked. They all moved into the office, leaving Din and Mamat guarding the two women. If a fight broke out, Maryam would have picked the women as the winners.

'They're crazy,' Rubiah stated as soon as they sat down. 'But they both agree poor Jusoh had nothing to do with this. He was misled.'

'I noticed that,' Osman said. 'Though he's old enough to know when he's killing his father, isn't he?'

'Alamak! Of course he is. What is this new religious angle to the will? It's just unseemly, that's all. I won't have our religion dragged into this, this, mud hole,' she finished lamely. She couldn't think of anything bad enough to call it while keeping her language clean.

'You're right. I think they both worked on Jusoh, maybe on Razaleigh as well. They seem to me to be the guiltiest ones.'

'What about Yati? Or Afzan, if you prefer to think of it that way.'

Maryam shook her head. 'That seems to be Zulkifli's secret. I think he regretted telling her about it and wanted to take it back. Frankly, I don't think he needed to worry much about it. She never really believed him, and I don't know if she'd ever try to get any money. Can you imagine the disgrace of it if she pursued it? I can't imagine her doing anything.

'No,' Maryam continued. 'He could well have left that alone and never thought about it again. He killed an innocent woman, and underestimated Afzan. Really such a waste.'

'Do you think because they didn't like Zulkifli no one would tell us who killed him?'

'Of course,' Rubiah said tiredly. 'They were all happy enough to be rid of him. Why get in the middle of it? And that family is so awful.'

They all nodded, suddenly tired and discouraged. 'The one thing I like about this case has been no magic. No black magic, no *bomoh*, no spells. Everything comprehensible. I don't remember a case like this before,' Maryam said cheerfully.

'You're right!' Osman said. 'Just good, old-fashioned murder. It's really delightful, don't you think? I was beginning to think that would be impossible here, but I'm glad to see it can happen.'

There was the sound of chairs turning over, and indistinct arguing. Maryam did not get up, but everyone else did and rushed into the interrogation room, to find, just as Maryam predicted, Din and Mamat overpowered and outguessed by Halimah and her daughter-in-law, who were fighting each other with their fingers wrapped in each other's hair. Mamat was open mouthed with disbelief, and Din trying his best to pull them apart, but they ignored him. Fatimah, younger and perhaps stronger, had begun banging Halimah's head on the table while cursing her. There was blood staining the table, and Osman got his arm around Fatimah's neck and tried to drag her away. Mamat recovered himself and pulled Halimah in the other direction.

Just as they thought they'd gotten them apart, Fatimah stamped on Osman's foot hard enough to make him let go of her, and went back in to finish what she'd started, pulling Halimah's now lolling head by the hair and smacking it down on the table again. Rahman grabbed her hands behind her back and handcuffed them and was then able to drag her back and shove her into a chair.

Halimah's head was strange, somehow out of alignment. Din

had already called for the ambulance, who came to take her away. One of the attendants commented that the police station was now their most common destination. Din found nothing to say.

Osman, Rahman, Din and Mamat sat in the interrogation room, watching Fatimah as she collected herself. 'What do you think you're doing?' Osman finally asked.

'She deserved it. She deserved it long ago, if you ask me. See what she's done to her family?' Fatimah said haughtily, though the blood on her clothing detracted from her *grand dame* air. 'Asking a simple son to kill his father. Never in my life …' she let the sentence hang as she ostentatiously moved her shoulders to show how uncomfortable the handcuffs were.

'Never in your life what?' prompted Maryam, who could not wait to hear.

'I never thought I'd see a mother do that to her own child. It's unnatural.'

'Tell me,' Rubiah leaned forward in a confidential way, 'did she mention any of this to Razaleigh? Was he at all aware of what she was doing to his little brother?'

She was confused, as if this was one part of her story she'd never considered. She was silent, not knowing which way to jump. Should she claim Razaleigh had no idea? But then, might Razaleigh say otherwise? Could she admit he did know and did nothing? Unable to decide, she sat silent.

'*Cerdik, tak akal,*' Rubiah whispered to Maryam. 'Clever but not wise, as children may be.'

Maryam nodded. 'It's going to be interesting checking her story with "the boys", you know. I wonder why they both talk about them like they're small children. These are grown men! Is that supposed to make them more innocent?

Rubiah shrugged. 'So,' she continued, 'Am I to believe Razaleigh knew, or didn't know?'

'Razaleigh didn't know anything.'

'But you did?'

'I noticed it, yes.'

'And never thought to mention it to your husband. Really, Cik Fatimah, I find that hard to believe.'

'Here's what you should believe,' she said, 'that woman corrupted Jusoh and made him murder his own father.'

Maryam rose from her chair, and Mamat stood behind her. 'I think I'll be going,' she said. 'I'm afraid this isn't good for my heart.' She turned to leave, Rubiah following with her eyes. The door closed behind her, and Rubiah turned to Fatimah. 'She's very sensitive to lies, you see, and it upsets her. I think I'll leave as well.'

Half an hour later, after Fatimah had returned to the cells and demanded more tea and curry puffs, the hospital called. Halimah had died, and now Fatimah was arrested for murder.

Chapter XXIX

Razaleigh was stunned and could not come up with a cogent response when informed. He stammered, he choked, he sat silent.

Jusoh, however, collected himself far more quickly. 'She killed her?' He turned furiously to Fatimah in the next cell. 'You killed my mother?'

'She deserved it, after what she did to you.' Fatimah tried to sound in control, but her voice shook. She'd killed her mother-in-law in full view of the police. There was no way out of it, and most of her bluster, as well as her spite, was dissipated. It really didn't matter whether Jusoh backed up her story that Halimah had pushed him into killing his father and was therefore responsible. Now, it was only the straight charge of murder, which neither of them could avoid. Even if Jusoh said Fatimah was the mind behind his murder, it could hardly make things worse for her. She slumped on her bench against the wall. She started to cry.

Razaleigh was bereft of words. The future appeared clearer now, without his wife, without his parents, without his brother. He'd be alone, to take care of his children. He'd have to rebuild his life. Although he was still sitting in a cell, it didn't seem such a bad prospect for him. He studied Fatimah and Jusoh without feeling, and they seemed very far away. He already felt separated from them. They had their fates, and he had his, and although he'd never considered they would be taken from him, he now accepted it as *fait accompli*. How quickly everything had changed, as if a kaleidoscope had just moved, the pattern erased and a new one came into being. He settled back against the wall silently, watching the two around him who would be moving down an unhappy path while he waved goodbye. How strange.

Jusoh was raging. Razaleigh could hear it but didn't try to understand the words. He didn't care. There seemed to be a good bit of wailing in the cells now, but not from him. He relished the quiet in his own mind.

Osman scrutinized him, wondering what he was thinking. He knew all too well what the other two thought, they were howling it throughout the station. He walked back into his office, to find Maryam and Rubiah waiting for him. 'We decided to stay,' Maryam told him. 'I just couldn't listen to her anymore. So we came in here.'

'She died in the hospital.'

'No!'

Osman nodded. 'I'm afraid so. Right in front of us.'

'Alamak! I can't believe it!'

'Neither can I,' Osman said. 'So now we have two of them. Murderers, I mean. In the same family. And the father killed Yati, I'm still confused about that.'

'I can't really understand it.' Maryam said in wonderment. 'I just ... well, I don't know what. But how awful.'

'No wonder you had a heart attack working on this case,' Rubiah said in her practical manner. 'They could drive anyone to that. Just be careful, Che Osman,' she added, 'and keep them well apart. Otherwise who knows what will happen next.'

'All three …' He stared down at his desk. 'At least there might be someone left to take care of the children. Or will they go to Fatimah's parents? It wouldn't be much of an improvement, I'm afraid. Did no one consider them?' He asked rhetorically. It was apparent no one had.

Maryam stood up but remained a bit shaky. Mamat took her arm. 'It's time we went home. I don't know what those people are capable of, but I don't want to see any more.'

Rubiah pulled Din aside for a quick chat, or interrogation, depending upon the point of view. Rubiah appeared friendly, Din was bewildered and maybe a bit fearful. Rahman watched him with sympathy. Din would be probably be getting married.

'We just witnessed a murder!' Maryam fussed at Rubiah. 'And you move right in to check out bridegrooms.'

'Life goes on,' Rubiah told her, feeling extremely satisfied. 'Should my niece not find a husband because of those two? Be reasonable. And I think he's a very nice man. Rahman, you know him best. What do you think?'

'You couldn't do any better,' he said, pulling the car out in traffic on Jalan Ibrahim. He was surprised to discover he really meant it.

'I'll tell Dollah to speak to his sister right away,' she said, more to herself than to Maryam. 'We can get things moving so something good comes out of this. And Rahman, you'll be related.

Somehow.' She frowned slightly, unable to really explain how that worked, but did it matter? They were family.

Chapter XXX

Azrina awaited the unavoidable arrival of her mother-in-law as a sacrificial ox awaits a religious ceremony. She'd tried, she really had, to talk to Osman and explain why she dreaded her mother-in-law's visit. How she'd take over everything, making her a visitor in her own home, and a not particularly welcome one at that. 'Don't make me hand over my baby so that I can't even be his mother,' she begged him.

Though Osman could be impressively perceptive about many things, when it came to his mother, he was often dim-witted. He assured his wife that would never happen, that his mother was in fact incapable of such actions. Of course, she was forceful and competent, there was no denying that, but that was hardly a defect. And she loved Azrina as a daughter (this was patently untrue: she was fond of Azrina as long as she was doing what she wanted. This was the case with almost everyone, even Osman from time to time). Besides, his mother was determined to come to Kelantan, and Osman was no match for his mother in determined mode. The juggernaut could not be stopped.

And upon her arrival, it was just as Azrina had feared. She was back at work, and when she got home, her mother-in-law had taken over little Azman, announcing his naps and his meals with no consultation with his mother. Azrina was scolded for attempting to upset his schedule for even a few minutes, and Osman sat mute while this lecture was delivered. However, Azrina was no longer the pliable girl she'd been in Perak. She'd learned from Kelantan's finest, and she would stick up for herself.

She stopped at Maryam's house on the way home from work, to discuss the situation and receive some advice. When she explained the problem, Maryam was of two minds. First, she believed Azrina should tell her mother-in-law, in the politest way possible, that this was her house and she could actually run it according to her own lights. Second, however, was the precept that elders should be respected. Instructing Azrina to tell off Osman's mother would be tantamount to *ajar anak harimau makan daging:* teaching a tiger cub to eat meat. If she were encouraged to disrespect her mother-in-law, would it not lead to her disrespecting all her elders? An impossible state of affairs!

She considered the issue for a while before replying. 'Azrina,' she said slowly, 'rather than confront your mother-in-law, you must speak to your husband. If you challenge her, she'll be insulted for the rest of your life, and she'll make sure you know it. It would be rude. I'd advise against it.' Azrina looked beaten, now believing there was no way out.

'But you can work on Osman. You know you can convince him, and it's important you do it. He can approach his mother in a way you can't. And if does, she'll know he agrees with you and that will convince her. There are people with whom you can be direct, and those you must approach by another road.'

Azrina looked newly energized. 'Mak Cik, I knew you'd tell me what to do. Osman hasn't wanted to listen to me but if I can make anyone hear me, it's him, right?' Maryam nodded. 'And his mother will forgive him no matter what he says, while she'll never forgive me for saying anything.' She thought for a moment, and Maryam realized Osman would soon be caught in an avalanche of discussion and would no doubt capitulate. He adored Azrina and would hate her being unhappy. She could not predict whether his mother would become more accepting and stay or return to Perak in high dudgeon, but she was certainly looking forward to finding out.

***

'Are you still not sure about being a policeman?' Aliza asked while she and Rahman were walking home from Maryam's house. The emergency arrangements, as Ashikin referred to them, were scheduled to stop at the end of the week. Maryam was definitely on the mend and was now impatient to do things her own way again. Mamat swore he'd be able to provide all the help she'd require. Ashikin accepted his protestations, but also remained ready to jump back in if necessary.

'I'm feeling better about it than I was,' he said thoughtfully. 'When we wrap up a case and get dangerous people out of the way, I believe it's worthwhile. But sometimes, I feel like it's just too much. I think we did some real good. That family! It was only a matter of time until they started branching out and killing people they weren't related to. But when I went to see that older man who was limping, and thought I'd have to ask about his child, I just couldn't continue. I'm going to pull back from that kind of thing. It isn't just that I can't do it. It shouldn't be done at all. Do you see?'

Aliza nodded. 'I do. I think you're right, but maybe, well, maybe you shouldn't announce it as your policy. Just do what you think is right. Not that Osman is the type of boss to force you. But it isn't worth making it public, right?'

'Right,' he said, and smiled. Aliza smiled back and pulled on his hand, wanting to get home as soon as they could.

Amin had gone back to doing dikir barat but refused anything in the general Bacok area. He couldn't bear to be near the place where he'd lost Yati. Though he planned in the future to bring his children back to live with him, right now they were still with their aunt, who provided a real family for them. She was only a few doors away, he thought, so it wasn't as if he couldn't see them. In fact, he saw them every day.

He'd met Maryam once, when he was wandering through the main market on an errand. He was grateful to her, for solving the mystery around Yati's death but the truth now seemed ever more meaningless than he could have imagined. Yati died for no reason at all: a mistake due to near sightedness. He couldn't think about it. And seeing Maryam brought it all back, and so he hoped to stay away from her. He thought it would be easy to do; their paths were unlikely to cross again.

And yet, one balmy night in the midst of the dry season, Maryam and Mamat sat in the audience while Amin performed in a kampong close to his own home. A wedding, at which he entertained the guests. Maryam had only seen him in the depths of mourning, and it was a revelation to watch him perform. He was witty, he was pointed, he was articulate and as well-informed about kampong gossip as any market woman. It was hard to reconcile the two sides of Amin she'd witnessed, and yet, here he was in front of her, drawing a crowd, holding them in the palm of his hand. Some enterprising teenager was taping the performance, and would no doubt be selling copies of it in the local market tomorrow. They left without greeting Amin, not willing to bring down his well-earned triumph with a reminder of his tragedy.

Maryam was glad to be back at the market, selling her fabrics. Back to the usual rhythms of her life. The heart attack had frightened her more than she cared to admit, and there were times when she sat still and just listened to her heartbeat, in case it stopped. It took some of the confidence out of her and thinking back to those moments when she staggered into the police station, unable to breathe, with the world fading away from her, she wanted to cry. But she hoped that would go away, and she would no longer revisit that time, perhaps even forget about it. Let it slip away so she could again be confident in her strength and not doubt it at every turn.

Razaleigh went to jail with the rest of his family, though it would not be for as long as his wife and brother. Ex-wife, he should say, since he pronounced all three *talak* at once, while still in the Kota Bharu jail. He therefore considered himself well and truly divorced and found it hard to believe he had once been married. Their children were taken by Fatimah's family, and Razaleigh was resigned they'd most likely be just like their mother. He'd been that way too, once – maybe not as completely, but still, it was what he'd grown up with. And where had it led them all but to intra-family murder and finally to no family at all.

He had time to think in jail, and was almost happy. He felt free now, though alone, and resolutely never considered what his life might be when he got out. He was comfortable where he was, and agreed he deserved it. In that, he was one of the few prisoners who never griped about his sentence, or proclaimed his innocence, or planned what he'd do when he was finally free. The prison present was all he wanted, and he embraced it.

And Ashikin, who knew it even before it happened, was expecting her fourth child, whom she hoped was a girl, so as to have two of each gender. She'd wanted four children, just like the family in which she'd grown up. And it would soon come to be.

Acknowledgements

My thanks to Zdena Nemeckova and Bonnie Tessler for their tireless proof-reading. Ashikin Mohd Ali Flindall and Puteh Shaharizan Shaari for their insights into Malay culture and correcting my spelling. Shahmim Dhilawala for her help and encouragement. Thank you all.

Vol. I: Shadow Play

Shadow Play is the first in the series of Kain Songket Mysteries set in the northern state of Kelantan, Malaysia during the 1970s. Mak Cik Maryam, a smart and take-charge kain songket (silk) trader in Kota Bharu Central Market, discovers a murder in her own backyard, shattering the bucolic village world she thought surrounded her.

While the new chief of police, a pleasant young man from Ipoh whose mother's admonitions about the wiles of Kelantanese girls still ring in his ears, wrestles with the bewildering local dialect, Maryam steps up to solve the mystery herself. Her investigation brings her into the closed world of the wayang kulit Shadow Play theater and the lives of its performers—a world riven by rivalries and black magic.

Trapped in a tangle of jealousy, Maryam struggles to make sense of the crime in spite of the spells sent to keep her from secrets long buried and lies woven to shield the guilty.

Vol. II: Princess Play

In Volume II of the Kain Songket Mysteries series set in Kelantan, Malaysia, Maryam once again finds crime close to home: someone is killing the women of Kota Bharu's Central Market. Police Chief Osman has made little progress understanding Kelantanese, and seems at a loss where to begin his investigation. Although Maryam is loathe to examine any further crime, when she discovers one of the victims herself she must act. Murder is compounded by spirit possession: a Main Puteri ceremony is performed to find the killer and heal a quiet village that has been plunged into chaos.

Vol. III: Spirit Tiger

Tiger spirits prowl Kampong Penambang in the third novel of the award-winning Kain Songket Mysteries detective series set in Kelantan, Malaysia. Amateur sleuth Mak Cik Maryam volunteers to investigate the death of a village reprobate, convinced it will be a quick investigation with clear suspects. But her detection soon spirals out of control with a plethora of suspects who wanted him dead, including almost everyone he knew.

Maryam falls victim to a hala spell turning her into a were-tiger, terrifying her and her family, and leaving her vulnerable to any number of evil influences. Join Mak Cik Maryam in her latest adventure, *Spirit Tiger*, as she investigates Kelantan's gambling underworld.

Vol. IV: Moon Kite

In the fourth installment of the award-winning Kain Songket Mysteries detective series set in east coast Malaysia, amateur sleuth Aunty Maryam investigates the death of a winning contestant at a kite flying contest. With little experience, the winner is found to have beaten some of Kelantan's best competitors, but no one knows why he suddenly took up the sport. Aunty Maryam's investigation leads her into a labrynth of unexpected relationships in a seemingly peaceful village.

Vol. V: Spinning Top

Mak Cik Maryam and Rubiah once again investigate murder in a small Kelantan town. Someone has been killed at a top-spinning contest, hit by a *gasing*, a heavy metal spinning top, that had no business flying as it did according to all laws of physics. Malaysia's most famous female amateur sleuths suspect not only foul play, but black magic, and are determined to rid Kelantan of the source of evil. Join them in their fifth adventure assisting the Kota Bharu Police Department, or vice versa, in *Spinning Top*, the latest in the award-winning Kain Songket Mystery Series.